The eX and whY

by

Louise Burness

Published by Charpollo Publishing.

Cover illustration by Louise Burness, design by David Spink.

www.louiseburness.info

To David,
for all your tech support, ideas and encouragement.
Now get those bloody kitchen shelves up.

Chapter one
Helen
November 1993

'So, that's one watermelon Bacardi Breezer and a double Malibu and pineapple. That'll be three pounds and seventy-five pence, please.'

The barman places the drinks in front of me on the bar.

'Sorry, how much did you say?' I struggle to hear over the loud music and the racket of bartenders, as they make their usual whoop of Neanderthal, mating call sounds. It's all getting pretty irritating now. Every time I buy a round, this hairy rocker geezer is right there, it's like there's some unwritten code that says only he can serve me. He leans in closer, staring right into my eyes as he repeats the amount.

'It comes to three seventy-five, Helen,' he smiles.

How on earth does he know my name, the creepy stalker.

'Hey, I took the liberty of writing down my phone number, just in case you change your mind and fancy that date after all.' He gives me a cheeky wink and coyly slides a beer mat forwards.

For goodness sake, I can't believe he's asking out me, yet again. Which part of no is this guy having difficulty in understanding? I give a deep sigh and glance up from rifling through the few coins in my purse, trying to hide my exasperation as he gives me his hopeful smile. The dazzling white teeth and the long, permed hair, he's for all the world like something the eighties barfed up. A sad leftover of the decade that taste forgot.

It's my own fault, I knew I shouldn't have worn my White Musk perfume tonight. A dog tied up outside the offy tried to hump my leg earlier. I'd only gone to pat it; it took two men several minutes to get him off me. Yes, I'd have been better sticking to Samsara. It doesn't have quite such an extreme reaction on men and dogs as the fragrance I'm wearing.

'Just as I told you last week, I'm seeing someone. Thanks for the offer, but please do take this as an ongoing and final no.

Just in case you're ever tempted to ask again.' I politely, but firmly, push the beer mat back towards him. I'm pretty sure he has a whole stack of those by the till, ready to hand out at every opportunity. I roll my eyes at the song that's playing. Mr Vain: yeah, that's definitely you, mate.

It may sound like I'm being mean, but I know for a fact that this barman is known for hitting on several different girls, every weekend. He's pretty blatant about it too, because I can see him glancing at me when he thinks I'm not looking. It doesn't make me think he's some in demand super-stud, it makes me think he's a prick. This is the fifth time he's asked me out on a date, and I couldn't be less interested. Players are so not my type. I pull out the straw from my Breezer and place it on the bar. I'm twenty-one, for goodness sake, not five. His eyes momentarily fill with disappointment, but then as usual, he's turning on the charm for the next girl in the queue. Before I've even picked up my drinks, he's asking how her evening is going and telling her he loves what she's done with her hair tonight.

It is actually true that I've been seeing someone. Peter Forbes, one of the doctors from work. It's early days, but he's leagues above some wannabe rock god, who should stick to pulling pints instead of women. I wouldn't be interested in this Jon Bon Jovi lookalike, regardless of my relationship status.

When I say I'm seeing this doctor, it's a little up in the air at the moment. Peter told me he'd separated from his wife, months ago. She popped in to see him in A&E last week and it appeared to me that she hadn't quite got that particular memo. She had straightened the lapels of his white coat and stared longingly up into his eyes, in a way that made me think he could be on a promise later. It really unnerved me. It was the uneasy glance he gave me over her shoulder that made me feel most uncomfortable, like he'd been caught doing something he shouldn't. There have been a few rumours flying around the ward, about some alleged flirtatious behaviour with other nurses. I don't listen to gossip. However, the wife turning up did bother me. I confronted him about them still being together and he denied it. So, when I was off last Sunday, a day that he told me he couldn't see me because he had his kids, I decided I'd hang out in Fulham. At one point I just so happened to be walking past the park near his house. I gave him a cheery hello, as he and his wife pushed their children on the swings.

'Who's that?' I was just close enough to hear her enquire.

'Just some nurse from work,' he'd casually replied, shooting me a cautious glance.

I've been wary of Peter's claims of separation since then, because let's be clear about something, I'm no home wrecker. I have absolutely zero interest in being the other woman. Not that I have anything to feel bad about yet, it's all been pretty innocent so far. We've been out for dinner once, to some posh place down the riverside in Richmond. Last week we had a few drinks after work. We've held hands and had a very brief snog, but nothing more. Peter has asked me to go and see that new Tom Hanks movie, *Sleepless in Seattle,* next week. I need to do a bit more delving before I say yes to another date, I can't continue with this relationship if his marriage is still ongoing. I overheard him on the phone at work last night, arranging to take his kids to Hamleys, tomorrow afternoon. We're both on an early shift, so I'm just going to happen to coincidentally be up in town, getting some early Christmas shopping in.

I negotiate my way through the crowded club and place Susan's drink on the table in front of her. She's currently getting off with a bloke who could double as a Chesney Hawkes lookalike. This Jimmy geezer, he's her on and off current shag. Although there have been a few in the past, this one unfortunately seems to be going the distance. I sigh as I glance around, everyone else seems to be having a great time. All except me. As usual, I feel like the fat friend sat on the side lines. I never used to be conscious about my size ten curves, but Susan would make Kate Moss look obese. She's constantly surrounded by admirers, which means she then tries to palm me off with the dorky mate. Like this one, currently sitting opposite me, smiling awkwardly every time I have the misfortune of catching his eye. Susan finally comes up for air, a look of surprise flashing across her face, as if she's only just remembered I'm there.

'Hey, Helen, did you know that Jimmy is off touring with Nirvana next week? How cool is that?' She wipes her smeared lipstick on the back of her hand and picks up her Malibu and pineapple, giving me a smug smirk over her glass.

'Is that right? So quickly off the back of the Guns N' Roses tour too, fair play to you, mate.' I raise an eyebrow in Jimmy's direction, hoping my comment comes across as sarcastic, and not that I'm actually impressed by this peacock display of utter bollocks.

It's a complete fabrication, Jimmy is full of shit and I can't understand why Susan believes him. She's an intelligent girl. Her exam results in nursing college have been consistently higher than mine. Yet here she is, believing the cock and bull story of some dickhead. Jimmy was seen out down Fulham High Street whilst he was last supposedly on tour. My theory is that he has a variety of girls on the go, all over London. He's concocted this elaborate reason for going AWOL for several weeks at a time, as he does the rounds of them all. When I checked out their dates, Guns N' Roses were on tour for over a year and not just the three weeks that Jimmy was allegedly away with them.

'Come on, Helen, you gettin' up?' Terry, Jimmy's idiot mate yells over at me. Ebeneezer Goode; how would you even dance to that? Out of curiosity, I glance over at the gormless bunch flailing around hopelessly under the strobe lights. Not very easily, it would appear.

'Nah, you're all right,' I shout back, giving him a disdainful side eye.

Bloody lech, I've been keeping a safe distance away from him tonight. I made the mistake of hitting the dancefloor with Terry, last weekend. He's way too familiar, if you catch my drift. He basically sees asking me up to dance as an opportunity for him to have a good grope. Like a randy octopus, he was all over me like a rash. I took none of it. I grabbed his hand and held it aloft.

'Excuse me,' I shouted over the slow song that was playing. 'Does anyone know who this belongs to? I just found it on my arse.'

He'd looked at me in horror as the nearby couples turned to stare at him. I had stormed off the dance floor, grabbed my bag and coat, and left the club. I've since heard elaborate stories about what happened that night, people have been rushing up to me asking if I really sprayed perfume in his eyes, decked him with a swift punch, or I got some honchos onto him when he left the club. The gossip was rife. In reality, I only said that one thing and stormed out.

Unfortunately, it doesn't seem to have put him off me, even though tonight I intentionally dressed in a manner that would make a nun look like a slapper. He has still unabashedly stared at my boobs for the past two hours, when he thinks I'm not looking. I wasn't even going to come out this evening but Susan promised she wouldn't ignore me. Yet here she is again, stuck to Jimmy like a limpet on a rock.

I slump grumpily back in my seat and suck the dregs from my bottle. That's it, I'm almost out of cash and bored shitless. Fifteen quid I've spent tonight, counting the entrance fee and cloakroom charge. What a waste. Well, I won't be doing it again, no matter how much Susan begs me. She basically just needs someone to walk in with, so she doesn't look like she's some sad loser sniffing about for Jimmy. I'd rather sit in my tiny digs on my own, with a nice bottle of Mateus Rosé and a takeaway, watching Casualty. Which I can technically define as studying since it's a medical TV show. Right, there's no point in wasting any more time sitting here watching those two suck the faces off each other. I'm up for an early shift at half five and would much rather be in bed.

'I'm just popping to the loo,' I mutter to anyone who may be interested.

Susan doesn't even notice me pick up my coat and bag. Terry opens his mouth to protest at my departure, but the look on my face halts any pleas from him. Without a shred of guilt, I make my way towards the door. The past two weekends, I had hung around so we could walk back to our nursing digs together. My so-called friend had abandoned me to make my own way, as she headed back to Jimmy's gaff. I refuse to sit around and be spare part anymore. I count out my small change whilst waiting in the cloakroom queue, I have just enough cash left for some curry sauce and chips on the way home. Bonus!

I'm rudely awakened by Haddaway, when the radio alarm kicks in at ten past five the next morning. "What is love?" Fucked if I know, mate. I'll let you know if I ever find it. Besides, if Charles and Diana can split up then is there even such a thing? What girl could possibly believe in fairy tales after that? Charlie boy has allegedly been sniffing around that Camilla Park-yer-Balls, or whatever she's called. Proper devastated me did that. What was he thinking? He was totally punching by pulling Di in the first place. She's way out of his league, with the added bonus of not looking like she'd been bred with a racehorse, like some of that lot who hang around with the royals.

Anyway, Diana is way better off without him, she will find a *real* Prince Charming to take his place. I just know my favourite princess will go on to find the happy ever after she deserves.

Shivering as I pull back the flimsy duvet, I switch on the electric blow heater to warm up my tiny, shabby room. I stare at the panda in the mirror, a throbbing spot is newly blossoming on my chin. Bugger, I should know not to eat crap and go to bed with make-up on, particularly since my last bit of training was in dermatology. Now I have to face Peter with this beacon shining in his face. Warning him off like a bright red lighthouse beam. I think of his skinny, effortlessly grungy wife. She's groomed, of course, but in that dressed down kind of way. You could tell she'd spent an hour with the diffuser, fluffing up her highlighted blonde hair to look like she'd just stepped off a surf board. Nobody over seven stone could ever get away with a tied at the waist, plaid shirt. Her strategically ripped, baggy jeans revealing just a glimpse of perfectly toned and tanned thigh. She smelled expensive too, I got close enough for a sniff whilst passing her by, when she popped into see Peter one day. There would be no way that it was a cheap Body Shop oil, like I wear. One day I'll be able to afford Chanel, but not on my current pittance.

With a cursory glance at the alarm clock to see just how late I am, I take a quick shower and look out my best, clean outfit. I need to look good for running into them up in town later. Peter rarely sees me in anything but my nurse's uniform, although I'm never short of guys asking me to wear it for them.

'Would that be with the puke, shit and blood on it, or without?' I always enquire. With hindsight, it's fairly obvious why I'm still single. Well, sort of.

The shift is insane, as Saturdays always are. There's still a backlog of leftover patients to clear from last night: the accident prone drunks, the ones that came off worst in fights, the young women desperate for the morning after pill. The waiting room reeks of stale alcohol and is littered with drunken bodies. I'm put on cubicles, with a particularly scary senior nurse. Even though I'm only a first-year student, she expects me to know so much more than I do and is often frustrated by my lack of knowledge. Twice she's roughly moved me aside today, just because it was taking me a little longer than it takes her to put on a dressing.

'Get out of my way,' she had barked at me. Immediately followed up with another dig, whilst I stood and observed her.

'Good God, what's wrong with you, girl? Are you just going to stand there and do nothing?'

Yeah, she's one of those types.

'Make your mind up, love,' I'd muttered under my breath, passive aggressively, as I refilled the dressings. I'd certainly not normally take this kind of shit from anyone, but she's in charge of writing up my reports, and I won't give her the satisfaction of putting in any comments about how rude and disrespectful I am. She's very old school and has no time for the antics of the more fun senior nurses, including the hilarious one who sent me upstairs to gynae for a set of fallopian tubes. I still can't believe I fell for that one, but to be fair, it was my first day. Just to add to the fun, by the end of the first hour I've been thrown up on. I can't believe I'm going to have to shower again before I go into town, I desperately wanted to leave on time.

I don't see Peter the entire shift, but I did hear his voice a couple of times. The confidence and authority in it had made me smile. Of all the nurses in the hospital, he had chosen to take me out. I have to give him the benefit of the doubt, if he says his marriage is over, then I'm sure it is. Today is the day that I prove to myself, once and for all, that he really is only putting on a show for his kids. Just like he'd told me he was. When I see them in Hamleys, I'm going to walk boldly up to him and enquire if he still wants to go and see the movie next week, right in front of his wife. This will show me for sure that he's single. I'm not doing anything wrong in asking him, because he told me he was separated. In the unlikely event that he has lied to me, he has nowhere to hide. It's an infallible plan.

The tube is hot and a little claustrophobic, crammed with early Christmas shoppers and tourists. I manage to squeeze myself into the last remaining end seat, trying in vain to not to get irritated by the idiot next to me, territorially splaying his knees out and invading my personal space. I'm exhausted from my late night, followed by an early start. I won't be going out on working weekends again, it was fairly obvious I was a little hungover today. The scary senior had glared at me, as I cleaned up the particularly nasty and infected wound of a homeless gentleman we attended to. To be fair, I would have gagged on a good day at an oozing sore like that, and I did apologise for almost throwing up on him. I made up for it by trying to get him admitted to a ward. I hated the thought of sending him back out there to the streets. Poor man, he was real funny too, he kept flicking the bird behind bitchface's back when she was mean to me. The senior nurse was having none of it, she accused me of wasting time and stretching NHS resources. She simply prescribed antibiotics and gave him the name of a shelter. When the doctor came to sign off the patient, he had agreed with me. The man was a vulnerable person and certainly not guaranteed a bed if he was discharged. So upstairs he went. Brilliant, yet another reason for nurse arsehole to be a cow to me, on our next shift together.

The familiar sounds of the underground lull me into a light doze, the low rumble of the wheels on the track, the hiss of the doors. I awaken with a start, as we arrive into Oxford Circus, and join the queue of commuter cattle waiting to get off. I smile contentedly to myself as I stand on the escalator. I rarely come up into town, but I always look forward to seeing it near Christmas. The anticipation of the stunning lighting displays on Oxford and Regent Streets, the welcome blast of cold air after that sweatbox of a tube train. I love this time of year, it's full of promise and excitement. Even better, I just got my shifts for the festive season and I'm on an early Christmas Eve, then off until the twenty-seventh. I have no idea how I pulled that one off but I played possum, just in case it was a mistake. Normally, all the good shifts go to the parents of young children. The ones with no kids, like me, always seem to end up with the shitty end of the stick.

I arrive at the top of the escalator and feel the chill of the outdoors again. The Christmas atmosphere doesn't disappoint and I blink in wonder at the festive scene before me. Even though it's only late November, Oxford street is like a movie set. The shop windows are emblazoned with stunning displays of gifts, toys, and party dresses. The frosty air creates a glittering haze around the streetlights and a few delicate flakes of snow whirl around me as I walk. It's making me feel slightly dizzy and disorientated. Mind you, that could be the anticipation of what I'm about to do. Pulling my faux fur coat tighter around me, I walk determinedly out of the exit and take a left down Regent's Street.

'Daddy, I'm freezing,' a cross little voice comes from the corner, outside Liberty. 'Why didn't we bring the Audi? I don't want to go to Hamleys, I want to go to the Disney Store.' The little boy of around five scowls at his father, his arms folded in defiance.

'No,' wails a slightly higher pitched voice. 'We *are* going to Hamleys. It's my birthday and I said so,' the small child of around three years old, stamps her foot angrily. I gather myself; I hadn't quite expected to bump into them so soon. Not while I was still rehearsing a speech in my head. Peter crouches down in front of his children. 'We can do both, my darlings. Mummy and Daddy are going to take you to Claridge's for dinner, that's why we took the underground.'

'And Mummy and Daddy can't handle going into town without wine as a reward, my sweets,' chuckles Peter's wife.

'We don't even like Claridge's, you two do. it's my sister's birthday, she should choose. Tell them you'd like to go to Pizza Express, Ella.' protests the boy. Both children stare challengingly up at their parents.

I stop in my tracks, bracing myself. It's now or never. 'Oh, my goodness. Hello, Doctor Forbes,' I exclaim. 'Fancy meeting you here. Are you Christmas shopping too? I thought I'd get it in early, before it gets *really* crazy up here.' Oh, my God, shut up, I internally chide myself. Where the fuck did that high-pitched giggle-snort combo appear from? We are so not starting *that*.

Peter stares at me in complete shock.

'H...Helen,' he stammers.

'Pete, who is this woman? We seem to see her everywhere. What's going on?' His wife eyes me with suspicion. The doctor pulls himself to his full height, dumbstruck, shaking his head in denial of any association with me. 'It's funny, we do seem to keep bumping into each other,' I'm indifferent in my response. 'I was actually thinking about going to see *Sleepless in Seattle* later. I thought I'd best mention it, just in case I run into the pair of you again. I wouldn't want you to think I was stalking you.' I stare at the doctor pointedly as I turn away. That look of horror on Peter's face said it all, they're very much still together. His wife will find out, she's not stupid. I could see the questions in her eyes.

'Helen? What a coincidence bumping into you up here.' I turn back, towards the sound of a voice that I vaguely recognise. 'I've been shopping for my cousins' Christmas presents and was just about to grab some dinner.' The man holds up two large carrier bags as if to confirm he's telling the truth.

'I know that you don't want me to ask you for a date again, so please consider my request only as a friend.' He gives me a gentlemanly bow of the head. 'Would you care to join me?' It takes me a moment to recognise the barman. His long hair has been cut into that trendy style, like the guys from Take That have. Curtains, I think that's what you call it. Now, there's a style that will never date. Gone is the Bon Jovi hairdo weirdo, this new look is revealing some seriously chiselled bone structure. He gives me a wide smile before glancing at Peter and his family.

'Sorry, I didn't mean to interrupt. How rude of me,' he blusters.

'Not at all,' I laugh, a little too maniacally. 'This is just a work colleague I've bumped into whilst doing my Christmas shopping. Actually, I was just thinking about grabbing a bite, so I'd love to join you for dinner. That guy I told you I was seeing, he's history now. God, what a total loser. I don't know what I was thinking, to be honest. Once

I noticed the bald spot, it really put me off him.' I give a musical laugh.

Peter touches the top of his head, self-consciously. Which doesn't go unnoticed by his wife, who glares at him accusingly.

'Anyway, it was nice to meet you all. Bye, Doctor Forbes. Bye...I'm sorry, I don't think I caught your wife's name?'

My words hang in the air for a few long seconds.

'Olivia,' blusters Peter. 'My wife's name is Olivia,' he finishes smugly.

Of course it is: glamorous, elegant and polished. She could only be called Olivia.

'Hey kids,' I lean down to stage whisper. 'Did I hear you say you're going to Hamleys and The Disney Store?' The children give me a shy nod each.

'Well, you can't come all the way into town and not go to the Christmas toy market too. It's down near Leicester Square and it stays open until ten o'clock,' I squeal, excitedly.

The children's parents stare at me in horror. I'm far too nice to go for true revenge and tell Olivia her husband is a cheat. He blew his cover, all by himself. This belter will be enough to keep me chuckling all night.

'Oh dear, that was a little naughty of me,' I grimace. 'I bet Mummy and Daddy can't wait to get indoors and have a lovely glass of wine.' I blow on my hands and rub them together, the vapour from my breath makes clouds of steam around me. I wonder if it gives me an old Hollywood, soft focus haze.

'Talking of which, I'm just about to have a glass myself. It's far too chilly for me to hang around out here.' I turn to the barman with a smile, linking arms with him in a rather jolly manner. 'Come on mate, let's go and get that drink. I have the whole weekend off now, so do your worst. Oh, aren't you on an early tomorrow, Dr Forbes? Such a pity.' I give Peter a sly smirk and his face flames.

I am so glad it worked out this way and I didn't have to give my pitiful rehearsed speech. I just pulled a hot bloke who admits he's been asking me out for ages. I heavily insinuated that there may be a little more action than just dinner on the cards. He's also way younger than Forbsey, with hair, and that will really piss him off. Plus, I totally got to tell him he's a loser, right to his face. Best of all, the Forbes parents will now have to trawl the outdoor market, before traipsing home sober. I can't imagine it will be much fun on a packed tube train, with two clearly rather spoiled children, who have swung from hyper to exhausted. This couldn't have worked out better had I planned it. Without a backwards glance, I skip off down towards Piccadilly Circus with my hot new friend.

Chapter two
Steve
November 1993

I don't know what was going on between Helen and those people she was talking to outside Liberty, but it struck me as a rather uncomfortable conversation. The man looked shocked and sort of guilty, the woman suspicious and wary. Helen looked fragile, it's a look I've never seen on her when I've served her in the bar. Normally she's confident, if not a little haughty. I thought she'd been seeing that Terry guy, who's mates with Susan's boyfriend. Not so, I had discovered last week. One of the glass collectors told me how Helen had humiliated him on the dance floor for grabbing her arse. Apparently, it was hilarious, I wish I'd seen it. She thrust his hand up in the air, to show everyone what he'd done, then slapped him and told him to have a fucking word with himself. Then she grabbed a nearby guy's pint and threw it into Terry's crotch, to cool down his rampant manhood. She then ever so coolly placed two quid on the table, for the guy to buy himself another pint.
'Keep the change,' she had said casually over her shoulder. The music had gone off by this point and everyone watched in silence, as Helen collected her bag and coat. She walked out to a huge round of applause.
Of course, I would have to have been on my break at that precise moment.
To say I was over the moon about hearing this was putting it mildly. Fair play to Helen, Terry is a lecherous creep and he's on his last warning with the club. Just one more complaint is all it'll take for him to be barred, then I don't have to serve the slime ball ever again. As a bonus, I assumed it meant that Helen wasn't taken. She was either playing hard to get, or just plain didn't fancy me. Anyway, armed with my new knowledge, when I saw her in the club last night, I took another punt and asked her out again. It was another no, with a firm instruction not to ask again. I finally admitted defeat. It seems that she is seeing someone,

just not lecherous Terry. Her refusals have only served to intrigue me more in the past, but I really wasn't planning on asking her out for dinner when I saw her in town. Not only does it make me seem a bit of a dick for not being able to take no for an answer, but maybe me backing off would spark her interest. I don't know where my request came from, just a knee-jerk reaction to seeing her, I guess. Someone in the club told me that she's a nurse, that already stunning package in uniform was something I definitely wanted to see. I even considered slamming my fingers in my car door, just to have a reason to go to the casualty department at Chelsea and Westminster. I figured that knowing my luck, she wouldn't be on shift. I'd end up with some big, burly matron type instead, plus some serious and permanent damage to my guitar playing digits. If Helen did happen to be working, she'd likely call security on me for being a stalker. Anyway, I wrote that idea off as a lose-lose situation.

I had initially decided I was going to pass on by this awkward group of five people on Regents Street, to not intrude on their conversation. For some reason my instincts told me to stop and thank God I did. Talk about synchronicity, it proper paid off. After asking Helen out unsuccessfully for weeks, she finally jumped at the chance when I mentioned it was just as friends. It almost felt like she wanted to be rescued and I couldn't believe my luck that she said yes to dinner.

I've fancied Helen for ages, ever since she came in with that Susan girl that Mick the manager pulled a few weeks ago. I'd see her standing there patiently waiting to order her drinks, purse open, hands resting on the bar. The breeze from the fan under the optics catching her hair every ten seconds. It made her look like a sexy rock chick, in a Def Leppard video. You know the kind of girls I mean, that slight aloofness they have that screams,

"I know you fancy me but I'm far too good for a shit-show like you."

The truth is, I've only been chatting to half the girls I meet across the bar in the hope that it would make Helen jealous. Because she turned me down every time I asked her out, I'd chat away to other girls, just so Helen could see I was in demand. I know that makes me sound like a complete tosser, but there was just something about her that I just couldn't get out of my head. You know what I'm talking about, right? We've all been there.

Anyway, now here we are arm in arm, heading towards Piccadilly Circus. It was a completely genuine, happy coincidence me running into her. I thought maybe she'd think I'd been following her, so thank goodness I'd already been shopping. I made the excuse it was all Christmas presents for my young cousins. I thought it would make me look immature if she knew I'd bought a Super Nintendo for myself, while I was in Hamleys.

We head to a curry house, down a dingy back street off Piccadilly Circus, one that Helen says is a real hidden treasure. All the while that we walk, she's pointing out clubs she's been to and the best takeaways she's found that stay open late. Despite my job, I'm really not a party animal, but I feign enough interest to make out I'm not some saddo who looks forward to heading home for a cuppa at the end of the night. Helen's chatting away non-stop and I like that. Her closeness makes me nervous and I don't want to put her off by saying the wrong thing. I'm happy for her to do all the talking. We walk into the restaurant and the front of house manager asks if we've reserved a table, despite there being no other customers seated. He peruses his bookings then picks up two menus, asking us to follow on. He takes our coats from us and a slight silence ensues after he leaves. Helen and I smile nervously at each other.

'Shall we share a bottle of wine?' She glances awkwardly at me from over the top of her menu. I stare at her in awe. Those beautiful, brown, sparkly eyes are like melted chocolate. She is a stunner. God, but what do I reply to her

question? Sorry, Helen, I never touch alcohol?
'Sure,' I reply.

She gives a friendly wave to the waiter, who's dressed in full Indian attire, and expertly orders a bottle of something French and posh sounding.

'So, what's with the new hair? I have to say, it looks really good on you,' Helen batts the thick lashes over her Bambi eyes.

I run my fingers self-consciously through my curtains. I still can't get used to the chill on my neck.

'I'm joining the Metropolitan Police, I had to have it cut short for my training. I'm glad you like it,' I smile awkwardly. 'I'm taking bad having no insulation from the cold weather.'

Helen's eyes widen.

'You're going to be a police officer?' She gasps.

'Well, hopefully. I've been accepted for the next intake and I think I should pass. I've spent hours in the gym, training for the fitness test.' I take a sip of the dark red liquid the waiter has poured. It's gross. I never have been a drinker, I just can't stand the taste, let alone the dizzy feeling it gives me. I've also seen more than my share of complete states in the bar. There's nothing quite like watching someone so fucked up that they'd argue with their own shadow, to put you off. Then there are the ones who think they're hilarious, cruelly pointing out the people in the club that they find least attractive. Even worse are the ones who will then ask those people up to dance, just to humiliate them in front of everyone. I overheard one guy describe that so-called game as pull-a-pig. It's just dreadful. I've regularly seen people throw up over themselves, and on a couple of occasions, even shit themselves. Drinking never has been and never will be for me.

We finally order, and our early awkwardness dissipates along with the first glass of wine. I say first, but I'm less than a third down mine. Helen tops her own up and I politely refuse the offer of more, with the excuse I may have to drive later this evening. Our meals arrive and Helen digs straight into her tikka masala. She's so skinny, yet clearly enjoys her food. I like that in a woman. I love to cook and if we get on well tonight, I'm going to suggest I make her dinner at mine as a follow up date.

'I'm sorry,' I give an uncomfortable laugh. 'I have this weird, annoying injury that means my jaw clicks when I eat. I was punched in the face taking down a mugger on Acton High Street, last summer.'

'Oh, my goodness, are you for *real*?' Helen squeals, staring at me in awe.

'Tell me all about it.'

I shrug, nonchalantly. I did want to point out the irritating sound, but I wasn't completely unaware that the story I was about to tell made me sound hard as nails.

'It's nothing, really. There was this old dear who had just withdrawn her pension. This guy had been following her since she left the post office, the police later told me. I heard her scream and just took off after him. I chased him down and managed to restrain him until the cops arrived, but he did get in a few good punches. Until then, I hadn't been sure I'd make a good policeman, but the officers bigged me up so much that it gave me confidence. It looked good on my application and the cops from that day verified what happened, so every cloud and all that.'

'My, you really are a hero,' Helen smiles flirtatiously. 'Don't worry, every time I hear that cute, little jaw click, it will make me smile. It'll remind me what a big, tough guy you are.'

The next few weeks pass by in a flurry of dates. It feels like Helen and I have known each other for much longer than we have, she's so easy to get along with and really goes out of her way to make me feel good about myself. Confidence is something I've lacked all my life, but she makes it seem like I can take on the world. She's encouraging of anything that I mention I've always dreamt of doing, insisting that I really can make it happen. She listens patiently to the songs I write and play for her on my guitar. Every dinner I make for her is met with great enthusiasm. It's like having my own, personal little ray of sunshine with me, wherever I go.

Helen stays over at my flat every night now, as she can't stand her draughty, shabby nursing digs. After a desperate, late-night call, two weeks into our relationship, I had driven over and picked my girlfriend and all her belongings up. There was no sign of the mouse she had seen. To be fair, I wanted her home with me, so I didn't spend too long looking for it. In fact, I told her there was never just one mouse, there were probably at least five nearby, if not more. So that's how we came to live together. I was delighted. Helen has completely made herself at home. These days, my SNES console is nothing but an ornament, but I don't really mind. We spend our evenings watching Coronation Street, Eastenders and Brookside. I've quite got into them now. My girlfriend is not the greatest at taking her turn of the housekeeping, but she works so hard and I know she's constantly exhausted. With me only working part time in the bar for now, I really don't mind doing more than my fair share. Maybe once I'm working full time too, we'll have a better balance of chores. It's nice to have someone to cook for again, I was head chef when I lived here with my nan. I've been on my own a year now, since the lovely lady passed away. I'd been really lonely and I enjoy having the company again. I'll be off to Hendon soon, for my police training. I'm dreading the residential part, but I like knowing that Helen will stay on here. The house is like Fort Knox, as Nan had insisted on upping our security after Betty down the street was burgled. Although the guy actually came off way worse. Betty had a good few belts of him with her walking stick and he left empty handed. A busted lock to the back door was the only damage done. Helen lights up a Regal King Size and has a few puffs. She holds it towards me and I reluctantly take it. I don't know why I feel the need to impress her by acting like I'm into all these disgusting habits. I guess I know that I'm way out of my league by dating her and I want to appear a little more edgy and dangerous. I take two drags, without inhaling, taking the taste away with a sip of the beer that Helen brought through for us in the last commercial break. She tucks her legs underneath her and gives a contented sigh. 'I love being with you, Steve,' she smiles up at me. 'I've never had so much in common with a boyfriend before. Say we'll never split up.' She twists her hair into a knot and ties it into a bun, with a leopard print scrunchie. She looks even more stunning with her hair up. It makes those big, brown eyes pop all the more, like a beautiful little elf. 'We will never, ever split up, Helen.' I pull her to me and fondly kiss the top of her silky head. 'I can see us being married and having beautiful babies. We'll have a lovely home that we'll do up, like something you'd see in the Habitat catalogue. We will keep this flat too, obviously, and rent it out to make money for our retirement fund. Then we'll work hard at our careers and make loads of money. After that, we'll spend our retirement travelling all over the world.'

Helen stares up at me, quizzically. Shit, I took that way too far for a relationship of only two months.

'I'm just kidding,' I laugh nervously.

'Don't be, please,' Helen smiles wistfully. 'That sounds so lovely and I'm touched that you've thought about our future. Really, I am. It's exactly what I want too. I know it's not been long but it feels right, doesn't it? Oh, bollocks, was that the last beer?' She holds her empty bottle up with a little pout.

'Have mine, I've hardly touched it,' I offer generously, secretly happy to offload the bitter tasting stuff. 'You're off tomorrow, I'll go fetch you some more from Vicky Wines.'

I begin my Met Police training and I already know I'm going to absolutely love being a cop. The residential part, as predicted, is agony. I hate being away from Helen and I spend every night in the phone box, making sure she knows this. Knowing that I'm working towards our future helps a lot. We have gone from just talking about our dreams to making firm plans. We are even looking at buying a house together. For the first time in my life, I feel like a proper grown up. I am a police officer, I have a duty to protect those around me and I take my responsibilities most seriously. London is under threat again, after another recent bombing. It's a city that's always had its complicated issues as a target spot, but it feels particularly vulnerable out there right now. I feel strong and prepared enough to deal with this, but I know Helen is really scared for me. She won't go anywhere near the town centre at the moment and I don't want her to. For me, this is my life now. Rushing in where others rush out. Facing danger head on to protect the civilians of my home town.

That, and I look fit as fuck in my uniform and have a six pack for once, thanks to a punishing physical training regime. Helen had looked stunned when she first saw me in full cop gear. I prefer to keep my private life discreet, but let's just say, we didn't get much sleep that night.

Helen was out looking at houses yesterday. She's found a really nice one near Acton Central train station, perfect for links into London and really affordable too. It has three bedrooms, and this makes me smile. It shows me she's as serious as I am about our future. No one bedroomed starter flat for us, just straight in there with enough room for two, maybe even three kids. She also mentioned that it's right next to Acton Green Common, for picnics and family days out. There are also a couple of pubs, one right across the road and the another one practically next door. This doesn't particularly interest me, other than I hope that doesn't mean we get any hassle at chucking out time, but I made the right noises to keep the missus happy. I'm thinking so far ahead now, right into our future. I've never wanted anything more in my life, just me, Helen, and our future babies. Maybe a dog too, once the kids are up a bit and can handle themselves better.

My nan always said to me that when you meet the one, you just know. I didn't really believe her at the time. I was painfully shy when I started working in the bar, most of my chats with girls was just banter. A confident outer layer to protect the crushing insecurity I felt inside. Drunk girls are easier to talk to, they just come right out and say what they're thinking. My confidence grew, thanks to the ones who flirted with me over the counter. All the, 'hey, you're really cute,' comments helped to boost my self-esteem no end. Still, I never took advantage of it. I didn't do what most of the other guys in the club did. They used the attention to lead girls on and notch up their shag portfolio, whilst simultaneously criticising the same girls who slept with *them* on the first date. I found it all pretty disgusting, to be honest. I wanted a long-term relationship with one girl, and I knew who, the second I saw her. Helen. Sure, I may have chatted with others over the bar, while I was patiently waiting for her to say yes. I'd only admire their hair and outfits, or crack little jokes, I never took them home or led them to believe that I was a potential boyfriend. In fact, I maybe took the compliments too far. I overheard one girl tell her friend that I was cute, but with my eye for fashion, I was clearly gay. That made me laugh but I didn't mind them thinking that. I only had eyes for one girl. I upped the flirting with other ladies a little more when Helen was at the bar, just to try and show her what a fun guy I was. I'm not particularly proud of that but it was fairly innocent.

I never for a second thought I'd find what I have with my girlfriend, but Nan was right. She and Granddad had been besotted with each other. Even through the devastating challenge of nursing him through a long battle with Dementia, she had acted like they were still loved up teenagers. Nan had still insisted on taking him to their favourite restaurants and to the ballroom dancing classes they enjoyed. Even when Granddad could no longer walk, she'd have me push him in his wheelchair along the canal tow path near his childhood home, to feed the ducks. She would walk by his side and hold his hand, singing their favourite, old tunes. She knew this was the way to tap through his Dementia, the songs they loved meant their connection bridged his memory loss and made them a couple again. Like my grandparents, Helen and I will never tire of each other's company. We won't split up like my folks did. I detested the frosty atmosphere at home. The awkward silences, my mother and father eating and even sleeping separately. I remember thinking at the time that they didn't even try to make things work, it was like they intentionally went out of their way to piss each other off. It was a constant battle of one-upmanship in that house. As an only child and sick of their shit, I ended up living with Nan. It was an absolute pleasure to stay at my grandmother's house, in fact, I wished I had done it years before. With me gone, my parents seized the chance to divorce and moved out of London, desperate to put as much distance between each other as possible. Mum ended up in Scotland, Dad in Southampton. Both have married again and I rarely see either of them. Then Nan went, bless her soul, and I was all on my own. She did leave me the flat in her will, for that I will always be grateful. It's not cheap to buy around Fulham Broadway. She gave me the best start in life, in so many ways. Nan made sure that I'd never want for a home again, ever in my life.

I will always miss her, but with Helen, I feel like I have a new family and a fresh start. This makes me happy beyond words. Her parents, and her older brother and sister, they're all still with their spouses. They are warm and welcoming, I was treated as if I was already part of the family, the one and only time I've met them so far. This fills me with hope, my future wife knows what a secure and loving relationship is. I don't see Helen ever leaving me, with such fantastic role models in her life. I've never felt more sure of anything than I am of us.

Chapter three
Helen
April 2019

'Excuse me, are you all right, my dear? You look as white as a sheet.'

The voice snaps me from my thoughts. I glance up to see an elderly lady sat opposite me, smiling kindly.

'I wish I knew. I have my appointment in a few minutes, so I guess I'll find out. I just hate all this waiting around,' I sigh.

'Sorry, I'm so distracted that I didn't even hear you come in. You must think me very rude.'

'Not at all, it must be these soft soles I have on. They're new,' she chuckles and holds out her feet proudly, to admire her navy-blue slip-ons.'

'They're lovely, they look very comfortable. Are you here for your own appointment?' It's very sweet of the woman to ask about my nerves, but what about hers?

'No, dearie. I'm just here to offer my granddaughter some moral support in her time of need.' She indicates towards the door of the consultant's office.

'That's nice of you. What a lovely thing to do. With hindsight, I kind of wish that I had brought someone along, but I never even told anyone that I found a lump.'

'Why ever not?' The old woman looks at me with concern.

'Just because…you know. I don't like to worry them. It may be nothing,' I shrug.

'Well, don't you worry, you can talk to me while you're waiting.' She takes a seat next to me and pats my hand.

I may be a nurse, but I've never been good with handling emotions. We were all rather, stiff upper lip, in my family. Whining was for babies, by five years old you were expected to have stopped all that silly nonsense. Now I know, first-hand, how frightening waiting on a diagnosis can be. If one good thing comes out of this, then it will be the lesson in empathy that I'm learning. To this day, I cannot handle sympathy. If I'm feeling fragile then please do not be nice to me. Tell me I'm being pathetic or have nothing to worry about, but don't get emotional about it. It makes me feel a hundred times worse. I don't want to deal with someone else's feelings about my issues, or to have to comfort them. I just want to get on with it. The elderly lady sat next to me is full of warmth and kindness. I know she means well but I find it all a little suffocating.

'You're very sweet and I'm so grateful for your support, but I'm OK, thank you. I think I'll just pop to the loo and freshen up,' I whisper. 'I hope you're about to hear some wonderful news about your granddaughter's health.'

'You do that, dearie, a little splash of cold water will work wonders,' the woman smiles benevolently. 'Thank you. My girl will be just fine. I know it.'

I stare at my ashen reflection in the mirror of the bathroom. Get a grip, you silly cow, you deal with this kind of thing every day. I pull a paper towel from the holder and run it under the cold tap. Breathe, Helen, either way you're going to cope fine with things. Just like you always do. You're the rock of the family, the one that everyone comes to if things need fixing. You're the one who never panics, who keeps a calm mind and thinks things through in an orderly and rational manner. You've got this. Now, for the love of God, stop dicking around in the bogs and take what's coming to you. The little pep-talk works wonders. I take a deep breath and wipe over my face with the wet paper towel. I pinch my cheeks to get some colour back in them. There, that's better, you almost look healthy again. I pull my phone from my bag to check the time, it's just gone five to ten. How on earth can the consultant be running late already. I must only be the second appointment today. I hope that doesn't mean that it's bad news for the lady's relative, because I'm pretty sure the clinic opens at nine, appointments with positive news don't take *that* long. Forgetting about my own issues, I head back out to the waiting area. I should've been more supportive instead of wallowing in my own self-pity. Perhaps that lady approached me because she herself needed someone to talk to. See what I mean? No empathy chip in me at all, I'm surprised I haven't made it to a management position with my ruthlessness. That makes me smile wryly, we nurses constantly bang on about seemingly soulless middle managers, who only appear to care about stats and punting people from their hospital beds. I know it's not necessarily true, but we do love a good bitch about it all on a busy shift.

Right, take back your power, Helen. Go sit out the rest of your wait with the old dear and give her the support she needs. With my many years of experience, I will know the instant that I see her granddaughter's face what the results are.

To my dismay, they've already left. That was extremely selfish of me, being all wrapped up in myself while that poor woman fretted for news on her loved one. The consultant stands in his doorway, looking a little irate at being made to wait.

'Helen Brown?' he sighs gently, as if this is all a major inconvenience to his day. He turns and walks back into the room. I'm just about to follow him in when something catches my eye. A little sprig of white heather sits on the seat that I vacated earlier. The elderly lady must have left it there for me, for luck. I can only imagine that she originally got it for her granddaughter, who then received happy news. She must have decided to pass on her good wishes, now that her loved one no longer needed it. With a smile, I pick up the tiny sprig and glance behind me, down the corridor. I'm so thrilled with this kind gesture. Knowing it was good news for the pair delights me. Now to face my own diagnosis. I scurry forwards into the room and take the seat opposite the oncologist, an icy hand of fear clasping itself around my heart. I daren't breathe until he tells me the news.

Mr Henderson shuffles my notes, completely devoid of any concern that my fate, quite literally, lies in his hands. Finally, he removes his spectacles and looks at me directly. 'Helen, I can conclude that all of your tests have come back negative.'

'Dear God, I'm going to die,' my panic escapes as a high-pitched squeak, my years of medical training and good sense escaping me in the moment.

'Negative good, Helen. You don't have cancer.' He almost smiles, most likely at my stupidity than his delivery of my good news. He doesn't seem to remember me, but I've encountered Mr Henderson a few times during my years of working for the NHS. He's not known for his bedside manner. Nor for having much tolerance towards us in the so-called lower ranks, even though I would class us nurses as the backbone of the hospital, along with the domestics and porters. You wouldn't catch him emptying a bedpan or cleaning a toilet, that's for sure. He's more the hand on brow, pen-pusher type, who's quite happy to let others do the donkey work. Mr Henderson has the weariness of someone who has done this job for far too long and would quite happily retire to the golf course. I know the feeling, minus the golf.

I can't quite believe what I'm hearing. I don't have cancer. Not only is this the best news possible, it's a game-changer for me. A second chance. How long have I been thinking of leaving Steve? Easily going on five years now, around the time that Jenny left for university and Matt changed his mind, yet again, about what to do with his life.

'Do get back in touch with us should you have any further concerns, Helen.'

The oncologist snaps me from my reverie.

'I will. Thank you so much, I can't tell you what a relief this news is, I've barely slept in a week.'

I bid Mr Henderson goodbye and walk down the corridors of The Royal Marsden, looking out in vain for the elderly lady and her granddaughter. I never want to see the inside of this place again. I dearly hope that they won't have to either.

The relief washes over me, as I wait on the bus back to Acton. See, I congratulate myself, you were right not to tell anyone about this. Steve and Matt would have completely freaked. They are most definitely the panicky members of the family. My daughter, Jenny, she's just like me, level-headed and methodical. The girls in our little family of four are tough, we assume things will work out because we feel in control. The boys are the worriers, they crumble under pressure and look for Jenny and me to fix things. My son is a total flake, although he is extremely smart. I was so proud when he went to med school. He made me feel nostalgic for my own training, especially the daft things we had to do like practising injections on an orange. I smile fondly as I remember him telling me that his orange wasn't peeling well, it had got pithed last night. Daft bugger. After a year, Matt quit, without warning or reason. Now, he's had around ten jobs in his twenty-three years and has dropped out of two university courses. I was patient in the beginning, while he found his feet, but this is his last chance. I refuse to fund him through any more. He left behind his dream of becoming a surgeon, declaring that his calling was to be a DJ, in Ayia Napa. Inevitably, he moved back home to save up and practice. The peace of the house was broken with a constant thud of bass from his decks, reverberating through the walls from the bedroom next to mine. His hero of the moment was Eminem, so Matt did the odd stint in a club, as a rapper. God love him, but he wasn't the best at it. His sister referred to him as a "crapper." I remember the great hilarity of Steve and Jenny ripping the piss out of the boy. They would have a new name ready every day, for Matt walking in the door. Steve referred to him as Slim Shitey and Kanye please-shut-the-fuck-up-now. Jenny came up with Dr Nay and The Notorious T.I.T. They would crease up on the sofa as they tried to outdo each other with their latest wisecracks. Poor Matthew, I felt truly sorry for him. He tried to retaliate in the beginning, saying they'd be sorry when he was rich and famous. Jenny just laughed sarcastically.

'Matthew Brown makes number ten thousand in the charts. What a time to be alive.'

I called a halt to it, when he stopped coming into the living room to say hello when he arrived home. He'd head straight up to his bedroom and hide away. I went in to see if he was OK and he looked so disheartened by their behaviour. He told me that he never had private jokes with his father, Steve always seemed to view him as either a laughing stock or a major inconvenience. It was always Daddy's little princess that his father had fun with. On hearing that, I lost the plot with the juvenile pair and stopped the bullying. Daddy's little princess Jenny may be, but nobody fucks with the queen.

So, it stopped, or at least they didn't do it in front of Matt and I any more. For a few more days they still chuckled quietly between themselves, until they got a scary Mum stare from me.

Jenny, on the other hand, is used to doing things and being automatically skilled at them. Matt has always been a little slower in his learning processes. It's lucky that he was the eldest, I'd have hated to see him try and follow any trail that his sister blazed for him. Anyway, he lost confidence in being a rap artist and gave it up, along with his degree. As a back-up to his rapping career, he had been studying Physics, at King's. While I have every patience and actively encourage my children to follow their dreams, I realise now that I may have been a bit lenient with the boy, just because he was the fragile one. Now he's decided to become an artist. A piss artist may be more apt. He considers himself a free spirit, I would now describe him as a workshy lout.

Jenny has always been the sensible one. She always knew she wanted to become an accountant. She hasn't given us much in the way of trouble, other than a seventy-four-hour labour and that pregnancy scare she thinks I don't know about.

With Matt, although he was super intelligent he could often be fairly scatty, as academics often are. I remember us all going out for dinner one night. Steve and Jenny, on perusing the menu, decided it would be hilarious to wind the boy up.

'Hey Dad,' Jenny had that glint in her eye, the one that always spelled trouble.

'Yes, my dear girl,' Steve had replied.

'Did you know that there's an orchestral performance playing up in town next week, by Fettuccine? I thought you'd probably enjoy that.'

'I would indeed, Jenny. I love Fettuccine, as you know. Have you looked into getting tickets?'

'I haven't yet, Dad. Matt, would you be interested in going to see it too?' Jenny asked her brother enthusiastically, with just a soupçon of smug.

'I think your brother is more of a Crostini fan, Jennifer. Isn't that right, son?'

I had just opened my mouth to tell them to stop, but Matt beat me to it.

'Actually, I'm a fan of both of their music, so kindly stop trying to make me look stupid.'

'Matthew,' I said gently. 'They're Italian foods that are on the menu, dear. Take no notice of them.' I glared at the hysterical twosome across the table.

'We're just pulling your pisser, Matt,' Jenny chuckled. 'But in all seriousness, we are going to a Porcini recital, aren't we Dad. You're welcome to come along, Matt. Although, it is a fairly small venue, so there's not mushroom.'

Steve choked on his beer and sprayed it right across the tablecloth. Everyone turned to stare. I was bloody furious with the pair of them.

I raise my head from the laptop, as the roar of Steve's game kicks up again. He's gone from fighting crime for real on the streets of London, to kicking virtual ass on the fifty-inch telly. The one that I paid for and never get to use. Instead, I squint at my soaps from the corner of Matt's old bedroom, on the portable TV that Jenny kindly brought back for me to use. The booster doesn't really work; Steve was going to look at it for me but it's yet another thing he hasn't gotten around to. It had taken me a while to get used to seeing my favourite characters with two heads, but it's funny how I've grown accustomed to it. The urge to escape has been overwhelming me of late, particularly since my cancer scare. There's nothing quite like facing a possible terminal illness to make you feel like you've wasted so much of your time. I couldn't bring myself to tell any of them about the lump I had found. Not Steve, nor the few friends I have. I never wanted to worry my kids either, not that I ever see the reasons I have no pelvic floor, these days. My offspring are way too busy with their own lives. Everyone just carried on, oblivious to my personal trauma. I certainly didn't want to give my husband any reason to be nice to me. Especially not when I was planning to leave him.

In the early days of his time off, I did try to get Steve to do more in the house. I'm not that fussy, even a ready meal would've been a welcome sight after a hard day at work. My husband had once been a fantastic cook, combining ingredients with the confidence and banter of a TV chef. Now he flatly refuses to do any chores. Everything is down to me, from shopping and cooking, to cleaning and laundry. As a result, I'm now at the leave him or kill him stage. I thought things would be so different for us. We spoke about early retirement and dreamt of empty nest syndrome. We envisioned waving to our little darlings from the front door, watching with barely disguised glee, as they crammed all the shit they'd left lying around the house for years into every crevice of their cars. Those same vehicles that we saved up for and bought for them when they first passed their tests. My kids leaving home, it was the stuff of fantasies for me. I love my children to bits, of course, but is there anything wrong with now wanting to love them from a distance? To have something nice to eat left in the fridge the day after a shopping trip? To not have to take a bloody number and join the back of the queue for the bathroom in the morning? I don't think it makes me a bad mother, I've done years of the raising bit. There's a fine line between being supportive and having the piss ripped out of you.

Anyway, off they finally fucked, and I thought this new chapter could draw my husband and I closer. Steve and I even looked at moving abroad, as so many cops seem to go into running bars once they retire. What will the future be like now? Our joint savings are non-existent and I'm effectively enabling him to be a drunken, chain-smoking layabout. A cock-lodger: that's what they'd call him on Mumsnet. I click on to my secret savings account and give a satisfied smile at the balance. I do feel a bit bad about hiding it from my husband, but this is all my own hard-earned cash. I shrug off the tiny pang of guilt nagging at me. The thought of all that money I was squirrelling away warmed me up on those cold, winter mornings, back when I dragged my reluctant arse out of bed at the obscene hour of five in the morning. I'd give Steve's drunken lump of a body a disgusted look, as I passed by what used to be our shared bedroom. He had refused to leave the marital bed and I couldn't bear to be in such close proximity to his noxious, boozy breath. I had no choice but to move out of it in the end, yet even from two rooms away, I could still hear his snoring. I give a shudder of displeasure and turn back to my screen. Fuck it, I've earned all this money, it's not like I've pilfered from our joint savings. He's the one who's drained it with his endless supply of fags and booze. Feeling a little rebellious, I click my laptop lid shut and step into my slippers. Let's see what joys await me in the fridge for dinner.

Without enthusiasm, I throw some pre-packed chicken into a pot. I add a jar of curry sauce and stare blankly at a packet of basmati rice, rotating in the microwave. Like Steve, I too used to take pride in my cooking. Back when the house rang out with my children's laughter and I had a husband who'd sweep in, plant a kiss on my lips, and pour me a glass of wine to say thank you for my efforts. With a sigh, I squeeze my middle area. No appreciative audience means I've put on a couple of stone. I wanted Steve to stay away and he has, it's the one thing he has done well at. The last time the earth moved for us was when we went on holiday to Cuba. It wasn't even the kind you're thinking of, we got caught up in an earthquake. 7.8 on the Richter scale, if I remember correctly. It was back in the days when we still shared a bed, my first thought was that Steve had done one of his pyjama-ripping farts.

'Come and get it,' I yell, slopping the bland goo onto a plate. I pick up my dinner and sit at the table alone, watching the steam rise from Steve's food. We never dine together now. I want to punch him when I watch him eat, that clicking noise his jaw makes as he chews his food, it drives me insane. I shiver with revulsion at the mere thought of it.

Will you look at that; the lazy twat can't even manage to come through for his dinner. A rage builds up inside me. I swear that man would have me breathe in and out for him if it was within my capabilities. I reluctantly get up and carry the plate to him, like a glorified waitress. The living room curtains are closed, despite the gloriously warm, spring day outside. The room smells musty, of stale cigarettes and beer. I wordlessly place the plate on the edge of the sofa. Steve's eyes never leave the screen, nor does he acknowledge my presence with a thank you. I return to the kitchen and pour some white wine into a glass. I wasn't going to drink today, but I swear to God, that man would drive a saint to it. I pick up my own dinner from the table. I'll have it outside on the patio, away from the constant drone of a car chase.

I sit up in bed, and for the umpteenth time today, I stare at the balance on the screen. Seventeen thousand, three hundred and sixty-four pounds. This is the harvest of many extra shifts and almost five years of squirrelling away cash. The second Steve quit his job, I started saving small amounts on pay day. In the beginning it was to afford life's little luxuries for us both. I had a lot of sympathy for his trauma back then, it was a devastating loss that he had suffered. As I saw our joint balance dwindle further, I decided to open an account of my own. My escape fund, that's what I called it. I'd match him pound for pound, on what he spent from our joint finances on booze and fags. It made me feel less helpless, having this secret account. The mortgage, bills and shopping are still covered from our combined savings, but it's quickly being depleted. I log out of my banking app and close the laptop lid. I'm so exhausted and overcome with the relief of my positive diagnosis, that my eyes close like a child's doll, the second I lie down.

At one in the morning, I'm rudely awakened, thanks to one of Steve's late-night music sessions kicking off. We've never shared the same musical taste, so the sudden blast of Whitesnake has just added insult to injury. I stare at the ceiling, trying to control the anger building in me. He is so inconsiderate and it's getting worse by the day. Leaving Steve would end life as we all know it, but I really can't go on any longer. With a few deep inhalations to calm myself, I walk downstairs to talk to him. He's still gaming away, his bloated face red and sweaty, a half empty bottle of whisky sits on the side table. I turn down the music and he gives me an irate tut.

'Hey, do you think you could turn your game off for a moment. I'd like to speak to you.' I take a seat awkwardly on the edge of the sofa.

'Hang on, it's taken me ages to get to this level,' he mutters. I stand and pull open the curtains, pushing the windows out as far as they will go. The mustiness of the room is making me feel queasy, but perhaps that's just what I'm planning to say next.

'Now, Steve.'

'Helen, what the fuck?' My husband throws down his controller and glares at me in disgust. I switch off the TV and sit opposite him.

'I'm leaving you.' When did this strange calmness come over me?

'Don't be stupid, of course you're not leaving me,' Steve gives me a cautious, sidelong glance.

'I'm sick of being the only one working, especially when you do sod all in the house to help out. I've had enough of running around after you, coming home from a shift to make dinner, picking up groceries, doing all the laundry and housework. I can't even sleep without being wakened with your bloody awful taste in music. What must the neighbours think? Some people have work and school to get up for in the morning. I mean it, Steve, I'm done with all your shit. It's over.'

He shakes his head dismissively, struggling to focus on me. 'Fine, I'll keep the music down. That's what you really want, isn't it? God forbid I be allowed to enjoy myself in my own home. Go to bed, Helen, we'll talk in the morning,' he slurs. I'm pretty sure he won't remember any of this tomorrow, but at least I have the silence I need to mull over my decision, as I try to drift off.

'Do it.' Sandra, my next door neighbour, smiles wickedly when I tell her of my plan the next day. We're enjoying the warm, spring day in our local beer garden. It's a favourite hideaway of ours, where we get together and have lunch and a good gossip. No men, no kids, just a couple of perimenopausal women, trying to find the answers in the bottom of a bottle. We may not find them, but it doesn't hurt to have a bloody good look. Sandra pours us another glass from the bottle of Chablis on the table.

'Quite frankly, I'm amazed you haven't left before now,' she shakes her head in disgust. 'Steve has been taking the piss for years, Helen. You've been saying that you're going to leave for over half a decade. Trust me, it's time.'

'Well, Matt was home, on and off,' I shrug. 'I didn't want to put him through the grief, you know how delicate that boy can be. Now he's away again I should make my escape, before his inevitable return.'

'Damn straight,' Sandra lights a cigarette and takes a long drag. 'It's about time both your men stood on their own two feet. You're not a maid, Helen.'

I envy Sandra. My neighbour has the perfect husband. When I arrived on her doorstep at lunchtime, she merely called out to William to ask if she could take off for the afternoon?

'Of course you can, you've had the kids all week,' he'd replied. 'Go and have fun, I'll tire the horrors out down the park later. Don't worry, I'll see to dinner and keep you some aside if you're not home by then,' he'd added with a chuckle. What I wouldn't give to have a Sunday roast cooked for me again, I'd thought nostalgically. It's like farting against thunder arguing the point to get my lump to do anything for me. Somewhere along the line, I just gave up trying.

'You don't think me leaving is a bit hasty?' I grimace, eyeing up Sandra's pack of lights.

'Have one,' she pushes the cigarettes towards me and I quickly shake my head. I quit way back when I found out I was pregnant with Matt, and although times of stress still test me, I'd never start again. One person in my house with disgusting habits is plenty. It's lucky I lead a fairly healthy lifestyle, otherwise we'd be bankrupt by now.

'Helen, how can five years be described as hasty. Even if you just put the wind up him for a couple of months, it would be worth it. It may just give him the rocket up the arse that he needs.'

'Maybe you're right,' I sigh.

'I know I am. Why not just see it as a holiday?' Sandra continues. 'You could tell Steve you're leaving whilst knowing full well that you could come home any time you wanted to, not that you will when you see what's out there waiting for you.'

My stomach flips over with anticipation at the thought of leaving my home. Not Steve, but my home.

I remember the pure joy that I felt when I found our house. I actually squealed when I saw it advertised in the window of the estate agent. The perfect abode to raise our family to be. By the time I'd looked around it, I had visualised exactly how I wanted it. The master bedroom was so large that it had room for an en suite. A smallish nursery, which could one day become an office, once our children had left home. A bigger room for an older child, with both kid's room overlooking the garden, so they'd be nice and quiet. I'd completely remodel the 1980's style kitchen. It even had a gorgeous bay window that I saw a six-foot Christmas tree standing proudly in, with dilapidated homemade ornaments hanging on it, from my children's latest craft project. Life seemed rosy and full of opportunity back then. But we never got around to building an en suite, Matt's room was now mine, and the remodel of the kitchen remained unfinished. The only part of my dream that still occurs is the tree that stands in the bay window, every Christmas.

I look up to see Sandra watching me with concern.

'Come for dinner, Helen. William always makes enough to feed an entire army. We're having roast chicken and his Yorkshires are far superior to mine, although don't tell him I said that.' She blows out a cloud of smoke and jabs her cigarette into the overflowing ashtray.

I smile at my friend gratefully. She's one of those types who never seems to gain weight, regardless of the amount they eat. Her glossy, blonde bob and immaculate dress sense have always made me envious. Goodness knows why she'd want to hang around with a fat, old frump like me. Maybe this *could* be a turning point for me, perhaps I too could get in shape and clean up my act.

A new life, a new me. Steve would shit a brick if I left, but he needs to get back to work and he won't if I continually provide for him.

I awaken early in Matt's old single bed. It's going to be another cracking day. The sunlight streams in through the pale curtains, as I bound over to open the window. Just imagine being somewhere hot and sunny, all by myself, for two whole weeks. I hum tunelessly to myself as I rifle through the wardrobe, mentally ticking off my garments. Too fat, too old, not a stripper. For goodness sake, I really do need to go shopping. Half my wardrobe is older than my firstborn. I pause in my rummaging to think properly about what I'm doing. I sit heavily on the single bed, clutching on to my favourite garment. The pale blue shift dress fit me several years ago, but I'd be unlikely to get it up past my thighs now, let alone zipped. What was it Steve said when I moaned about my weight gain? I remember him glancing at the box of chocolates on my lap.

'What is that old proverb, Helen? Oh yes, abstinence makes the arse grow smaller.'

He had chuckled for ages about that. I had laughed too, but his words stung. I had already been feeling increasingly insecure about my weight gain. I'd dearly love to be one of those people who can't eat when they're under pressure. Instead, I'm a binger. I'll take my stress with a side order of fries, please. Fuck it, stick some cheese and mayo on top while you're at it.

Can I really just up and leave? I'm agency nursing for now, the extra money from a higher hourly rate had been useful, and I was never short of shifts. I never agreed with those nurses who would sign up with agencies. I'd work alongside them in my salaried role, thinking how grabby they were. The NHS isn't exactly loaded and yet we had no choice but to pay more than double, just to fulfil our staffing criteria. Then Steve left his job. I became one of those mercenaries too, as a result. It will have served me well if I do decide I want to make a sharp exit, I only have to give a twenty-four-hour notice period to cancel a shift. Agency staff are ten a penny, my scheduled day of work will be snapped up in minutes, so I needn't feel bad about it. I give up on the wardrobe and chuck on a kaftan, before heading downstairs. At least it hides every one of the lumps and bumps I so detest.

I sit at the breakfast table and absorb everything I can about my home, saving it to my memory. The half-finished kitchen with a few wires sticking out of the wall That was where the under unit lights were supposed to go.

We had workers in to do the main part of the new kitchen install, but Steve had insisted he could finish the rest himself. Why waste money we didn't have? That was many years ago. Irritating myself all over again, my mind turns back to work. Where's the harm in signing off from the agency for now and giving Steve the shake-up he needs? I don't want to dislike my husband, maybe I'll even miss him and we won't split up forever. It could be that with a bit of appreciation towards me, we could rekindle. I give a snort of derision at the thought, I'm extremely doubtful of this. It's not like the kids will even notice I'm gone. When did I last see them? Matt, two months ago when he needed to borrow some money. Jenny, probably Christmas. She sent an apologetic text on both mine and Steve's birthdays. I don't recall that she even sent a card, just one of those e-thingummies. Matt hadn't even sent a text. It was the first time ever that I had received nothing at all on my birthday. Sandra had brought round a card and some chocolates the next day, Steve had horsed into them, leaving only the toffees for me. I discovered this when I got in from my late shift that night and fancied a couple with my bedtime cup of tea. For some reason this creates a rage in me that becomes the deciding factor. Nobody messes with a fat woman's chocolate. I head back upstairs to my laptop, I'm booking a holiday right this second, before I have a chance to bloody well calm down.

Chapter Four
Steve
April 2019

The bitch left me. Helen *actually* bloody well went
and did it. She threatened to go, but then absolutely nothing
more was said about it the next day. I assumed it had all
blown over and that she just needed to rant it out, as usual,
then we'd just go back to how we always are. Then William,
that smarmy twat from next door, knocked to see if she was
ready to leave. I've never liked that idiot; he has zero sense
of humour. For a start he's a bookie, which is akin to being
a crook to me. He told me his occupation when we first met,
at a neighbour's barbeque.
'So, you're a bookmaker? What are the odds of that?' I'd
joked. Nothing. Not even a flicker of a smile. Just a slightly
perplexed and dismissive glance in my direction, while I
stood there laughing like a right twat.
Plus, he lets that wife of his away with murder. She swans
about spending all his cash and won't get a job, even though
their kids are in school all day and they have a Polish au
pair. In some sad, apparent attempt to look as fit as her hired
help, twenty-one-year-old Iwona, Sandra has spent an
absolute fortune on plastic surgery. To the point that when
she dies they won't be able to bury or cremate her, she'll
have to be recycled.
Anyway, I digress. I assumed that Helen was off out with
the pillock from next door and that piss-head wife of his.
Not so, it seemed. I heard a clattering as she brought a case
down from upstairs, and then another.
'Goodbye, Steve.' That's all I got, for twenty-six years of
marriage and two kids. I stood at the bottom of the stairs
and watched her leave. I know I should have begged her not
to go, but I was completely dumbfounded by her departure.
Besides, I wasn't giving that William the satisfaction of
seeing my desperation. Where has she gone? I'm buggered
if I know. Probably just next door so she can get hammered
every night with that Sandra one. I've since checked, she

hasn't touched the joint bank account, so I know it's not a permanent thing. There's no deposit paid for a flat rental, not even a B&B or a hotel has been booked. She'll be back, she's just trying to scare me. Well, it won't work. I'm not even going to text her.

Helen never answered any of my texts. None of them. Not the, "Helen, I'm sorry," one. Nor the, "come home so we can talk about this," one. Not even the one that said, "I'm applying for jobs, right this very second."
I wasn't looking for work, but she doesn't need to know that. Of course, I was aware we'd been drifting apart for a while, but isn't that how all long-term relationships are? No couple I know can maintain that first flush of romance and why would you want to? It's exhausting. We all gradually slide into a settled routine, it's perfectly normal. Expected even. Sure, I haven't been too attentive, but it's been that way for years and she's never moaned about it before. My quip that marriages were like a three-course meal, with the pudding at the start, probably didn't help. Considering she knows that dessert has always been my favourite. The thought of food makes my stomach give an urgent rumble. That's it, I'm calling next door. There's nothing in the fridge and I'm not able to go down to the supermarket. The very thought of driving the length of the high street gives me chills. The phone rings out for several minutes, they must have caller ID, and I can almost hear Helen urging them to ignore it. I hang up and call my daughter. I know she will help her old Dad out. There's no answer from Jenny, so I try the boy wonder. I'm just about to hang up when I hear his familiar grunts.
'Matt, hey son. I half expected you to be in uni.'
'Er, no, Dad. I'm uhh…I'm actually having a rethink about what I want to do for a career. I don't think I'll make enough money as an artist.'
'Well, they do reckon they're only rich after they die,' I give a forced laugh.

Part of me is furious that he's dropped out, yet again, the other part is relieved that he can be on hand to help me out. I can't be pissed off at him or he'll flat out refuse to do anything for me. He never quite got over the tantrum stage and requires delicate handling.

'Thanks, Dad. I knew you'd understand,' I hear a smile in his voice. He sounds partied out, a little stoned too, if I'm not mistaken.

'Have you heard from your mum?' I try to sound nonchalant in my enquiry.

'Nah, I'm still owe her money so I'm avoiding her calls. Don't tell her I've quit again; she'll drop a bollock. I want to have something lined up before I speak to her. You know what she's like.'

'Well, your mother has gone away for a few days so I wouldn't worry about that.'

'Where has she gone?' Matt sounds aghast that his mother would dare venture further than the back green to hang out the washing.

'Just a little break is all she told me,' I lie. 'Thing is, son, I'm going to need some shopping fetched for me.'

'Aw, Dad. Can't you just pop down to Morrisons? My car is in the garage and it'll take me an hour to get to yours, what with the rail replacement. I really should be looking into new courses.'

I have long suspected that this car of Matt's has been sold off to fund his rather dubious lifestyle choices. It's been three months since it allegedly went into the garage.

'Never mind, I'll ask your sister. I'll speak to you later, Matthew.'

Since he's refusing to help me out, I decide to take a more authoritarian role. 'By the way, your only option now is to get a job. You know fine well that your mother said you were on your last warning with uni. As you'll no longer be a student, we'll be renting your great-nan's flat out again.' I hang up the phone, feeling a sense of one-upmanship. That'll teach the work-shy lout to take the piss out of me and Helen. I try Jenny a few more times, then give up and look in the freezer. Settling on some unidentified item in an old Chinese takeaway tub, I chuck it in the microwave to defrost. I peer out of the kitchen window looking for signs of my errant wife. She's on a day off and the sun is splitting the sky, why aren't they sitting out the back of Sandra's house with a bottle of wine? That woman next door has far too much to say about me. I've overheard her on numerous occasions, hissing to Helen that she really shouldn't put up with my shit. I don't think it's any coincidence that Helen leaving has come just after one of their boozy, pub lunches. She's poisoned my wife's mind against me and has interfered in things that are absolutely none of her business. I distractedly watch the two lots of builders across the street, working on neighbouring houses. They've been a great source of entertainment to me recently. I see them sometimes from the bedroom window, fighting over parking spaces for their trucks. It's a narrow street and there's not a lot of room for cars, let alone large work vehicles. Builders on opposing sides: Brixit, that's what I'd dubbed it. I thought that was a clever joke with an amusing political reference, it didn't even crack a smile on Helen's miserable face. I may as well try her mobile again. I strain to hear for it through the wall to next door, over the pneumatic drills. It rings out and I hear nothing at all from the neighbouring house. She's probably put it on silent. The microwave gives a cheerful ping and I head over to see what my surprise dinner will be. Apple crumble, what a bonus. I search the cupboard for some custard and pour the entire tin over the top. That's it. There's nothing else now, even the freezer is empty. Jenny has no choice but to go shopping for me tonight.

I sat up until three in the morning finishing the last of my beers. As usual, I fell asleep on the sofa. Normally, I'd awaken around six in the morning, but it seems I'd only just dropped off when I woke with a sudden jolt. A loud noise outside makes me sit up sharply. Shit, just what Helen has always warned me about, I had a lit cigarette dangling precariously from my fingers. Another loud clatter in the front garden sets me on edge. I stub out my cigarette and head carefully over to the window, adrenaline coursing through my body. Who the fuck is outside? I peel back an edge of curtain and look cautiously around. A fox and its mate jump over the wall and take off down the street.

'Bloody things,' I mutter to myself, before realising they probably just saved my life. I need to be more careful with my cigarettes, I can't have Helen being right. I envisage her ranting at my cold, lifeless body, from six feet above. This makes me chuckle, but I'm secretly more than a little ashamed of myself. That's it, no more smoking whilst lying on the couch. I clearly can't be trusted to stay awake long enough to extinguish it. I sit heavily back in my seat. I'm too wide awake to even consider sleep now. Maybe I'll have a whisky.

I'm disorientated when I waken again at one in the afternoon. I'm in bed but I don't remember getting here. My head thuds, I vaguely remember hitting the hard stuff in the early hours. It all goes blank after the first double measure. I glance at the half empty bottle on the night stand, that had started off unopened. Even by my standards that's a pretty hefty session.

My daughter eventually graced me with a call back, she says she will pop over today with a shop for me. She's the only one who really understands, I know I'm lucky to have her. I've emailed her a list and I'm now sat eagerly in front of my game, awaiting her arrival.

I know you probably think by now that I'm some kind of lazy misogynist, but you couldn't be further from the truth. I haven't even told Helen the full extent of how things have affected me. Since I lost my partner, just over five years ago, I've been off work with stress. Luke and I had been partnered up for nine months, he was a lovely lad and had a brilliant sense of humour. He was going to go far in the force, I always had a good feel for the ones who'd climb the ladder. We had a call out, to what we thought was a disturbance of the peace. These are usually pretty straightforward as shouts go. Luke was a confident boy and you'd be forgiven for thinking he had way more experience that he really did, but Luke was still a rookie cop. I failed in my duty to protect him during what turned into a drug related arrest. He was fatally stabbed at the scene. Unable to forgive myself, I went off on the sick. Helen couldn't have been more understanding back then, she made a huge fuss of me and made sure I didn't lift a finger. Then, when six months had passed, she started to make noises about me getting back out there. My bosses had been great, giving me full pay and counselling, until even they too reckoned I should be fit to go back to work. That's when I quit the force and Helen went absolutely ballistic. I'd lost my partner and all she cared about was not affording some bloody holiday home she wanted. Home is forever in the ground now, for that young lad, he wasn't much older than our Matt. Helen's comments did not sit well with me. I think back to that horrific day, which is something I don't let myself do often. There had been an incident at a nearby tube station, a woman had reportedly fallen down an escalator. Someone had called an ambulance and the police had arrived on the scene too, for crowd control purposes. I was so fortunate that there was back-up close by. I hate to think what would have happened if I'd had to tackle that knife-wielding maniac alone, I probably wouldn't be here either. The guilt festers in the pit of my stomach. For experience, Luke had wanted to take the lead role and I had actively encouraged him. We had no idea the guy had a knife in his back pocket. He moved so fast. I saw the glint of metal and I tried to get to Luke. I was only a few feet away from him but it was too far. I was too late.

The sound of a key in the lock gratefully distracts me from my thoughts.

'Helen? Is that you?' My voice echoes strangely in the empty house.

'It's me, Dad.' Jenny stands in the living room doorway, laden down with carrier bags. 'Where's Mum?'

Where's Mum? That's all I ever sodding hear from these kids.

'She's gone away for a few days.'

'What do you mean she's gone away? She never said.' Jenny's pretty face creases into a frown. She looks so like her mother did at that age. The shoulder length, black hair with the too long fringe. The huge, brown, Bambi eyes. She's skinny like Helen was too. Although Helen filling out a bit didn't concern me at all, I know it really bothered her. She'd had two kids and often had no choice but to eat whatever crap she could get out of the dispenser at work. I'd always tried to lighten the mood with a few well-placed jokes, just to show her I didn't care about how she looked. She would laugh, but it never really seemed to help raise her spirits or her self-esteem. That Sandra one never helped either, prancing about in her bikini in the back garden, the second the thermometer hit double figures. A woman being that skinny isn't attractive to most men, but try as I might, Helen would never believe that her curves made her way sexier than that Sandra could ever hope to be. After having the kids, Helen was never a big drinker, until *she* moved in next door. I cannot stand that insufferable woman, with her fake tan and HD brows. She looks for all the world like Crash Bandicoot, from that PlayStation game Matt and I used to be obsessed with.

'Your mother just said she needed some time out. I don't know where she's gone, love.'

'That doesn't sound like Mum,' Jenny gives a scornful laugh. 'Oh, my God, she's not having an affair, is she?'

I look up sharply. This hadn't occurred to me. Surely Helen wouldn't do that, would she? She has been prattling on about some doctor at work. One that she knew from years ago and had run into again, whilst doing the rounds of the hospitals with that agency. She blushed a little when she said his name. Forbes, was it? I wish I'd listened now. I was concentrating on my game at the time, it was a really tricky bit. I'd made a few noises and had hoped they were the right ones.

'No, of course she's not having an affair. I'm sure it's just a little break from work that she needs. She'll be back before we know it.'

'OK, I'll try and call her later. Dad, you couldn't check my tyres for me, could you? One of them seems a bit flat.'

This is just an excuse to get me to leave the house. My daughter tries it often. I frantically think of a reason why I can't, settling on my pressure gauge being busted. Jenny gives a shrug and says she'll pop into the petrol station on her way home. She heads off to the kitchen and I hear her putting my groceries away in the fridge and cupboards. I follow her through, aching for some company. It's not like Helen and I talked much, but it was comforting to hear the sounds of someone else around. Our home has been lacking that since she went away, it's been eerily quiet and I've never enjoyed staying on my own.

'Oh, what's this you got me? That looks fancy.'

'It's dauphinoise potatoes, it'll go lovely with the lamb chops,' Jenny smiles.

'Toffee-nosed potatoes? My goodness, that is posh.'

'Dau-phin-oise, Dad.' Jenny gives a chuckle and nudges me in the ribs.

'Why don't you stay over? You've bought enough food for an army here.'

The edge of urgency in my voice unnerves me slightly. I sound pathetic.

'Sorry, Dad, I can't. I have a date tonight,' she wrinkles her nose in that cute way she did as a toddler, giving my heart a nostalgic squeeze.

'Do you now. Is this fellow good enough for my daughter? What does he do?' My heart sinks at the thought of another night alone.

'He's an accountant too, he just started at the firm last week,' she smiles

wistfully, blushing a little. I feel a ball of anger in my stomach. I know it's a typical Dad response, but he won't be good enough, he'll only be after one thing. Plus, every father wants to think he's the only man his daughter will ever love.

'Right, I'd better be off, the traffic is shocking tonight. Do you want these carriers or shall I take them away for next time? Look, I even splashed out and got you a bag for life.'

'I got one of those when I married your Mum,' I wink at my youngest and she suppresses a smile.

'I'm totally telling on you for that. Dad, you'll be OK, won't you?' My daughter gives me a concerned look, the one that all of them gave me when I was first signed off work.

'I'll be fine. You're a good girl. Thank you, Jenny-henny.'

She chuckles at my use of her childhood nickname. My son's had been Bat-Matt. He was obsessed with superheroes as a kid. We had great hopes that he would eventually grow out of his fantasy world. We still do, actually.

'Well, if you're sure,' she's already pulling on her coat. She doesn't want to hang out with her old man, not when she has a hot date with this dirty accountant fellow. I wave my daughter off from the bay window, watching as she kicks her tyre and hoping she'll make it to the garage safely. I head back to the fridge and take out one of the ready meals Jenny bought for me. I choose a beef stew with dumplings, and crack open a beer.

Still no word from Helen this morning and I've left three voicemails. She hasn't even answered her daughter's call. Jenny phoned her mother last night when she got home, just before she checked in with me. I tried to ignore the background sounds of a cork popping and the girlish squeal she gave, like that creep was tickling her. It's far too soon to have him round at hers, or for her to be at his house. That can only mean there's one thing on his mind. My face flames. I remember back to when Jenny was sixteen and desperately wanted a tattoo. She needed parental consent at that age and I said she could only get one if it was a picture of me on her thigh, waving a threatening fist at any man daring to want to go any further. Unsurprisingly, she declined. By eighteen, she had grown out of the idea. By her late teens, my daughter's way of rebelling was to be as straight-laced as possible. She would react scornfully to us badly behaved elders, deigning to have a glass of wine with dinner at the weekend. I miss the days when my daughter acted like a prim, maiden aunt. She wouldn't have entertained that creep back then, that's for sure. I drag my thoughts from some geezer manhandling my youngest, to ponder on reporting Helen as missing. It's a bit of a myth that you have to wait twenty-four hours, and being an ex-cop, they'll probably take me more seriously and pull a few strings. It'll have the added bonus of making her sit up and take notice. I type out a quick text to her, declaring my intentions. I've even checked her Facebook page and there have been no updates since last week. No tags or check-ins to anywhere either. My phone buzzes and I make a grab for it, narrowly missing spilling my coffee. It's a text from Matt, looking to borrow yet more money. Ignoring my son, I type out another message to my wife.

"Where are you, Helen? I've contacted the police now and they're making enquiries. The kids are worried and need their Mum."

Perhaps I should have said that I need her too, but my pride won't allow it. She should be back at work tomorrow, I think, although I can't remember which hospital she's scheduled to be in. She's all over the place with that agency. Damn it, why do I never listen to her. I check the side of the fridge for a work schedule. She usually keeps it stuck there, under the magnet of a pair of flip-flops that we picked up in Tenerife. She must have taken it with her when she left. I sit at the computer and try to log in to Helen's email account. She gets the schedule sent to her from the agency and always prints off a breakdown of her next week's shifts. I try a variety of names of long-gone pets, her maiden name plus birth year, the word "password," in both lower and upper case. JennyMatthew, MatthewJenny, jennymatt, mattjenny. Nothing works. I glance at the clock; it's not even lunchtime and I'm thinking about when it will be acceptable to have a beer. I click onto the Met Police website and scroll through the information available to the public. Just looking at the familiar uniform makes my stomach flip over. All these smiling pics of cops, looking like it's the best job in the world and they couldn't be safer. Well, I had loved my job and so had Luke, which ended with that young man in the ground and me with a crippling anxiety disorder. Don't get me wrong, they do amazing work and they do their utmost to support and protect their staff. I just think that had I known what was in store for me and my partner, I may not have chosen that career after all. I can never forgive myself for what happened to him and the nightmares haunt me to this day. His parents and brother came to meet me. It was kind of them, they assured me that they knew I had done everything that I possibly could to save him. They said he died a hero, and that I was one too. They said I should go on in Luke's honour and stop the kind of criminals who would deign to take another person's life.

Fuck, I felt like such a fraud. Apart from trying to stem the blood flow from Luke's wound and calling for back up, I really didn't do much. I'd yelled at the crowd around us to step back, to take descriptions of the perpetrator and the registration of any vehicle he got into. It was thanks to a member of the public, who did just that, that he was arrested. Nothing to do with me, I just put that poor lad in the line of fire. Washing Luke's blood off that evening was the hardest thing I've ever had to do in my life. I felt physically sick as I watched it flow from my body and down the plug hole of the shower. How could I go back to work after that? I slipped on a t-shirt and some sweatpants and they became my new uniform. Then I poured the mother of all whiskies and sank deeply into the bottle, and a funk of a depression. That first night, Helen actively encouraged me to have a drink, she said it would help with the shock. How ironic that she now looks at me with disgust when I pour one up.

Despite my many happy years on the force, I know that Luke may have been alive today with a different cop in a supportive role. Not someone like me, a coward. The guilt kicks in once more and I feel my breath quicken with panic. I hastily click back to Helen's email page. After a few more tries at guessing her password, I give up and head downstairs. I can't believe she would just up and leave me like this, knowing full well that I can't look after myself. The former panic I felt is replaced with anger. Really, how could Helen do this to me? I'm practically an invalid, I can't go outside, shop, or do anything for myself anymore. I don't even know who our energy or broadband suppliers are. She has dealt with everything, for over five years. Helen is a nurse; she's supposed to have a caring attitude towards sick and vulnerable people. What a joke that's turned out to be. Just fuck off when things get tough, why don't you?

That's it, she's made me need a drink now. It's all her fault that I need to start early today.

Chapter Five
Helen

My signal returns and my phone gives an irate beep, announcing the arrival of a voicemail. I type in my passcode and listen to the message.

'Mum, it's me, Jenny. Where are you? We're all really worried. I got Dad some shopping in today and he looked dreadful. Come home, Mum. There's nothing we can't sort out. Love you, bye.'

I click to save my daughter's message and play the next one.

'Mum, where are you? You can't just up and leave us all. How's Dad going to cope without you? Call me as soon as you get this.' Matt has that wheedle in his voice that he had as a toddler. It was cute then, on a grown man it just sounds a bit pathetic. My son has always been very full of his own self-importance.

'Mummy, me can't do it by mines self.'

It flashes back into my memory, that little boy, clinging to my leg and looking up at me with those chocolate button eyes. God, he was cute, but I feel now that I made him too reliant on me. Jenny was little miss independent, there was nothing she thought she couldn't do for herself. Steve and I pretty much permitted Matt to be that way, helping him put on his shoes and tidy his toys away. He was our first and I was terribly overprotective, I'm sure it's why he's like he is now. Still looking for someone, usually me, to bail him out. Steve and I had tried to chat to him after he last quit his so-called lifetime's dream. I took the gentler role as usual, telling him that we loved and supported him and wanted him to be happy. I told him that we appreciated he was confused about his future, but that it really was time to think about getting his ducks in a row. Steve lost it at that point.

'What ducks? He doesn't have any fucking ducks. He's probably not only expecting us to buy him some, but to organise them for him too. Get your head out of your arse,

Matthew, for all our sakes.' With that Steve had stormed out of the room and I heard him clattering in the drinks cabinet.

'Pot, kettle,' Matt had sniffed disdainfully.

I'm afraid I had to agree with my son on that.

My phone buzzes again, a text this time.

"Mum, I'm skint and Dad hasn't got back to me. I know I'm still owe you money but can I borrow another twenty?"

I tut irately at my son's message. He's clearly got over his earlier concern of my whereabouts and has crawled back up his own arse again. Maybe I shouldn't have always played good cop to Steve's bad one. We really should have stood united. I type out my reply.

"Matthew, I will not be giving you any more handouts. Sort your bloody self out, son. I'm having a bit of time away, that's all you need to know. Keep it to yourself, you need not concern your father with my affairs."

There, that's told him. I ignore the text messages from Steve about calling the police. He wouldn't dare waste police time, nor would he face the humiliation of anyone on the force knowing that I've left him.

'So, Sir, your wife has gone missing? Yet she packed took two suitcases and told you your marriage was over?'

They wouldn't take that seriously in the slightest. The fact that he thinks I'm stupid enough to believe that nonsense just irritates me. He's making desperate, pathetic attempts to get me to come back. I don't care, I refuse to enable him anymore.

I head through the baggage check-in to passport control. I'm annoyed with myself for switching my phone back on again. I already need some respite from the shitstorm that has ensued by me leaving. I've been away for little more than twenty-four hours and those who have had no interest in me for days, weeks even, suddenly have this great urgency to know where I am and what I'm doing. I ignore the further phone beeps and switch my phone back off. It was only more messages coming in from Steve. This time is all about me and I have no need to communicate with those back home, unless it's a dire emergency.

I enjoy the tranquillity of the flight. The attentiveness of the air stewards makes me feel like royalty. I'm so used to pandering to the needs of my patients and family, that it's lovely to have a bit of me time and spoiling. I smile into my glass of wine and look out from my window seat, stretching out my legs and congratulating myself on the sheer luck of asking for extra leg room, and getting it. There are some added bonuses of travelling alone. Who knew? Through the clouds I can see the stunning blue sea. This was a great idea, a two week chill out, just me and my audiobooks. I have so many that I've intended to get around to listening to, but I just never seem to have the time. Every day that I'm away, I intend to sleep until I waken naturally, before relaxing by the pool or on the beach. I will eat out every evening without quibbling over which restaurant to choose, and go sightseeing to places that interest only me. Peace and solitude, for fourteen whole days. I really can't wait.

I spent a few hours shopping for holiday clothes yesterday, floaty sundresses for evening, swimsuits and wraps for daytime. I really enjoyed my little spending spree. For so many years I thought I'd never see an end to the constant saving. When the alarm went off at five, on those chilly, winter mornings, it almost seemed a pointless exercise. As if one day I'd end up having to dip into in it anyway, for bills or to pay the mortgage. It wasn't until yesterday that it actually felt like mine. I could buy what I wanted, rather than critically looking at the price tag and deciding if I could justify paying the price. I got a gorgeous sundress from Monsoon, which was an eye-watering seventy-five quid. I would never have dreamt of going into that shop before, knowing it's a bit pricy, especially when I could get four dresses for the same cost in Primark. But I saw it in the window and loved the floaty, seventies style, tie-dye effect. It skimmed forgivingly over my generous shape; I could almost feel my confidence growing by the second. For once I was selfish. I bought the dress and smiled warmly at the pretty and well-dressed salesgirl, as if me being in Monsoon was a normal, weekly occurrence. Even better, when she told me there was ten per cent off everything this week, I ran back and got the hippy style, slouchy bag that I'd been eyeing up too. It felt good to be kind to myself for once. I got quite a buzz out of only considering me, for once. My skinny size ten days may be long gone, but I turned a blind eye to the label on my new clothing. Who cares, I'm happy. Most importantly, thanks to my recent all clear, I'm *healthy*. One day I'll have the whole of eternity to be a size zero.

The heat hits me immediately, as I step out the front of the airport. I've never been to Greece before but I've always fancied visiting. Steve doesn't like the sun so much, although he hasn't left the house since he went off sick anyway. If I hadn't been temping all over London, I doubt I'd have even made it out of Acton in all that time. My husband has needed so much careful supervision lately, many a time an eerie feeling has come over me whilst I've been lying in bed. On occasion, it's even woken me. It's almost like I'm being watched, something unseen urging me to get up and see if everything is OK. Every time I've gone to check on him, I've caught him passed out drunk with a burning cigarette dangling from his fingers. I shake off the heebie-jeebies and the image of that scenario unfolding, without me there to stop it. I had lost out on a much higher rate of pay by turning down night duties, just to make sure I was on call at home when the danger times would occur. As the drinking sessions crept earlier into the day, even a late shift became a problem. I half turn back towards the airport. This is a ridiculous idea. I think of the minister's words on our wedding day: for better, for worse, in sickness and in health, until death do us part. I'm dismissing the vows I once took so seriously.
'Taxi?' A tanned gentleman with a shirt unbuttoned almost to his navel, points towards his cab.
I can't go back. All I will have achieved is wasting a ridiculous amount of money on flights and the hotel

reservation. Sandra and William always hear our smoke alarm. There have been several occasions when they've knocked to see that we were OK, when all that was to blame was my lousy cooking skills. Anyway, I need this time for my sanity. Why should I feel responsible for a grown man who should be capable of caring for himself?

'St. George South, please.' I smile broadly as the rather fit looking driver takes my cases.

I lay on the sun lounger in my one-piece swimsuit. There's no way I'd be brave enough to wear a bikini, not at my age and weight. I had checked myself over critically in the hotel mirror. The supportive bra and stomach flattening panel, that was advertised, has not in the slightest bit kept its side of the deal. I think enviously of Sandra; her size eight figure was made for a bikini. She would often invite me to sit in the hot tub with her and enjoy a glass of wine. I couldn't bring myself to do it, not next to her. Especially since that summer day I saw Steve glancing out the window at her, he was probably thinking how unfair it was that he ended up with the chubby wife. I certainly didn't need to give him a side by side comparison, in glorious, pissed up, technicolour. Thanks to my looming menopause, the slightest bit of heat turns me bright red. Combine that with alcohol, and I look like a little, fat baby beet. No, there are some things even a husband of twenty-six years doesn't need to see.

I take a sip of my colourful cocktail. I can't remember the last time I felt this relaxed. The sound of the waves soothes my mind and my cheeky afternoon tipple emboldens the fear of being here alone. There are no kids around as it's term time. Not that I would have minded watching the little ones enjoy themselves, seeing them build their dilapidated sandcastles and have a paddle in the sea. Although, there's something about the nurse in me, or perhaps the mother, that makes me feel constantly on duty around children. It's like I've never been able to fully relax since I had my own two.

The agency had been fine with my so-called personal emergency when I called.

'Oh dear, is there anything we can do to help, Helen?' The gossipy secretary had said with mock concern. I thanked her kindly and said that everything would be just fine. Never trust someone who discloses information to you, they will most certainly be telling others all about you. She had tried to dig a little more, but I was giving her nothing. I just knew it would be all over the office, moments after the call had been disconnected.

I hear a kerfuffle a little along the beach and sit up to see what's occurring. For years now, Steve has used his fear of terrorism as an excuse not to go away. You weren't safe wherever you went, that was his opinion. It kind of stuck in my head, although I'm not usually a nervous type. I see some youngsters a little further along from me, messing about. I say youngsters but they're probably not much off the age of my two. They sound drunk already, although it's only early afternoon. Oh dear, knowing my luck I'll have booked a hotel filled with club eighteen to thirty sorts. I read a few reviews online, I thought all the rowdy resorts were over in Kavos.

Despite numerous attempts to switch off my mind, my thoughts turn back to Steve. Life seemed so full of promise when we first got together, I really thought I had found my soulmate. I didn't immediately fancy him; he was a slow burner to begin with. It wasn't until he got his hair cut short that I finally noticed how good looking he was. It's funny how when you're not attracted to someone, their flirtatious behaviour makes them seem like a creep. Suddenly, when you're into them, the exact same things they were doing before makes them appear attentive and romantic. Can I fancy Steve again? It'll take more than a bloody haircut this time, that's for sure. He used to make me laugh so much. He was shy the first night we went out. We were at that Indian place down by Piccadilly, if I remember right. On our second date he cooked for me at his nan's flat, the one that

Matt now lives in, currently rent free because he's a student. I had walked into the rich aroma of lasagne, Steve's signature dish. He had poured me a glass of red wine and seemed very at home in the kitchen. My new boyfriend seemed so grown up and sophisticated. The fact that he had his own place impressed me no end. He had a stack of bills with dates on them; when they were due and when they were paid. His home smelled fresh and clean, with laundry catching the last of the light, out on the line. Not sheets, pillowcases, and a duvet cover, that would have really pissed me off. It would seem as if he was hoping to get lucky and changed his bedding in anticipation. Women notice things that many men would be oblivious to. No, the washing on the line was just everyday stuff: boxers, t-shirts and pyjama bottoms. I liked that he appeared to have no agenda, nothing was hidden from his normal, everyday life. He had kitchen utensils I'd never seen before, they looked more like some kind of torture implement, or something I'd use for a medical procedure at work. This man was mature, he knew how to take care of himself and that made me smile. It meant he could take care of me too. He made me come over all Vivien Leigh, in *Gone with the Wind*. I'd found a proper grown up, at last. Not like any of those other guys I'd dated, who still lived with their parents and threw a strop if their mother dared ask that they bring their laundry down. One mum even told me to make sure I didn't marry her son, as he was a lazy shit who couldn't even run the loo brush around the toilet after he'd used it, or clean his hair out of the plug hole. It's difficult to fancy someone again once you've heard things like that. Particularly in the very early days.

Steve had proper artwork on his wall. Not some scantily clad, young woman with nipples like rivets, pouting suggestively down from a poster. No, he had classy prints, water colours, and family photographs on his walls. He turned back to his cooking and I surreptitiously ran a finger along the shelf above me. There was not a speck of dust. This man made *me* look slovenly. I glanced away sheepishly, as I saw Steve suppressing a smile in the reflection of the window. Dammit, he caught me good there. Like a true gent, he said nothing. He just reached into a nearby cupboard and handed me a bar of chocolate.

'This is in case I get flustered and run out of things to say tonight. I'm naming this the "Topic" of conversation. Feel free to use it too.'

He'd smiled and blushed a little, when I laughed.

'I know, it's a silly idea. I just thought it would be a bit of fun,' he'd shrugged.

'Actually, I think it's genius,' I had smiled benevolently. 'It's my favourite chocolate bar too. You'd maybe best hide it.'

After that, whenever we fell out, one or the other of us would turn up, Topic bar in hand, as a making up gift. The year we went to see *Basic Instinct* at the cinema, our gift graduated to an ice pick. He had refused to tell me the relevance and it drove me bonkers for two weeks. I'd startled him in the middle of the night when it occurred to me why.

'It's an ice breaker,' I'd shrieked.

I started to get his humour, so I hadn't been flummoxed when he'd come home with a cheese and pickle sandwich, after another fall out. His nan being Scottish, he used a lot of her funny little words.

'Is this a "peece" offering,' I had smiled.

I sit up in alarm, as a sudden shout along the beach pulls me abruptly from happier thoughts of my past. Something in the urgency of one of the young women's voices unsettles me, she's repeatedly calling a name that I can't quite make out. Then I see a girl around my daughter's age, slumped over on the sand, her friends crowding around her urgently. I climb awkwardly out of my lounger to get a better look. I probably resemble a badly set blancmange: all boobs, arse and wobbly thighs. But somehow I'm up and running towards her, in a most inelegant manner.

'Can everyone move aside, please,' I say breathlessly. In what I hope sounds like an authoritative, matronly voice. I crouch down in the sand and take the young woman's pulse. It has striking similarities to that of a startled hamster's.

'Has she taken anything? Drugs or alcohol?' I glance around at the sheepish faces of the group. 'You won't be in any trouble; I just need to know so I can make a proper diagnosis.'

'She's only been drinking,' one of the young men volunteers. 'We all have, we're on holiday, innit.'

'Tell me how you're feeling,' I remove the girl's sunglasses and peer into her reddened eyes.'

'Like I'm gonna hurl,' she says weakly.

'What's your name? How old are you?'

'Millie. I'm twenty-one. Well, I will be tomorrow. That's why we're here.'

Her friends acknowledge the information as correct, with a few nods. She's fine, they're starting to lose interest now and a few are indicating towards the bar. The invincibility and irresponsibility of the young. I give an irate tut, but I vaguely remember being the same, once upon a time.

'Have you eaten? Had any fluids today that aren't alcohol?' I enquire, trying not to sound too judgemental.

'No, we had shots for breakfast,' she gags a little.

'Woah!' her friends give a collective chorus of warning and take a step back in anticipation.

'OK, Millie. I think you could be dehydrated, with possible heatstroke. We need to get you to hospital so they can get you sorted out.'

A shadow falls over me. I glance up to see a man in around his early fifties, watching on with concern.

'I saw what was happening from a little way along the beach there. Would you like me to call an ambulance?' he says in a soft Irish accent.

'Yes, if you wouldn't mind.' I smile my appreciation. It's then that it hits me: a projectile stream of vomit. It's certainly not the first time I've encountered this, but the crowd gasp in horror.

'Shit, I'm so sorry.' The young woman retches again.

'It's fine, love. Don't you worry, I'm a nurse and a mother. You're not the first to pebbledash me and you certainly won't be the last. Removing all that alcohol from your system has probably just saved you a stomach pump. Every cloud and all that...' I smile gently at the girl, stroking back her hair from her clammy face. One of the young woman's friends arrive back from the beach bar, with a bottle of water.

'Thank you, dear.' I accept the bottle from the girl. 'Take tiny sips, Millie,' I advise. 'It's important that this stays down and gulping will only upset your stomach further.'

'Maybe clean you up a bit though...' she gives a hoarse chuckle.

With a proper grown up in charge, some of the friends begin to drift away from us. I give them a disappointed shake of the head, the one I once reserved for tantrums and poor school reports. Matt's of course, never Jenny's. I help Millie into the shade and sit down next to her, taking her pulse and respirations every couple of minutes. A few concerned friends follow on, including a guy that seems to fancy her. She tells me this information in a whisper. She starts to settle down a bit and we chat about her holiday and birthday celebrations. She confides that she's not a big drinker, but has been trying to keep up with the others in order to look cool. Now they'll all know what a lightweight she really is. I try to reassure her that alcohol is a poison, that it's natural for the body to want to expel it.

We hear a short burst of a siren, as an ambulance parks up. Two paramedics rush towards the small remaining group of us. That was quick. I'm used to things taking five times as long back in London. The amount of rush hours I've sat and fretted, with a blue light in my rear view mirror, stuck in a line of traffic with nowhere to go. It's such a dreadful, helpless feeling, and one reason why I prefer to take the tube to work when I can. The medics arrive on the beach and help Millie to her feet. I give them the lowdown and watch as what's left of her crowd of friends follow on behind her, intrigued by the drama. I stand up as dignified as one can in a rather revealing outfit, discreetly trying to simultaneously tuck in a buttock and a rogue boob, that are trying to make their escape.

'Good work there, are you a doctor?' The Irish man had been sat a little away from us. His blue eyes crinkle with amusement, as I look in horror at my hands, now covered in the young lady's stomach fluid.

I smile benevolently at my imaginary promotion. Men usually assume that other men are doctors and women are in nursing.

'I'm a staff nurse,' I smile. 'It's been a while since I've been vomited on, I was long overdue that one. Sorry, I haven't introduced myself. I'm Helen.'

'Tom,' smiles the man, holding out a hand for me to shake, before quickly pulling it back on seeing the state of mine. 'I guess formalities can wait. Are you here on holiday?'

'I am indeed. It's only my first day here and I'm already one swimsuit down,' I laugh, instinctively covering my near nakedness as he glances at the state of my costume. 'Anyway, I think I'll head back to my room for a shower. It was nice to meet you, Tom.'

I head back up the beach with my belongings, displaying all the elegance of a cart-horse and feeling extremely self-conscious at the thought of being watched. I don't mean to be rude to anyone, but I don't particularly want to get involved with niceties and making friendships on this trip. I'm here to think about the state of my marriage, and I most certainly don't need any interruptions in the process. Decisions need to be made. Despite being covered in vomit, thanks to the sunshine and a cocktail, I do already feel like a weight has been lifted from me.

Chapter Six
Steve

Helen has been seeing other men. Thanks to Matt, I've had confirmation of this now. I had initially dismissed Jenny's question about her mother's fidelity as ridiculous, of course my wife wouldn't cheat on me. Not only from a moral point of view but where on earth would she find the time? It turns out I was wrong. It wasn't just the one indiscretion either, she actually admitted it in a text message to her own son. I can't believe the bare-faced cheek of her.
"Keep it to yourself, you need not concern your father with my affairs."
That's exactly what Helen said. Cold, heartless words, and to her own child too. I pop a piece of gum in my mouth to hide the strong smell of whisky. I need to speak to that Sandra sort, next door. Although it's none of her business if I fancy a lunchtime drink, I don't need her judgment. She always makes that face when she sees me, the one where her mouth resembles a cat's arse. She gives me that look any time I have the misfortune to catch her eye. I know *she* drinks in the day too; I've seen her sat out on their patio on sunny weekend afternoons.
'Why would it be OK on a Saturday or Sunday, but not on a Monday?' I mutter defensively to myself as I head to the door. But she's just the type to have double standards like that.
The strong scent of jasmine mixed with diesel hits me, as the front door opens. It's a very London smell: sweet and pungent, the mix of flora and pollution. The doors are always locked. I don't even open the windows in the house, they're way too easy to pull from the outside, allowing entry to people who may mean me and my family harm. The familiar scent takes me by surprise. It reminds me of summers when my children were young. Of bike rides and picnics, games of catch on the green. It triggers a nostalgia in me, and I realise that I've missed the outdoors. I glance up anxiously as an overground train screeches into Acton

Central Station. You're fine, you silly arse. I take one pace forward onto the doorstep. Dizziness and nausea wash over me. I step quickly back as people troop out from the station and pass the gate. I'll hang off until they've gone, but I won't go in past the threshold, I'll lose my nerve. A couple of minutes pass by and I take a deep breath, steering myself towards Sandra's door. I glance anxiously back towards my sanctuary. Five steps down the path, a left turn, four steps along the pavement, another left turn and five paces to Sandra's door. What's going to happen to you, stupid man? Get a grip. You were tackling criminals just a few years ago and now you can't handle walking next door? Mind you, that Sandra is well fucking scary, more so than most of the hoodlums I've ever encountered. I chuckle at this thought, I take two steps forward and stop. Feeling hot and cold at the same time, I force myself on. I've just reached the bottom of the path when a car pulls up beside me.

"Scuse me, mate, 'ow do I get to Park Royal from 'ere?' The man throws a cigarette end on the ground by my feet. He leans out of his rolled down window, with a smirk. The beanie hat, the dark shades, the skinny arms covered with tattoos. He looks familiar and not in a good way. I back slowly up the path, he shrugs and pulls away muttering, 'wanker,' under his breath.

Was it him? Was he the one, who as he stood over my partner's bleeding body, shouted that I'd be next? It's always in the back of my mind that one day he will be let out into the community again. Not after five years, surely. He claimed self-defence and said we were harassing and threatening him, but he still went down for life and even the best of behaviour couldn't see a release yet. Unless he's an informant? My booze addled brain can't remember all the agreements and rules we had. I do recall that taking other criminals down means that you can renegotiate terms of imprisonment and secure a lighter sentence.

Fuck, what if it really was him? Surely he just looks similar. He had the perfect chance to off me there, with nobody around to witness it. I feel the cool familiarity of the front door behind me. I pull myself back in and quickly shut it and lock myself in again. That was an unfortunate occurrence to have on my first trip out of the house in years. I shakily pour another large drink and spit out my gum. Who am I hiding the booze from? Myself? Well, there's no need. No family or friends will be visiting me today. They don't really care anyway, so why should I? I stare scornfully at the amber liquid in the glass, as if somehow all this is the whisky's fault. Alcohol is the only thing that can curb the panic I feel. All day I struggle by, waiting until it's deemed socially acceptable to drink. Usually around four in the afternoon is all I can handle. It's a long, drawn out existence until then, even if I don't wake up until lunchtime, as often happens. Basically, if I'm awake, I'm simply waiting for an opportunity to imbibe. The build-up to that first sip, it's what I live for. For that numbness that spreads through my body and dulls my senses. By the end of the second drink, the bravado kicks in. I'm thinking, just you try and come to my door, mate. I could take you down in no time. I've still got what it takes. It's an endless cycle, which culminates in me passing out on the sofa. I generally waken there and take myself off to bed. This is when the fear sets in again. I lay awake for hours, before I crash out once more and sleep until lunchtime. Then begins the endless wait to start drinking again. It's a cycle I'm sick of, and one I'm ashamed of too. I used to be so strong, mentally and physically. Now I'm like an old man. I look way older than my grandfather did when he died, and he was seventy-five. The puffy, bloated face; the reddened eyes. I hate to look at my reflection. I generally don't bother to anymore.

The doorbell goes and I start in shock. He's come back. He's realised who I am and he's going to finish the job he started over five years ago. I stand behind the stale cigarette scented, heavy living room curtains, leaning back slightly in order to look through the bay window. A man with a parcel propped against his leg glances at one of those hand-held devices in puzzlement. It'll be yet another package for that spoilt cow, Sandra. She's obviously not in anyway, so my journey next door would've been a wasted trip. Well, she can traipse all the way down to the sorting office for that one. Poor bugger, I give a sly smile. Imagine coming back from having your nails done, or whatever she's wasting William's cash on today, and looking forward to opening your new purchase, but it isn't there. I sigh with satisfaction that she'll know that I deliberately didn't take it in. It's not like I'm ever out. She just assumes that I'll pander to her wishes like every other man who has had the misfortune of being part of her life.

It's just gone six when my mobile goes. I sit up with a gasp from my prostrate position on the sofa. I had that dream again. The one I have every few nights, in which I relive the horror of the day that I drink to forget. I sit up disorientated, trying to physically shake the dream from my head. With a sigh, I admit to myself that it's never going to stop. I know that horrific scene is etched on my brain for the rest of my life. All the counselling in the world couldn't fix me now, I gave up on it a long time ago. There was absolutely no benefit to me in dredging it up repeatedly, and that's what the therapist wanted to do. My mind can do that all by itself. I've never understood how reliving something makes it go away, it isn't something you can simply desensitise yourself to. I blearily type in the phone passcode and ring my daughter back.

'Hello, love. Sorry, I just missed you call.'

'No problem, Dad. How are you today? Any more news from Mum?'

'No, she won't answer my calls or texts.'

'She will, she just needs a little time to get her head together is all,' Jenny says gently. 'Dad, have you been drinking already today? You sound a bit...pissed, pardon my French.'

'I just woke up, Jen. I've not been sleeping well since your mum left.'

I feel her sympathy crackle down the line.

'Well, I thought I could come by tomorrow and see you.'

She sounds excited at the thought and it makes me smile.'
'That would be fantastic. I'm not sure what I have in for such an occasion but...'
'It's fine,' she interjects. 'I'll get you some shopping in and pick something up for dinner. I thought I'd bring Joseph along. You know, the guy I'm seeing?'
'No, I'd really rather you didn't, love. The house hasn't been cleaned for over a week and I don't know where your mother has put the hoover. Besides, wouldn't it be nice to have dinner just us two? Actually, how about we invite Matt too. We can have a bit of a brainstorm on what to do about your mum.'
I feel a flame of anger ignite in my stomach, at the thought of a stranger coming into my home. I have no interest in meeting this Joseph. She knows virtually nothing about him, I'm betting.
'Leave it to me, Dad. I'll sort everything out,' my daughter says with a smile in her voice. 'Don't worry about Mum, she won't be having an affair, no matter what Matt says. I'm sorry I even put that thought in your head. Mum with another man, it's just *ridiculous*.'

I switch on the evening news, to see that yet another assault on a police officer has taken place up in town. The sound of the siren chills me, and I watch in horror. The cop has been seriously hurt, his injuries are potentially life-threatening. London doesn't feel like a safe place to me anymore. Perhaps it never has been and I was just better equipped to deal with it back then. I quickly switch over to some quiz programme. I can't watch the news; it only makes my anxiety rise. After muttering a few answers to some of the questions on the show, and congratulating myself on being right, I wander through to the kitchen and pull out another ready meal that Jen bought. A lasagne, which on further inspection looks bugger all like it does on the packet. Serving suggestion: put straight in the bin? I glance sceptically at the real suggestion of a side salad and garlic bread. What could possibly enhance this chewy, plastic looking item? I used to enjoy cooking, a long time ago. I'd play some 90s music, all the songs that remind me of working in the pub and first dating Helen. Those were good times. I'd pour myself a wine and blissfully immerse myself in the whole process. It was certainly a lot more interesting than piercing a few holes in some plastic. I eye the offending item in the microwave with suspicion. It was back then that I first discovered how alcohol seemed to calm and de-stress me. When Helen and I first got together, I couldn't stand the stuff. It made me feel sick and dizzy. I'd even surreptitiously decant some from my glass to hers, when she wasn't looking. Little by little it crept up on me. I began to associate booze with happy times. Alcohol meant time off, Sunday roasts, nights out at the local comedy club. It punctuated moments free from stress and marked our downtime. Bit by bit, I got used to the taste, and even seemed to notice and enjoy the different notes and flavours. I quickly became a wine snob and was known by many a host for my fantastic choices to compliment any dish. Once I discovered it numbed the difficult side of my job, it was like a door to a stress free world had opened up for me. I started to have certain drinks for set times of the day. A beer was innocent enough, barely alcoholic at all. That was acceptable at any time, for football matches or lunchtime barbeques, for watching the children splash around in the paddling pool and chasing them round the garden with the hose. Nobody even looked twice at a man having a beer. It was benign, somewhat expected at daytime gatherings, really.

Wine became my preferred choice. It was classy, the perfect accompaniment for food and that included the cooking of it, for posh dinners out and pre-theatre drinks.

Whisky, now that really was in a league of its own. I discovered that it was the fastest route to oblivion. No messing around with this stuff. I kept the hard liquor for those special times, when things were particularly bad and I needed a quick fix. That and any time I felt the beginnings of a cold, I could have a hot toddy even at 5am, for medicinal reasons. I discovered I had quite a lot of chills come on all of a sudden. I steadily developed a complicated relationship with alcohol. It went from meaning nothing to me to being everything.

Attended a horrific RTI? Have a drink.

Had to go clear bodies from a terror incident? Have a drink.

Witness rookie partner scream in terror as he's stabbed to death? Have many, many drinks.

Unable to leave the house due to paralysing fear? What else is there left to do but drink?

I was, quite literally, drip-feeding myself through the panic. Now what? I can't function properly without it. It's definitely not alcoholism though, it's merely a coping strategy. I pull my thoughts back to the present. If Helen came back, I'd think about cutting down the booze and stoking up my passion for cooking again. There's no point in making anything special just for me. I'm going to once and for all finish this bloody kitchen too, she'll like that. There's probably not much point in putting in an en suite upstairs, now that there's just the two of us again, but I'm going to do so much more than I have been. It's time I got my arse into gear once more.

I write Helen a lengthy text about our first date and the good old days. I told her I was looking forward to recreating some of them with her. She's right about one thing, I should have done more to help out in the house. It's not too late. I can see it, so surely she will be able to. I will struggle to get past her affairs, but I'm not letting some no-doubt flash pricks wipe out almost twenty-seven years of our lives. I think I'll go look at her Facebook page again. I need to see if she's friends with any doctors, particularly this Forbes one. In fact, any man working for the NHS could be a potential fling. I flip the lasagne from the plastic container onto a plate. It's pale and slimy, I can tell it's that fake cheese, like the stuff they put on the burgers from that dodgy takeaway along the road. I pull the chips from the oven, cursing as the tea towel slips from my hand and I burn myself. Ignoring the smarting and the blister that's appearing, I pour another whisky and sit down at the dining table. I open the lid of the laptop and refresh Helen's Facebook page.

'Thing is, Dad, we're worried about you. Aren't we, Matt?' Jenny looks apologetically across the table at me. I'm infuriated that she's choosing to tell me this in front of a lanky streak of piss that, until half an hour ago, I had never even clapped eyes on. I glare at my youngest child. How dare she humiliate me like this, in front of a stranger? She stares defiantly back. Stubborn little madam, just like her mother. Joseph shifts uncomfortably in his seat, taking a great interest in swirling his wine glass and checking the legs. He looks smarmy, the sort to be hiding something. Tax avoidance or a wife? Probably both. My cop instinct has never left me. We're trained to size people up very quickly, making snap decisions and assumptions on them. This slicked back, suited slime-ball makes me uneasy, he looks like a politician. I mean, who wears a suit to meet someone's father for the first time? We're not in the bloody 1950s. I ignore the fact that Jenny said they were coming straight from work and that my daughter is also in work gear, with a smart skirt and blouse on. She looks grown-up and professional. Matt has on some stained tracksuit bottoms and a Ghostbusters t-shirt. He's always been one to chuck on the first item he finds on his floordrobe, sniffing them like a dog to see if they'll pass as acceptable. He peels the label from his beer bottle and jiggles his leg under the table, it's a habit of his that has always annoyed me. He senses my displeasure and glances up self-consciously. Mistaking my irritation for me looking for his input. Always been sharp as a butter knife, that one.
'It's true, Daddy-o. You need to get help. You never go out and Mum has gone off with one of those dudes now. We can't really help you as much as you need,' Matt shrugs. Jenny glares at her brother.
'No, Matthew, it's that we care about our father and want him well again. Don't listen to him, Mum is *not* having an affair. Dad, Joseph's sister is a therapist. We were

wondering if we could book you in for a few sessions.' Jenny holds her hand up to silence my protests. 'She will come here to see you and I will be paying.'

'I'm not seeing a shrink and that's final,' I warn, jabbing a finger across the table at my daughter. 'We are not having this discussion. I had months of it from the Met and it didn't do a single bit of good. Besides, if I did feel I needed to see someone, I would not be requiring financial assistance from my child.' I pour up another wine and stare back at those familiar, brown eyes, sparking with tenacity. I can tell that she's trying to be polite in front of the new boyfriend, but I know for a fact that if he wasn't here, she'd be going off on one and ripping me a new arsehole right now. He'll find out how feisty she is soon enough, at the moment she's keeping up the pretence of being a mature and thoughtful young lady. I bite back a smile at the thought of the shock heading his way.

'Suit yourself, it was just an idea,' she replies, haughtily. 'Anyway, I won't be able to help out as much as I have been, so I suggest you start shopping online. I have a few new, big clients and it will mean working *very* long hours.'

The little shit that she is. She knows fine well that withdrawing help gives her back full control. I glance at Matt who shrinks, bug-eyed, in his seat. There's no chance he will help out, the work-shy waste of space.

We finish our dinner in a rather terse atmosphere, with Joseph occasionally breaking the silence with polite enquiries about my days on the force. I recount many of them with a nostalgia that I'm surprised to feel. I ignore the surreptitious glances between my offspring, with each top-up of my glass. Also, to the fact that they've had two small drinks to my five generous ones. I hear them whispering urgently amongst themselves, while I fetch the trifle from the fridge. I smart at hearing Joseph's mention of Alcoholics Anonymous. The bloody nerve of him, who is he to judge me when he's only known me five minutes. I make a mental note to speak to my daughter about this later, she has no business discussing her opinions of me with a complete stranger.

By seven o'clock, to my relief, they're off on their way. Jenny gives me a snooty peck on the cheek and I wave them all off from the bay window. I have enough food and beer for the next few days. Tonight will be my last big piss-up before getting my arse into gear and moderating my intake. Tomorrow, I'm having a massive clean-up of this house. I don't need their help, their judgement, or their quack therapists. I can get myself back to being the man I once was. I'll show all of them.

Chapter Seven
Helen

My family seem to have taken leave of their senses without me around. Steve left a puzzling message on my phone, something about a plastic lasagne and managing to walk to the end of the garden path. He also says he knows the truth now and he can forgive me, if I come home immediately. He's clearly found out about my secret bank account. I have paperless statements and I've reset my email password to something so obscure that even I struggle to remember it. So I have no idea how he has managed to come across this information. The only person I've told about my savings is Sandra, and there's no way she would drop me in it with Steve. She was so keen for me to escape that the SAS wouldn't have got any information out of her. No, I bet he's just putting some random, generic statement out there to try and get me to admit to something he assumes I've done. Well, I won't. He can get stuffed if he thinks he's getting any confessions out of me with his silly games.

Matt messaged to say that if I think he's going to call another man, "Dad," then I'm more insane than he thinks. Oh, and can he up his request of twenty pounds to fifty? I ignore this particular text, but I do reply when he messages again to ask when we can have a catch-up. I should reinforce his positive messages and ignore the negative. That's how I want to live my life from now on, embracing only the good in people. I reply that I'm only away for a couple of weeks, so it'll be soon. I'm expecting.

Jenny simply chatted away in her email, like nothing had occurred. All about work and the new man she's seeing. I will adore him, apparently. I email my daughter back, just to say I'm thrilled she's so happy. I don't give anything away, I know for a fact that her loyalties have always leaned more towards her father, than me. She wouldn't hesitate to tell him where I am and I need the space to think, not to be bombarded with his demands for me to return.

I take my seat in the outdoor restaurant and peruse the menu. The food here is amazing. All locally sourced, grilled meat and fish, salad served with every meal ordered. I even brought my pale blue shift dress, in the hope that I will fit into it by my last evening. It's doubtful, but as I mentioned, the new me wants to think more positively. I have walked a lot today and swam twenty lengths of the pool before breakfast. Already, I feel a little healthier. I'm lucky that my complexion seems to brown on contact with the sun. A year of backpacking around Australia and Asia in my younger years gave me an amazing base tan, one that my skin seems to remember and adapts to accordingly. I was so sceptical of Sandra's suggestion to take a holiday, but she was right, I feel like a huge weight has lifted from my shoulders. It's like I've been carrying around a heavy rucksack for months, maybe even years. It's a truly wonderful feeling. After making my food and drink choice, I tip my face up to the sky to feel the sun. I take long, deep breaths of the sea air and feel all my problems drift off, in my meditative state.

'Hello, Helen. Are you dining alone?' I'm pulled abruptly back from my moment of tranquillity, to see Tom standing over me. I try to hide my dismay at the interruption, and that he's managed to find me, once again.

'I am, but I'm fine, thank you. Please don't feel obliged to sit with me.'

'I don't feel obliged at all,' he takes the seat opposite. 'Are you holidaying all by yourself?'

'Yes, but by choice, I just fancied a little time away to recharge my batteries,' I answer carefully. 'You?' I feel it's only polite to ask.

He gives a large guffaw.

'No, I'm practically a native here now, I've lived here for many years. I bought a practice just up the road there, after noticing how many strays there were while I was here on holiday.' He points to a small, scruffy tabby, looking up hopefully at the people sat at the table a little away from us.

'You're a vet?' I smile, I can't help but notice the awe creeping into my voice. 'How wonderful, so you treat the local cats then?'

'I treat any animals that need me. I'm more a cat person, but I love all God's creatures,' Tom smiles.

'I'd imagine that most of them are feral, not pets, it must cost you a fortune to treat them all?' I bend to stroke the little cat who has wandered our way. She reminds me of the one I had in college, Tabatha, her name was. She was a pretty little thing. I had hoped to rescue a couple of cats when Steve and I got together. He said they would piss everywhere and we should get a dog instead. I was wary of having a dog when we were planning to have kids, my mum always said they could be jealous of a new arrival and their instinct was to hunt. I had no idea if that was true or not, but it stuck with me. After several months of arguing, Steve and I reached a stalemate and settled on two goldfish and a budgie instead.

'Did you notice a donation can on your hotel reception desk?' Tom enquires.

I nod politely, although I don't know that I have. 'Well, that's how I raise a lot of my funds, the leftover change of holidaymakers. I put every penny back in, once I pay for heating, lighting and medication costs. The public are surprisingly generous, I thought we'd make very little in the way of donations but they get to know the kitties over their stay. We have a feeding station a little away from the resort, as encouraging holiday makers to give food to the cats at the dining tables encourages snakes into the area. The station attracts a lot of people; the little ones seem to enjoy it the most.' His face creases into a smile. I beam back at him. I have huge admiration for medics who devote themselves to worthy causes. He loves animals and he clearly loves kids. That's my two main criteria in what I like in people. Anyone who treats either with disrespect isn't worthy of my time. Now, if he treats the waiting staff with kindness, he really is a top bloke.

'How on earth do you manage to survive with no income?' I enquire. I may have a bit of savings, but without those, I'd be in the gutter within a couple of months. 'My goodness, I'm so sorry, that was rather rude and none of my business. Please forget I asked,' I gasp.

'It's fine,' Tom waves away my embarrassment. 'I don't mind, it's something that people always want to know. Basically, I did pretty well out of selling my two West London practices. I don't really need much of a wage to live here. Then there's my private pension, a few ISAs, the usual guff. I manage Ok. This is basically retirement for me, and I love the island. It doesn't feel like work; I have a real passion for animals. I humanely trap, neuter, immunise and treat poorly creatures. Only here at the moment, but once I've sorted out Corfu, I'll look for a nurse to keep an eye out for future patients and move on to help out on another island. It was hearing a local describe them as vermin that spurred me on to help. In my opinion these beautiful creatures deserve respect, cats are incredibly intelligent. It's not easy for me to convince the community to keep them as pets, they are rat catchers to them. Although some kind-hearted souls will give them a few scraps as a thank you, in return. It wouldn't occur to them to seek veterinary care for these animals. There aren't a huge number of volunteers here. I can't not help.'

'West London? That's where I'm from. Originally from the Ladbroke Grove area but I now have a home in Acton. So, you moved there from the emerald isle, did you? I've been to Northern Ireland and I love it there, the people are so friendly, and I developed a bit of a penchant for your Dunnes stores.'

For someone who didn't want company, I'm certainly curious enough about this kindly man opposite me.

'Oh yes, you and my wife would have a lot in common with that.'

I start at the mention of a wife for the first time. I don't know why, but he struck me as single. He has a kind of sadness in his eyes, a loved and lost look about him. He takes up his story again.

'I moved to big smoke in my early twenties. I met a London woman on a training course, she was a veterinary nurse from Earls Court. After a year of us to-ing and fro-ing, I married her. Much as she loved the Dunnes store, she wasn't keen on moving to Belfast. Although it's perfectly calm now and is absolutely stunning, I think people still have a bit of an unfair assumption on what it's like. Personally, I think she would have loved it, had she given it half a chance. Anyway, she wouldn't come over, so I went to her.'

'Does she help with the practice too?'

There's something about Tom's set up here that intrigues me. I would love to have a job like that.

'Actually, my wife died of cancer, twenty years ago. I didn't feel quite at home in London without her, but I also didn't want to move back home with no family left there. I was at a complete loss on what to do next, so I came here on holiday to plan my next move. I finally felt like I'd found my spiritual home. Apart from tying up some loose ends in London, I've never left the island since. I don't need to, everything I could possibly want or need is right on my doorstep now.'

I was right about the sadness; I knew it wasn't imagining it. Poor Tom. It must have been such a devastating time for him. How funny that I ended up here too, planning my own next move. Thankfully in less tragic circumstances.

'I'd love to help you out while I'm here, Tom. If you're happy for me to do so, of course. I'm not a veterinary nurse but I know all about medication and caring. I've also had cats before, so I have a little experience of their quirky nature. I'm not quite sure how I'd fill my time here otherwise, all on my own. There's only so much sunshine and cocktails I can take. You'd actually be doing me a favour.' I can't help but want to be part of this interesting man's project for the next two weeks. The distraction from the chaos of my life would be most welcome too.

'Thank you, Helen, I would love that,' Tom sounds genuinely delighted by my offer and it gives me a warm fuzz. Be careful, my mind tells me. Mention you're married so he doesn't get the wrong idea.

'Excellent, I'm so pleased you'll let me help out. Actually, it's funny you should say that you came here to make an important decision. I'm at somewhat of a crossroads myself right now.'

'You are? How interesting that you chose the same destination as I did. It's a good place for getting your head together, being near the sea always seems to clear mine. Some sunshine and great food doesn't hurt either. Is it a career change you're in a dilemma about? Are you looking to leave nursing?'

Deep breath, Helen, I tell myself.

'Not quite, although nursing is taking its toll on me now. My issue is that I can't decide if my marriage is over or not.'

I glance up to see Tom's response. His eyes show an understanding and his smile is supportive, but I really do feel the need to explain.

'I know, especially since what happened to you, that I should be grateful to have the person I married in my life. It's a very complicated situation we've found ourselves in. Steve hasn't worked in over five years, he's also an alcoholic and agoraphobic. He won't admit any of it, he always says he's fine, which is probably the most frustrating part of the problem. My husband drinks excessively to suppress a trauma that occurred when he was a police officer, some years ago. I know it has been horrendously difficult for him and I do understand. Well, I did, back in the beginning. It's just a lot to do everything by myself. You know, being the breadwinner and keeping the house going. Things may not have been so bad had he taken care of the home and the cooking, but he did nothing to help me, he just drank and gamed constantly. I guess I just got overwhelmed by it all. As if all that wasn't bad enough, I hardly ever see my children. I know they have their own lives, but months can literally go by without contact, unless my boy needs money, of course. I guess I just feel worthless and undervalued by everyone. I wanted out, so here I am,' I give a helpless shrug.

A silence falls over us. I look off into the far distance, along the beach, anywhere but at Tom. I really shouldn't be putting all this on a virtual stranger. He listens patiently as I go on.

'Anyway, I recently found out that I tested clear of cancer and something in me just snapped. It had been a horrifically tense time, but I didn't want to burden anyone else with it, so I waited it out myself. I felt like the walls were closing in on me and I had to escape, regardless of what the results were. I'm so sorry that the outcome wasn't positive for your wife, like it was for me.' I smile my sympathy and give Tom's hand a little pat.

'That's very sweet of you to say. She gave it her best shot; she was a strong woman and fought to her last breath.' Tom looks lost for a moment, before snapping back to the present. 'Anyway, I'm so pleased it was a happy result for you, Helen. Please accept my most sincere congratulations on your all clear diagnosis, I'm genuinely delighted to hear of it.' Tom reaches across the table and returns my gesture with a squeeze. He talks so eloquently, like a true gentleman. I feel for all the world like I'm in a Jimmy Stewart movie. He makes me want to flutter prettily, preferably in soft focus.

'Maybe the therapeutic value of our patients will help you in your emotional recovery too,' he smiles warmly.

'I really do think so. I'm so sorry to put all that on you, you must be regretting sitting opposite me now,' I smile. 'Let's change the subject, when do you want me to start?'

'Not at all, I'm enjoying the company of someone who can communicate with more than a meow or a hiss,' Tom laughs. 'Well, surgery is over for now, although I will pop in later to check on the in-patients. How about we enjoy some time getting to know each other properly and you can start in the morning? No strings, obviously, I know you're a married lady. The last thing I want is for you to think I'm hitting on you.'

'That sounds like a plan. I would never assume such a thing, you're far too much of a gent. Right, shall we order some food now, I'm bloody starving and that Souvlaki over there looks amazing.'

'Let's do just that, but first, I'll let you into a little secret of the locals, Helen. I didn't know this for a good few weeks, and let's just say, it was life-changing for me. All you need to say to the waiter who comes over, is that Stavros sent you. Suddenly you'll find yourself with a special menu that makes the usual food choices seem like a cheap, ready meal. Oh, and it also comes with its own special wine list too, plus a fairly hefty discount. I'll show you all the ways to live like you were born and bred on the island. Of course, they do appreciate their tourists too, it's a huge part of the industry here. But trust me, only the best is reserved for friends of Stavros.'

'Who is he?' I lean forward to whisper.

Tom looks around cautiously, as if he's being watched.

'Promise you won't tell anyone?' He asks quietly.

I shake my head solemnly.

'I haven't got a fucking clue, Helen.'

I give a loud snort and look quickly around in embarrassment.

'Here comes the waiter,' Tom says urgently. 'Do it. *Be* that local.'

I smile up at the waiter standing by our sides.

'Are you ready to order, Madam?' He asks politely.

'Well, that depends,' I shrug, feeling a little foolish. 'Uh, Stavros sent me…'

There's a slight pause, as the waiter looks at me in a rather perplexed manner.

'Who, Madam?'

'Stavros?' I look at Tom in confusion. He nods his encouragement.

'Stavros sent me,' I say with more confidence.

Suddenly, our table is surrounded by musicians. They begin to play the Syrtaki, a traditional Greek song. It starts slowly, as it always does. I stare at Tom in puzzlement, but he simply creases up at my embarrassment, which is about to get worse. Within seconds, I'm pulled to my feet by the waiter, despite many protestations from me. He puts one hand on my shoulder and tells me to do the same to him. Oh, dear God, to my absolute horror, I realise that the whole place is staring at me. The music starts to speed up and we are joined by more waiting staff. They form a line either side of me, pulling me back and forth. The music speeds up again and they all break apart, squatting down and kicking out their legs, twirling all around me. To say I am suitably mortified would be putting it mildly. Tom is puce, slapping the table in mirth. I'm going to fucking kill him for this. People get to their feet and start clapping for us. How long does this song go on for? It seems endless. I'm passed around each dancer and instructed to copy their moves. I am going to be in agony tomorrow, trying to emulate this energetic routine. After what feels like an eternity, it finally stops. I can't get back to my seat fast enough.

'So, that's what happens when you say Stavros sent you, is it?' I can't help but laugh, breathlessly, now that the embarrassment is beginning to fade.

'I'm so sorry, Helen. I couldn't resist. I've seen it done to others, but I've never had anyone around to prank. The waiter did it to me on my fifth evening here.'

'I'm so glad to have amused you, Tom. You owe me a bloody large wine to steady my nerves.'

I reach into my bag and switch off my mobile. I don't need guilt tripped by those back home, today is all about fun.

Chapter Eight
Steve

"I'm only away for a couple of weeks, so it'll be soon. I'm expecting."

I read the text message from Helen yet again. Matt forwarded it on to me and I'm *stunned*. Helen is expecting? As in pregnant? Jenny says that's not what she meant at all, what she's saying is that she's *expecting* to be able to have a catch up soon and it's simply a punctuation error.

My daughter has accused me of overreacting and Matt of creating a drama where there is none. She says she certainly won't be letting me know of any messages she gets from her mother, if I'm going to freak out and read into things in such a ridiculous way. Well, I can hardly be reading into things that aren't there when those are Helen's very own, precise words. Besides, anything is possible, given that I also didn't expect my wife to have numerous affairs either. Helen is meticulous with her grammar. There's no way she'd have put a full stop when she meant to use a comma. Where the fuck is she anyway? Has she left me for this latest bit on the side? They'll be planning ahead for their new life and new baby, no doubt. It makes me feel angry that she will be sharing this experience with another man. I remember how special and exciting it was choosing buggies, cots, and teeny tiny going home clothes, for our two. Yes, I have been a bit of a dick, so for her to run off with someone else, I suppose I could see why. It's the baby thing that's the hardest to come to terms with. It almost tarnishes our own memories for me. This is all so much worse than I thought. Helen is in her late forties, how on earth has this even managed to happen, physically? She's had hot flushes for going on a year now. She kept prowling around in the night, desperate for some respite from the insomnia and the burning heat. It could be minus five and she'd be complaining the house was like a furnace. She was in complete denial of her symptoms and it got to the stage where she would often accuse me for causing her inability to sleep. It was my music, or the game I was playing, or my snoring. She would blame anything but face the truth that she was fast approaching the change, because that would make her feel like she was getting old. I had suggested she go to the doctor and have her menopause diagnosed. She said it was completely unnecessary.

'Don't be ridiculous, Steve. You don't go to the doctor when you *start* menstruating, do you?'

'I think you'd find I would, Helen,' I had patiently replied. 'It would be most unusual, seeing that I am a man.'

Mind you, didn't I read somewhere that on nearing menopause, women become super fertile? Like it's nature's last chance to procreate, or something. Well, it's not mine, that's for sure. I haven't been near her in years. If it really is true, and I hope to God that it's not, I'm going to have to find a way to be happy for her. As difficult as that will be, I owe it to my kids to maintain a friendship with their mother. I know only too well how awkward it can be for children stuck in the middle of a separation.

I think back to the absolute joy we felt when we found out Helen was expecting Matt. We had been trying for a while and were getting fairly stressed out by it all. Every month, we would have two weeks of what ifs and excitement. We pored over baby names and fantasised about our little one having Helen's eyes and my cheekbones. These were what we considered our joint best features, and we ended up getting lucky with that too. If she was a day late, we were convinced that this was it, then the cramps and crushing disappointment would start. Helen felt like a failure, but there was no way it was her fault and I refused to allow her to take the blame. We both had a week off coming up, so I suggested we get away from it all and go and stay in my Nan's old family home, up in Glen Coe. Now, I don't know if it was getting away from all the pollution and into the fresh, crisp air of the Scottish Highlands. Or maybe it was a week of no stress, lie ins, long walks and giggly dinners out. We were so happy and so chilled out, and just weeks later, we found out Helen was pregnant. To honour our little Scottish miracle, Matthew's middle name is Hamish. He's always detested it, I probably hadn't helped, to be fair. 'Hey, Matt, what do you call a Scotsman with one foot in his front door? Hame-ish,' I'd chuckled.

He wasn't impressed. It was a lame, Dad joke, he scornfully informed me. He also didn't find it funny when I tried to encourage him to embrace our Scottish roots on Burn's night.

'Here, son, try some haggis,' I held out a forkful to him.

'Urgh, no thanks. Isn't that offal?'

'You'd think so, but it's really quite nice,' I'd chortled.

When we decided we wanted to expand our family, back we went to Scotland. It worked and along came Jenny. We initially wanted three kids, but once we realised they were expensive and bloody exhausting, we thought one of each would do. So, after two successes and desiring no more children, we were cautious about going to Scotland again. I was instructed to keep well away from Helen, and off we'd trek on the ten-hour journey, for two weeks in the summer holidays. It was an attempt to get away from it all and take in the fresh air, with no games consoles and bad influences. By that I mean Matt, not Jenny. We would teach them to play chess and encouraged them to read classic novels. Matt used to say the games in Nan's cupboard were called board games because you'd have to be *really* bored to want to play them.

We actually all went back to Scotland a couple of years ago, with the kids now adults. It didn't go well. We all sat down to play Monopoly and it ended up in a massive argument, as the game often does in our house. Jenny accused Matt of cheating and freeloading from the bank of Mum and Dad. Just like in real life, she'd smugly added. Then when he had bought up Park Lane, Marylebone and Mayfair, she snidely commented that with all these expensive places to live, why was he still at home with his parents, like a sad bastard.

With that, Matt flipped the board, called his sister a sarcastic bitch and stormed out. He was missing for hours and we were frantic. Thankfully, he was finally found by a local, out walking her dog. He was lying pissed under a hedge, having got lost walking the two miles back from the nearest local. It was sheer relief when the police brought him home. Unfortunately, this was *after* we'd called out mountain rescue and they'd sent out the chopper.

We haven't felt the need to go back since.

Maybe that's where Helen is now. She probably had enough money on her for a top-up of petrol and a bit of shopping. Helen always has a full tank and at least eighty quid of cash about her person, in case of emergencies. It's a habit that has always annoyed me. She was more likely to lose the cash, or have it nicked, than actually need it. Especially in a city where there are ATMs on practically every second corner. That would explain why no money has been taken from our account. She's just upped and left, probably let herself in with the spare key under the bird house roof, round the back of the cottage. Either that or she's moved in with her new bit of stuff. That could be bloody anywhere. I pick up my phone and text my wife.

"Helen, I can't say I'm not shocked by your departure, it really came out of the blue for me. I wish we could have talked before things came to this. Anyway, I hear congratulations are in order. We both know that little ones are always a blessing. I'm trying my utmost to be happy for you. I just miss you so much. I hope you're enjoying your time away."

I give a sigh of defeat and place down my phone. I know the risks associated with older mothers and even though it's not mine, I care about my wife's welfare. Although, If Jenny's right and it's not true, I also want Helen to know that I'm compassionate and will leave the door open for her. I'm trying to cover all bases here, even though my instincts are to scream, 'what the fuck,' and demand an immediate explanation from her. You catch more flies with honey than vinegar, that's what Nan always said.

I cleaned the whole house today, and I've made the decision that I'm only going to smoke at the front door from now on. It'll do my confidence good to be nearer the outside world and probably make me cut down too. I've wanted to quit for years and I promised Helen so many times that I would try. The price of them is a joke, and there's only so long I can dodge the bullet of serious repercussions from puffing away all day. If Jenny is right, and Helen isn't pregnant, I may still be in with a chance to win her back. She would be delighted to see that I've stopped the fags. I know I haven't exactly been husband of the year, but I do genuinely care about my wife. I was proper punching above my weight with Helen, and lo and behold, she's clearly still the catch she always was. I just stopped noticing. I stand at the door with my cigarette, venturing out a few steps. It's not stressing me out as much as I thought it would. Each time I come out, I walk half the path. The smoke calms me, I think. There is less of a sense of foreboding out here with each puff. Maybe tomorrow I'll manage next door.

I could have kicked myself for not taking in that parcel, it would have ensured Sandra came to me and I could have grilled her about Helen's whereabouts. Heading back into the kitchen, I instinctively take out the bottle of whiskey from the cupboard. I glance at the clock, it's only ten past four. I put away the bottle and put on the kettle, I want to show my daughter that I'm not perpetually pissed. She's popping in for a coffee on her way home from work. If I can make small changes to my lifestyle, it will verbally filter back down to Helen. I'm only going to have beers on the weekdays from now on, I'll save whiskey for the weekends. I switch on the TV and open the windows a crack, to let some air in. Already the living room smells better. Not only because I haven't smoked in here all day, I also took off all the sofa and chair covers and washed and tumble dried them, with those fancy scented dryer sheets of Helen's. I polished and hoovered; I sprayed the curtains with an entire bottle of that fragranced stuff that Helen used to go nuts with in Matt's room.

I scrubbed down the kitchen worktops and units, vacuumed and mopped the floor. Tomorrow I will tackle the upstairs. Once all the cleaning is done, I will start on all those DIY jobs I haven't got round to completing in years.

I hear a key in the lock and my daughter's voice sings out merrily.

'Wow, Dad. The house looks amazing.' Jenny appears in the doorway, a wide smile on her lips. 'A cup of tea at five o'clock, I'm impressed that you're not on the hard stuff by now,' she picks up my cup and gives it a sniff.

Cheeky madam, she was checking I hadn't laced it. My daughter heads off to the kitchen and I hear the kettle boil. She rattles about in the cupboards, what is she looking for? Bottles? I know for a fact that a few have gone missing from where I've placed them before. I had previously blamed Helen, but maybe my daughter was the culprit. I never brought it up though, that would imply I had hidden them and make it a big deal. No, it was normal to keep whisky wherever you could find space, especially in this house where storage is limited. If that happened to be behind the loo rolls in the cupboard under the bathroom sink, then so be it.

Moments later, Jenny walks back into the living room with a tray of cups, biscuits, and the good milk jug and sugar bowl. She gives me a cautious smile and perches daintily on the edge of the sofa.

'What's going on, Jen?' I stare warily at my youngest.

'Nothing, Dad. Just some people popping over that I know you're going to love to meet. They'll be here in a minute.'

'Jenny, what have you done?' I glower at my youngest.

The doorbell goes and she darts quickly from the room, before I can grill her. I stare at the closed living room door, listening to the muffled voices in the hallway. Not that idiot again, surely. I'm trying to sort myself out and I do not need his interference.

'Dad,' Jenny says hesitantly as she comes back into the room. 'This is Joseph's sister, Sarah. She's the therapist I was telling you about. She specialises in...uh, your kind of issues.'

'What exactly are *my* kind of issues, Jenny?' My face flames at the sudden invasion. I should have known there was an ulterior motive at play. Since when does my daughter ever just happen to pop in to see me for a coffee? Even though her Ealing office means she passes through Acton on her way home, every night.

'Hello, Steve, can I call you Steve?' This Sarah one holds out her hand for me to shake.

'It'd be a bit late now if I had a problem, you've already called me it twice,' I grumble.

Uninvited, she takes a seat, bloody typical intrusive sort. Jenny stands to fetch the tea. She gives me a stern look, similar to the one I used to give her and Matt if there was any sign of misbehaviour, whilst in company. I can feel my irritation rising. The little shit is going all out to humiliate me publicly. I need a whiskey, sod my new good intentions. The second I get rid of this pair, I'm back on it.

'Steve, I'm only here to tell you a bit about what I do, there isn't any pressure on your part to have counselling. There is something I thought may interest you, I run a buddy system for people like yourself, suffering with agoraphobia. We have many people from all walks of life, who use our service with great results. The one thing you do have in common, is a phobia of leaving the sanctuary of your own homes, triggered by a trauma. Would you mind if I introduced you to Jacob? He's a firefighter with a similar experience to yourself. He's overcome his issues and now works helping others like him.'

I feel a little relieved that this busybody isn't going to poke her nose in where it's not wanted. Counselling has never solved anything for me, and I've had enough of it to know what I'm talking about. It would be good to be able to make changes to my life, it's not an exciting one anymore, but I need to do that in a positive way. Talking is not something

I relate well to; I leave the gabbing to the women. I tend to only communicate if and when I'm required to.

'What happened to Jacob?' I ask grumpily. I can't help but be intrigued but I'm trying desperately not to show it. Next thing I know, I'll be in some church hall happy, clappy support group, where you have to hug the person next to you, or some such bullshit.

'He attended a particularly horrific fire in which a family lost their children. It was around the same time a close friend of his died and the double blow made him spiral into a deeply depressive state,' Sarah hesitates. 'He is OK with me telling his story, I'm not being indiscreet.'

I give a brief nod to show my understanding and Sarah continues.

'Jacob began to use alcohol as a way of self-medicating. His issues began with a panic attack on the tube, not long after the bombings. To be fair to him, I remember it well and everyone was on edge at that time. Anyway, he saw some guys nearby acting in a suspicious manner, whispering to each other, glancing around. Then two got off to head to the other line, the guy remaining looked pretty anxious. Jacob got off at the next stop and ended up having to get a cab home. He never went back on the tube for years, it seemed to create a trigger in him that resulted in agoraphobia. With cognitive behavioural therapy, he was gradually able to go out to nearby AA meetings. He hasn't touched an alcoholic drink in years and that really had a knock-on effect with his feelings of anxiety. He now helps others to overcome their own circumstances. He really is a wonderful person, Steve, to look at him you'd never know he ever had his own issues.'

'Poor guy,' I frown. 'I can understand how he feels. I mean, I actually don't have a problem with the booze side of things. I like a drink, like most people, but I haven't had a single drop today.' I hold my mug up as evidence. 'There's a big difference between liking the occasional tipple and being an alcoholic, but I can relate to the trauma.' I finish firmly, glancing pointedly at my daughter, who had given a snort at the, "occasional tipple," part.

'Actually, Steve, I'm not a fan of the label alcoholic,' Sarah smiles. 'I find it unhelpful as it lays blame with the individual. I prefer to say alcohol misuse disorder, that doesn't put any judgement on the person. Alcohol is an addictive drug. Ethanol is a poison, unfortunately, it just so happens to be a legal one. The drinks industry invest vast sums of money to glorify and package a substance that would be better used only for sterilising surgical instruments.'

This sparks my interest, Sarah isn't judging me, she's blaming the toxic substance. She actually may be onto something with this self-medicating malarkey. As I said before, it helps calm the anxious feelings and palpitations that I get.

'Steve, do I look like a heroin addict to you?' Sarah states.

'No, are you?' I ask, intrigued.

'I'm not, but what if I told you that if I injected heroin for the next week, daily, that it's probably all that it would take for me to become one. Possibly even sooner than a week. Addictive substances are just that, they're *addictive*. Now, I'm not here to bullshit you and I'm not here to nag. You're a grown man and it's nobody's business what you choose to put in your body, but I am more than happy to help you, should you wish to rid yourself of these afflictions. Be it the agoraphobia or the booze to cope. It must be done safely though; you must see a doctor to check that stopping drinking abruptly won't be dangerous for you.'

I smart at her words, but resist the urge to reiterate that I do not have a problem with drink. Certainly not one that would involve a gradual detox under medical supervision. Her sort isn't the kind to be told though, I can't be bothered with arguing with her.

'I guess I could meet this Jacob guy,' I shrug. 'I don't need help with having the odd drink, I'm fine. But it sounds like your firefighter could do with a mate. I understand what he's going through, so I guess you can give him my number.'

Sarah and my daughter exchange a look of triumph.

'That's the spirit, he will be delighted to have your support.' The counsellor smiles warmly.

'Get my mobile number from Jen. I never can remember it.'

My daughter digs quickly into her bag, before I can change my mind. We avoid any more therapy talk but Sarah does ask about my cop days. In a strange way, it makes me feel valued to talk about it. I wasn't a sad, lonely recluse once. People tend to forget that.

I feel a little lifted when they leave. I have a new sense of purpose in knowing that I can help this poor guy. Us emergency services personnel, we see things that the normal person on the street doesn't usually see. We're the ones who rush in and deal with the aftermath of horrific things. The kind of stuff that you'd never see on the news. The ghosts of those visions stay with us afterwards, they creep up and haunt you when you least expect it. Its why we're known for our gallows humour, a rather twisted way of looking at things in order to process what we see. Never is it disrespectful, it's more like a safety valve to release the horrors of the reality. As a brand new cop, I had had a rather embarrassing emotional response to seeing my first jumper. I had been fully trained up in all aspects of police work, but nothing can teach you how to react when you see a horrific situation unfold in front of you. My Scottish partner, who we nicknamed Jock, called me a big Jessie for being so distraught. Yes, that person was someone's son, a husband, and a father too. He had found himself in a desperate situation where he felt there was no other way out. You can't let that stuff get under your skin, because you can't always fix people, and you sure as shit can't put them back together after a speeding tube train has hit them. You turn up at their front door to break the news, very gently and professionally, and then you're left to cope with the aftermath of how it affects *you*. It's a double trauma, assisting at the incident and then having to see how distraught their families are when they hear of the tragedy. 'Is there anyone we can call for you?' We say it every time, knowing that nothing but time travel could help that individual. This is why we have to find an element of humour in a situation where there clearly is none. Anyway, the name stuck, it continued to pass through the staff force, long after Jock retired. I was still known as Jessie till the day I went off on the sick. Ironic, really, it was my fragility to trauma and the inability to switch off from it that caused my leave. I am indeed the ultimate big Jessie.

On opening the fridge, I see that my youngest has taken it upon herself to buy some cook from scratch ingredients. She had been impressed that I wanted to get back into making proper meals again, I mentioned that I'd make a list for her at some point but she has obviously decided that time is now. I put on the radio and glance at the clock. Its 6pm, I can have a glass of wine as I cook. Whiskey feels wrong, wine feels classy. Social almost, although there isn't anyone here for me to socialise with apart from the Magic FM DJ, and he'll do. I pop the cork and pour myself a small glass. There won't be any plastic lasagne in this house tonight. I'm making my signature dish for nobody but myself. At the very least, if Helen is pregnant and shacked up with some other bloke, or decides she isn't coming back, she will see what she's missing. The new and improved Steve, who cooks and cleans and helps other people. I imagine her sat with her new family, a screaming, teething baby on her lap, reflecting on her good times here with me. She will eventually find out this new man is a pillock. Whoever he is, I'm confident of that. She always did lean towards the wanker type of man. She will hate going back to nappies and sleepless nights. She will see Facebook posts on our kids' walls. Me looking buff, maybe one day with a hot woman on my arm. The new me, who helps troubled emergency service and military personnel, because I *know*, I understand. I don't have to go back to the force to be a success. I could have a new career helping others. How much does a counsellor make? I bet it's a lot. I'm going to look it up on the internet later, maybe I could speak to that Sarah about what the best course of action would be. I could probably do a distance learning course too, I wouldn't even need to go out to a university. The clients would come to me too, I could build an extension in the back garden and have a clinic. There's plenty of space out there. I smile into my wine glass. A good counsellor needs to have been there too. Experiencing trauma creates empathy, and I am definitely that man. This is exciting, I finally have something in life that I can look forward to. I dip a spoon into my tomato sauce. Shit, that's good. I had forgotten what a great cook I was. I slice a baguette in half and root around in the fridge for some butter and garlic. Today feels good, I raise a toast to congratulate myself. I've turned a corner; I can feel it. It may appear that the bottom has fallen out of my world, but in reality, it feels more like a fresh start. Like I've wiped the slate clean and I'm starting over. I may have lost my wife, but if her head has been turned by another man, it probably would have happened at some point. I will show them all what a success I can be. Watch out, everyone, the old Steve is back in town.

Chapter Nine
Helen

I arrive at the veterinary clinic at nine the next morning. Tom really helped me to get my head straight yesterday. In an almost therapeutic way, he asked open questions about what I wanted from life and where I could see myself in the future. It's something I've mulled over myself, many a time, but there is something about saying it out loud that seems to clarify things. It feels as though there has been a cloud above me for a long time, maybe even years. It's been following me around and blocking out the sun. Over here, I don't feel it's quite gone yet, but it has parted a little in the middle to allow a small stream of light and warmth through. A tiny ray of sunshine that warms the top of my head and feels like it's gently being absorbed into my body, spreading its way through and making me feel happier than I have in ages. I like that feeling, it's one I recall from years ago, before the half-arsed existence of the daily grind kicked in. I didn't even notice my happy-go-lucky side disappearing; it was so gradual. I just got so settled in my role as a wife and mother, the old Helen had gone and I didn't even see her leave. Of course, I adore my family, but everything was always for and about them. My job has gone from being a vocation, to a means to an end, my body now feels too old to cope with the heavy, physical demands of nursing. I had such a passion about making a difference when I first trained. These days, the NHS resources have been stretched to breaking point, it has placed a much bigger pressure on the staff who work there too. I'm done, physically and emotionally. I'll happily pass the baton on to the fresh-faced young people, ready to embrace the challenges. With no means of escape from the daily slog, I realise now that I grudged Steve for not working and putting unfair additional pressure on me to be the breadwinner. I'd say it's there that things started to go wrong for us. We could easily have been mortgage free by now, had we both been working. I don't resent what I strongly suspect is his Post Traumatic Stress Disorder. He can't help that and he was certainly not to blame for that young lad's death. I just wish he hadn't let it consume him, allowing the alcohol to take a grip. Of course, that's very common in professions that see a lot of trauma and death. It's a way to let off a bit of steam, a gallows sense of humour also being a must. I think what had annoyed me most was that Steve had refused to see the doctor and had become irritable if anyone tried to suggest it. He may have let himself slide further into his misery, but I also feel that I contributed by enabling him. Neither of us are entirely innocent, a bit of space is showing me that now. Anyway, there's no point in pondering on what might have been. I've left, and going by the way I'm feeling right now, I can't see me wanting to go back to him. The freedom is exhilarating, I had wondered if I'd miss him, but I really don't. Perhaps we will sell our home, get a one-bedroomed flat each. It means Matt will have to permanently sort his shit out and stand on his own two feet, but that can only be a good thing. 'This is Miss Tilly,' Tom breaks me from my reverie. 'As you can see, this young lady is about to have her little family any time now.'

I reach my fingers through the cage and the cat gives me a hesitant sniff.

'She's a timid little thing,' Tom smiles. 'She will be spayed before she goes back out there. The little ones will be socialised in the hope we can find them homes. They too will be neutered when the time comes. It's important to control the population in Corfu, there are hundreds of cats here and unfortunately, I can't fix all of them. I found Tilly looking very poorly, not too far from here. She was covered in mange, flea ridden, with a bad case of worms too. She's only around six months old, still just a kitten herself.'

Tom takes me by each cage. I meet Hector the orange tabby, a grand old gent and very sociable. Another tabby, but grey, the very vocal Jasper. Then I meet Madeleine, a young and shy tortie, who gives me a warning hiss to stay back. All have been in some scrape or another, and are cage bound until they're well enough to be neutered and released again. 'Now, this is where I think I'll never get you away from, Helen.' Tom opens the back door of his surgery to reveal a massive caged pen. 'The nursery,' he declares with great affection.

I gaze around in wonder. There must be twenty-five tiny kittens in here.

'Your main job will to be to care for this little rough and tumble bunch.'

'Are you serious? Tom, you're never going to get rid of me now.' I scoop up a little ginger scrap, he must be around seven weeks old. I kiss his soft, little head and he gives my hair a playful swipe. 'I don't know what the collective noun is for a group of kittens, but I'm declaring it a snuggle,' I give a little squeal as the kitten jumps onto my shoulder.

'A snuggle of kittens, that sounds perfect to me,' Tom beams. 'Aren't they just precious? Life is so much easier for these little ones if they're socialised early enough. I'm trying to encourage people to see these fine creatures as pets. A few of my former babies have moved on to work in bars and restaurants.'

'Tom, stop it. I now have an image in my head of kittens in little waiting staff uniforms.'

'You have some imagination, Helen,' he laughs. 'Many Greek people aren't accustomed to keeping pets. Sure, they'll have goats and cows and other animals that provide a purpose, so that's where I started out. Come and get yourself a free mouser, who will also sit on your lap and give you unconditional love and company. I've had success with a few.' Tom picks up a little tuxedo cat and expertly checks her teeth, ears and eyes. 'So, Helen, do you think you could cope with twice daily hugs to each kitten, to feed and play with them and change their litter boxes? In exchange, I will buy you dinner every evening as a way of thanking you.'

'Are you kidding? I'll do this for free,' I exclaim.

'Please, allow me to, it means a lot to me that you're taking time out to help. Buying you dinner is the very least I can do, besides, we'll all enjoy the company here. They must get sick of seeing only my face every day. Right, I'm off to do my drugs round and to check over Miss Tilly. I shall leave you all to it. All their supplies are in the walk-in cupboard behind the back door there.'

I spend five blissful hours with my new, furry family. It's not that easy to remember who has been cuddled and who hasn't, so I grouped them into categories of ginger, tuxedo, tabby, and tortie. It's the only way I could keep track of them all. Tom brought me out some lunch, and a bottle of anti-bac, after seeing I was a bit of a victim to the claw.
'I'm fine, what's a few scratches amongst friends,' I had shrugged.
He was having none of it.
'I can't have my star kitten cuddler struck down with cat scratch fever,' he had insisted. 'Are you covered for tetanus?'
'Yes, of course, and I'm your only cat cuddler,' I'd chided.
'I suspect you'd still be my favourite.' Tom's face defied him with a blush and he gave an embarrassed cough.
I haven't been able to get that look he gave me out of my head since. I need to be careful not to encourage him in any way. Although, I have to say it's rather nice to have some male attention again after all these years. He is rather dishy, in an older man kind of way. Salt and pepper hair is something I've always found attractive on men. He smiles with his whole face, and is tall and muscular enough to make me feel rather dainty and petite. Two words that you'd certainly never associate with me normally.
'I can see that you and I are going to get along,' I whisper to the tiny, ginger kitten, currently resting on my lap. 'This is your third cuddle today. I'm going to have to let your friends have a turn too.' Rather than disturb the little one, I scoop up a black kitten, just within arm's reach. I can't bring

myself to move my little ginger, I'll just have to hug two at a time. The door opens abruptly, making me jump.

'Right, say goodnight to your brood and we'll switch the heat lamps on for them. It's time for dinner.'

Tom and I have a lovely evening out, it's wonderful to spend time with a man who not only is great company, he seems to be genuinely interested in my life and opinions. I discover that he's soon to be beginning his search in recruiting a veterinary nurse to run the shelter, while he island hops to see where his services are required. Part of me is tempted to say I'll stay on and do it, but that would be irresponsible until I know exactly what's happening in my own life. It wouldn't be right to mess this kind man or the kitties around. I glance around the restaurant and into the distance, along the beach. I sure could get used to living here. The Greek people have such a joy for life and a great work ethic. I glance over at the young waiter. He must be only around eighteen, but Tom says he's here every lunchtime, and back again for a shift in the evening. Always with a smile on his face and displaying flawless customer service skills. I can't help but make a critical comparison with this lovely, young lad and my own son. Matt's laziness and sense of entitlement drive me insane. He was an arse-ache of a teen, always hanging out in parks and drinking, occasionally he'd come home smelling of weed too. He constantly requested money that I'd never see again. It turned out that my eldest was also a bit of a jack-the-lad with the girls too. I had a couple of his conquests knocking at the front door, looking for him. While he hid upstairs, hissing at me to tell them that they had the wrong address. I told him that if he was going to partake in a no-strings shag, then he could deal with the repercussions himself. I nipped it in the bud quickly, in fact, it was all over by the second occasion that one of his ladies turned up. He hid upstairs behind the bannister, peeking around the corner to see which one of his harem had made an appearance.

'Matthew?' I'd said. 'Yes, of course, my dear. You must be a new friend; I don't think I've met you before.' I swept my arm out majestically towards the staircase. 'Please, go right on up. His room is the second door opposite, to the right. Oh, and if you'd like to stay for dinner, then you're more than welcome. I always make way too much food anyway.' I'd laughed heartily as the scuffle at the top of the stairs relocated itself down the hall, as Matt ran to tidy up the skip site explosion that he called a bedroom.

My darling son had glared at me across the dinner table, that evening. Two hours he had to play nicely, like a big boy, or Mummy would tell our lovely guest the truth about him. I made sure I seated them right opposite each other at the table too. Just so the dear lad had to see that in front of him was a real, living and breathing human being, not a sex toy. I'd walk by and ruffle Matt's hair, right in front of her, telling him to make sure he ate all his veggies or there would be no pudding.

At one stage, he even mouthed the words, 'fucking bitch,' at me. I raised an eyebrow challengingly at him and strolled over to the walk-in cupboard. I pulled out an old, family album. One that contains only embarrassing photos of Matt, be it in the bath or running naked around the garden, as he was inclined to do. I'd like to say these were all childhood events, but one happened to have been taken last summer, when he came home drunk with some friends and they decided to streak. The neighbours were not amused. Old Mrs Thompson, next door, wasn't long out of hospital after suffering a stroke. The family two doors down, were alerted to my son's nudie antics by the cackling of their twelve-year-old twin girls, who had a perfect view from their bedroom window. We took the photograph to ensure it would never happen again. If it did, I'd put it on Facebook and tag him. Matthew always had a fixation with his winkie, in fact, many childhood photographs feature my son having a good, old rummage around his undercarriage. This album is a joyous collection of bribery fodder, that I regularly change the location of, to ensure it doesn't go missing.

Matt had glanced from the album to me, bug-eyed. I wasn't planning to humiliate him; I was only going to show the lovely lady what she could expect their future babies to look like. I had such a great laugh at his expense. I never met another of his one night stands again, funny that.

Jenny, now she's a complete contrast, she doesn't really need me at all. She epitomises all that I'd hoped for my kids, but for her to rarely call or pop round, that's a bit unfair. She only lives a ten minute drive away too.

Jennifer wasn't a wild kid, just an irritating, know-it-all arsehole. I dearly love the girl, but she drove me to distraction with her continual challenges and corrections of my knowledge. The phrase, "because I said so," was invented purely for my youngest. I couldn't argue with her, she always won.

Her bedroom was immaculate, we had to take our shoes off before entering this pristine space. It had new freshly cut flowers, each week, bought from her own pocket money. We allowed the kids to choose how to style their own rooms, the décor she chose looked like something from a Victorian palace. She said it was tragic that we bought a house with high ceilings and then bastardised it with modern décor. You see what I mean? Imagine that shit spewing from the mouth of a ten-year-old. What chance did I have?

Jenny would not be fazed at all for me to pull out her photo albums, I have no dirt on the girl. *Nothing*. Jenny was a beautiful child and extremely photogenic. I once suggested that she start herself a university fund, by doing some child modelling. She made me feel two inches tall by retorting that she was not just some prize cow to be displayed at a market. That she would feel way more validated as an individual, if people would appreciate her first place in the spelling bee over her looks. She said I was superficial and that if I wanted her to develop a drug problem and an eating disorder, then please, just say so.

That shut me up.

I feel saddened by the sudden realisation that nobody would really miss me if I stayed on here. Maybe Sandra would, but she has tons of friends and would probably see it as a wonderful excuse for a holiday. With regards to work, I'm pretty much supernumerary at the agency. Once nurses realised that they could make more by not having a contract, the agency books were brimming with staff. Steve may be trying to get me back now, but I know that's only because he needs a cash flow source and a general dogsbody. It's not like he will make any changes to his life, and it's certainly not because he loves and misses me. I have to face the truth now, if I don't want to go home, we really do need to sell up. I refuse to pay a mortgage for a house I don't live in, plus the insane rent on a London flat. Isn't this all that I'd sit at the kitchen table and dream of, to just disappear?

We finish up our glasses of wine and Tom pays our bill. He says he is off back to the surgery to check in on Miss Tilly, as she's due any moment now. I too really want to be there when she has her babies. Her temperature dropped a couple of days ago, apparently that's a sign. Today, she has been restlessly grooming herself and nesting. I insist on tagging along with Tom, we walk the darkened streets back down to the surgery and he quietly opens the door, so we don't startle the cats.

'Listen, can you hear her?' he whispers into the half-light. 'I think her labour has started.'

Sure enough, there are low pitched yowls coming from the pen. We already put in some extra bedding and a box turned on its side, to keep out the draughts and to help Tilly feel more secure. We creep forward, making soothing sounds. A low hiss warns us to stay back.

'That's me bedding down here for the night, Helen. You may as well head back to your hotel. This could take some time, I just need to keep an eye out and make sure there are no complications.'

'Not a chance,' I exclaim. 'In for a penny, in for a pound.'
Tom chuckles and passes me a fold up camp bed, blanket and pillow, from the store cupboard.
'At least go and sleep in the nursery where it's warm. The kittens will enjoy you being there too. I promise I'll come and get you when the first baby is on its way.'
I open the nursery door to sleepy squeaks of welcome. I unfold the camp bed and lay down, pulling the blanket over me. Immediately, I'm climbed upon by several tiny, warm bodies.
'This must be what heaven feels like,' I smile.
Above the four little nesting areas, warm glows emanate from the heat lamps. The soft kitten purrs lull me off to sleep almost immediately. This is my ideal hotel room.

Around five in the morning, I'm gently shaken awake. Tom stands over me with a soppy smile on his face. His hair is tousled and sticking up in parts. He must have tried to catch some sleep on the little couch in the surgery.
'Come on, Helen, the first kitten is on the way.'
I gently begin to pick up the tiny furry creatures from my body. Tom holds his hands out and takes them two at a time over to the nesting boxes. Fifteen there were on me, we chuckle quietly as we count them. By the time we get back to Tilly, baby one is out. We leave her be as she sets about cleaning her tiny kitten.
'Tilly, you clever girl,' I whisper to her. 'I am so proud of you. Congratulations, mama cat.'
One at a time was a struggle enough for me, yet here this very young cat is unperturbed, no pain relief, kicking straight into her nursing duties. I can barely take my eyes off the tiny, squeaking creature at her belly, seeking its first taste of mummy's milk, but I have other little ones to feed and cuddle. I reluctantly tear myself away from the beautiful sight and head back to the nursery. An hour later and Tom is back.
'Here comes the second baby. I think this is the last one, she's so young herself and I could only feel two in there.'

We watch together in awe, at the beauty that is new life, calmly encouraging Tilly on. It makes me feel so sentimental, being a mum of two also. Although, I made a shit-load more noise than this girl here is, which included some rather unladylike language and threats for Steve to never come near my lady parts again. Oh, and the endless demands for pain relief, and gas and air. I'm amazed I ever did it again. They say the first is the worst but not for me. Matt would be an only child had I even suspected what Jenny was going to put me through. Tilly has been a trooper; she took it totally in her stride and is now dozing with her two little ones. I'm seriously considering staying over at the surgery every night now. Why lie in a lonely hotel room when I have a tiny brood who need me here?

I beam up at Tom, who is watching the new family with a nostalgic look on his face. New-born babies of any description do that to you. I wonder if he's thinking how different it should have been for him and his wife. They were just thinking about starting a family when his wife got sick. He would have been an amazing father. He has a calming attitude and a genuine warmth to him. This is the most amazing holiday I've ever had and this wonderful man is making it all possible. I hate to say it, but he too is growing on me more with every second I spend here.

Chapter Ten
Steve

I finally got a text back from Helen. I really wish she hadn't bothered. I sit down heavily on the sofa and read it once more.

"Hi Steve. It's kind of freaking me out that I haven't told anyone what's going on with me, yet you're coming out with things that you have knowledge of. If you have any of your cop friends tracing me, then may I request that you stop it, please. Thank you for your kind congratulations. It turns out it's twins. Now, I don't mean to be hurtful towards you, but please leave me alone to get on with my life. I will be in touch regarding what to do with the house, in due course."

What the actual fuck? First off, what way is that to announce your pregnancy by some random bloke? To a man who, *by the way*, you're still married to.

I was absolutely furious. The accusation that a cop friend was tracing her, that beggars belief. By that, I mean that I can't believe I didn't think of it first, how very annoying. I call Jenny, who tells me in hushed tones that she's about to go into a meeting and will call me back.

'She's admitted the pregnancy and told me she's having twins,' I manage to blurt out before she hangs up. I pace up and down the living room, unable to believe what I've just been told.

Stephen, stop wearing out the carpet. I can almost hear my nan's voice saying it. I get that a lot, especially if I'm stressed out. I think it's a comfort thing. If I don't know what to do in a situation, I imagine what Nan would say if she were here.

I try to call Matt but there's no answer. He's been keeping a suspiciously low profile these past few days. Flying under the radar generally means he's up to no good, or scared to tell us something. He's always been the same. I'm pretty sure he's building up to telling me about selling his car. I don't know why he's bothered; we may have bought it, but it's his to sell if he wants to. I just hate all the cloak and dagger stuff that surrounds my son. He currently has no job or college course, so I can't think what else it could be. Mind you, I don't know that anything would surprise me when it comes to Matt.

An hour later and Jenny's on the phone to me.

'Dad, what is wrong with you? Seriously, I'm really worried about you right now. These elaborate claims about Mum have got to stop. You're going to drive yourself demented. Let her have the space she's asking for and she will make a decision much quicker. You have to stop texting her because all you are achieving is to piss her off further.'

'How can she miss me if I don't go away, is that what you're saying?' I ask, sulkily.

'Precisely. Leave her be and stop imagining the worst from what is clearly nothing more than a misunderstanding. Now, I'm coming round later with that fireman guy, Jacob. Please try and keep your shit together in the meantime,' she scolds.

When I finally got through to Matt, he just pissed himself. He laughed his arse off and told me my life had turned into a soap opera overnight. He couldn't wait to find out what was happening in the next episode.

I hung up. He's stoned. Once he's come out of it, he will be shocked and wonder if he dreamt it. Then he will call to check it out and I'll ignore him.

Did I reply to Helen? Would *you*? No, I simply ignored her comment, poured some whisky into a glass, poured it back into the bottle, threw the glass across the room and watched it shatter into hundreds of pieces. Then I spent half an hour clearing it all up, made dinner, and grudgingly sat there with a cup of tea whilst eating it. There is no way I'll give my daughter the satisfaction of seeing me with a drink, when she brings that fireman round. She can accuse me of having a problem all she likes, but she'll have to prove it. I'm giving her no help with that.

At seven in the evening, the doorbell goes, followed by the sound of a key in the lock. The couple of rings is Jenny's way of announcing to me to be sure to hide any booze I have in my hand, from our visitor. I look at my cup and give it a smug smirk. Nothing more potent than coffee has passed my lips today. Suck it up, buttercup.

Jenny walks primly into the room with her, "we have guests," smile plastered across her face. She dumps her bag on the sofa before turning to the man behind her. 'Dad, this is Jacob, the firefighter that Sarah was telling you about.' She has her posh telephone voice on. Snooty little madam, she may live in Chiswick now but she grew up in Acton, for goodness sake.

Jacob holds out a hand for me to shake. He smells of fresh air and aftershave and his skin has a healthy glow to it.

'Hello, mate. Good to meet you,' he smiles.

'Likewise,' I nod. 'Can I get you a tea or coffee, Jacob? You, Jen?'

'Coffee, please,' Jacob says.

My daughter shakes her head.

'No thanks, Dad. I'm meeting Joseph at that new restaurant on the high road. Oops, ten minutes ago I should have been there. You guys have fun.' She heads off, with a friendly wave to Jacob and a frosty peck on the cheek for me.

'Play nicely,' she hisses into my ear and gives me that warning look again, the one I used to give her if it looked like she might be about to misbehave.

I take my guest's coat and offer him a seat. I make my way to the kitchen to prepare a tray, taking my time over it, so I can overcome my awkwardness and think of things to say. I hadn't expected Jenny to disappear off like that, to leave me trying to fill the evening conversing with a complete stranger. This won't be uncomfortable at all, I think sarcastically, shaking my head angrily at the cheek of my daughter. I open the cupboard to get the sugar bowl and stare longingly at the whisky bottle. No, Jacob is in recovery and it would be extremely unfair of me to have an alcoholic drink in front of him. It would make me look bad too.

'Here we are,' I announce, as I appear back into the front room. 'I hope a rich Colombian is OK with you. I mean, who wouldn't want one of those.'

I don't add what was also in my head: preferably with big tits.

Jacob gives a throaty chuckle and picks up the milk jug.

'A rich Colombian, I'll take that Sofia Vergara woman then, if you don't mind.'

I decide that I like Jacob.

'So, I hear you were a police officer, Steve. How long were you in the force?' He loads two large spoonfuls of sugar into his coffee and gives it a stir.

'Almost twenty years, mate. I take it you know why I left,' I offer up a sympathetic smile. I get straight in there with acknowledging our traumatic similarities, it can't have been easy for Jacob to come across those dead kiddies, nor to openly discuss it with a complete stranger. There's no point in skirting around the reason he's come to see me.

'I heard,' he gives a gentle sigh. 'It really isn't an easy thing to deal with, in our line of work. My kids are all grown up now, but those little ones I pulled out of that building, they looked just like my Samuel and Lily. The little girl even had corn rows and bunches, like my baby girl. When you tuck your little ones in and read them a bedtime story, it never occurs to you that it's the last time you'll see them, or kiss their little foreheads. The parents got out; they slept on the ground floor. I remember their father saying he wished they'd all been wiped out together. I totally get that. My colleagues had to hold him back from going in. He did what any good Dad would do, tried to risk his own life to save his children.' Jacob's brown eyes fill with sorrow, it's like he's been transported off to another place. He snaps quickly back.

'Anyway, the agoraphobia set in and it took me years to get out and about again. Unfortunately, it ended my marriage. I don't know what I'd have done without my kids being there for me. My ex-wife has now split with her new partner, we're meeting up once a week for coffee and I'm hopeful we will get back together. I'm not sure if she feels the same but the signs seem promising.'

The similarities in our lives is striking. We talk for two hours about the stresses of our old jobs, the drinking to cope, the paralysing fear of going out. Jacob is like how I want to be again: teetotal, a non-smoker, confident and secure. It's how I once was, and it's when I was at my happiest. Jacob tells me about the extent of his former alcohol consumption and even I'm surprised enough to give a low whistle. His drinking puts mine in the shade, it actually serves to validate what I already know, that I don't have a problem at all. I tell Jacob honestly about how much I booze in a day, he looks unsurprised. He explains that although I feel that the alcohol is calming my anxiety, it's actually increasing it. All those toxic chemicals are messing with my brain chemistry as well as my body. He didn't realise, until he stopped drinking, just how much his stress was being exacerbated by it. He was constantly exhausted and worrying about what it was doing to his physical health too. He tells me that it's like scratching an itch and breaking the skin. It's itchy, but now it's painful too. The more you scratch, the more it itches and hurts. Stop it and they both go away. It's an interesting concept. Not one I'm keen to try, but looking at Jacob, he has a calmness and serenity about him. A bit like a vicar has. It's a purity I recognise from my old days when I felt relaxed and free from the chains of addiction.

'Maybe coming from a place where you once hated cigarettes and alcohol will make it easier for you,' Jacob shrugs. 'It's just like being back where you started, nothing more. You didn't need it then and you don't need it now. I can do everything I used to, anything at all, except drink. I'm so much more at peace for that. I got back into reading and now I get the same buzz from sitting down with a cup of tea and a good thriller. I don't have to re-watch entire box sets now that I can remember what happened in each episode. Sure, I lost alcohol, but I gained so much more in its place. In fact, I now know it was actually no sacrifice at all. I know it can be the same for you, Steve. I'm happy to come round any night to offer advice and support, so please don't hesitate to call me.'

'Thanks, mate. I appreciate that. You know, I'd actually like to try and work up to getting out again,' I venture. 'It's been so long and I'm sick and tired of being stuck indoors. It's something I've wanted to do for a while now but I didn't know where to start. I don't know if I'm ready, but how will I know if I don't try? I don't suppose you'd like to help me with that, would you?'

'Of course, I've been there so I totally get it,' Jacob's face creases into a smile. 'Let me pop round tomorrow and we'll give going out in the car a whirl, we'll take it slow and build up your confidence.'

'Tomorrow? That's rather soon,' I give a long exhale.

'Why not? Or we can go now? No time like the present,' he laughs.

'No, thank you. I need a bit of time to get my head around it. About two OK for you? It should be fairly quiet then. I definitely can't handle the rush hour yet.'

'Deal,' Jacob stands to go, shaking me warmly by the hand. 'I'll pick you up tomorrow and we'll go at a pace you're comfortable with. Even if you just make it to the car and back, it'll be an amazing achievement. Well done, Steve. It takes a lot of guts to commit to that, quite literal first step, in getting back out there.'

Morning arrives and I feel like I have the mother of all hangovers. How strange, I didn't drink at all last night, not a single drop passed my lips. Jacob left around half nine and I toyed with the idea of having a whisky. Instead, I poured up a pint of water, downed it, topped up another and took it up to bed. The long talk we had felt therapeutic. For once, I didn't feel the need to numb it all away. An early night and a western on DVD in my bedroom, that's all I needed. I lay in bed feeling elated, I slept better than I have in years. Sure, I still woke at my usual time of four in the morning, waiting for the horrors to hit, as they always did.

Thoughts like shadowy figures surrounding my bed, ghosts of the past and fears for the future. Realisation crept over me, I was sober, and I felt so proud of myself. Today I feel like shit. Maybe I'm like Jack Hackett in that episode of Father Ted. The one where he finally sobers up and realises he's still on that fecking island, with the gobshite priests, as he so eloquently puts it. I chuckle at the memory of it. I haven't seen that in years, I'll maybe see if it's in the telly boxsets. It'll pass the morning and stop me from stressing about going out later.

I make myself a huge fry-up and a coffee, I have an amazing morning, chuckling along to the classic comedy featuring my favourite priests. I intentionally put off all thoughts of leaving my sanctuary, until it's almost time to go. Helen isn't coming back and I need to come to terms with it. A good start is to rebuild my life and be less dependent on my kids. I feel a surge of adrenaline course through my body at the thought of leaving the safety of my own home. I have to do it. it's been so long. I never expected that on the first day I decided not to go out, that it would be the beginning of a five-year, long stretch of being incarcerated by my own fears. I never should have let it happen. Helen said she understood, that it was OK to lie low for a bit and lick my wounds. The more she did for me, the less I felt inclined to do. I'm certainly not holding my wife responsible. She did what she thought I needed. I'm the one who should never have let it get out of hand.
I don't bother with lunch; I'm still stuffed from breakfast and way too anxious. That's one thing I have to change too, my diet is atrocious. I used to be a healthy eater but now most of my calories come in liquid form and sugar. I've developed a bit of a gut as a result. I stand in front of the hall mirror and pull my stomach in sharply. I used to be buff, with muscles and a six-pack. There's only one kind of those I have now, and it's currently chilling in my fridge. I'd like to get in shape again. It gave me confidence to be physically strong and look good. I bet they wouldn't even

have a uniform to fit over my gut now. I certainly couldn't pass the beep test, or that gruelling physical stuff we have to do. The puffy, overweight man in the mirror stares back at me sadly. Look at what you've let yourself become, his eyes say. Oh well, let's take the first step today and see where that leads. I could be back down the gym in a few weeks, if I can stay strong and get used to being out once more. At least I manage to resist the urge to have a stiff drink, to dull the anxiety I'm feeling about going outside.

The doorbell goes at five to two. I dig around for my coat in the cupboard under the stairs, finding it underneath several of Helen's. I haven't put it on in years and it's tight on me now, I discover. Fat, disgusting bastard that I am. I abandon attempting to do up the zip. It has a travelcard in the pocket, dated over five years ago, plus a long-forgotten tenner. That's a bonus. Knowing my luck, it'll not even be in circulation anymore. I open the door to see Jacob smiling at me.

'Ready?' He enquires.

'No, mate, but I'm going to force myself to do it.'

Jacob heads down the path and opens the passenger side door.

'We can start with a very short trip, if at any time you want to head back, we will. There's absolutely no pressure, mate. Just getting into the car is more than you've done in years. Please remember that.'

I nod, taking a deep inhalation. I pull the door behind me and notice that my hands are shaking uncontrollably, as I try to put the key in the lock. It could be the nerves or it could be the lack of booze. I hope Jacob thinks it's just that I'm scared. As embarrassing as that is, it's better that than him thinking I'm a raging alcoholic. Not that he's been the slightest bit judgemental towards me. I hurry quickly down the path to the next safest space outside of my home. I slam the car door, looking anxiously up the street and behind me. The old guy across the road is trimming his hedge, he lifts his hand in a cheery wave to me. I give him a nod and shakily put my seatbelt on. Jacob turns up the radio, I assume as a distraction technique. He indicates right and pulls out into the street. This is it, my first foray into the wilderness of London, in so many years. We stop at the first set of lights and I instinctively lock my door. Jacob smiles and asks if I'm OK. I give a barely discernible nod and focus on keeping my breathing steady. We drive around Acton in a comfortable silence. I look out at my now unfamiliar suburb, so many changes have taken place. New shops and restaurants have popped up, the pub Helen and I used to go to has changed its name, it now has tables and chairs outside it too. I see a couple of faces I recognise, all looking a little older than before. There's Anna, one of Jenny's old school friends over there, pushing a double buggy. How lovely for Babs and Joe, they've been desperate for grandchildren for years. We drive around for twenty minutes, until Jacob says what an amazing first trip out I've had. It really wasn't as scary as I thought it would be. Stopping at the traffic lights was a bit daunting, it's harder to hit a moving target, so staying still unnerved me a fair bit. I think it was the realisation that nobody really gave a shit about two middle aged guys in a car, that was so reassuring, I had kind of forgotten how anonymous you are here, and how disinterested many Londoners are in each other. In uniform it would have been different, then you were considered public property. Drivers would slam on their brakes at first sight of me, old ladies would come up to me, knowing I was a safe person. A staggering amount of people who were no doubt completely innocent, looked guilty when they saw me in cop gear. I found it hilarious, I remember being the same myself back in the day, before I became an officer of the law. It was also a good way to see who really was up to something. In my experience, the ones who played it cool in front of a uniformed cop were often guilty. Hiding in plain sight and trying to style it out, those types always made me suspicious. Along with anyone who would say, 'alright, Officer?' Usually in a very smug and smarmy way. As if to say, look at me, I'm drawing your attention in my direction so I can't have done anything wrong. These types were usually incredibly thick, they clearly thought we were too. If you did stop and search, the ones who blew up at the injustice of it were almost certainly likely to have been up to no good. The compliant ones never were. I was conscientious about not stereotyping people, unlike some of my colleagues. The young mum with a baby in the buggy, could be as much a shoplifter, as a track suited teenage lad who looked like he was high as a kite. You just never knew. I had very good instincts and was often approached about promotion. Being a boots on the ground type, I wasn't really interested in the department management type roles. I had finally relented, after realising I struggled to keep up physically with the younger cops. I was due to become an Inspector just before my partner was killed, but then I went off on the sick. I think that's why Helen took it so badly. My job description was about to become less front line but with a huge pay increase. I had lost all confidence in my instincts and abilities by then. I honestly wouldn't have trusted my judgement at that point to be a lollipop man.

Jacob turns back along the High Street and indicates left towards my home. I'm proud of myself that I actually went through with it. Helen and the kids would never believe I'd achieved this. We pull up outside my home, this time I have to get out into the road side and that makes me feel vulnerable. I hesitate on opening the door and Jacob notices. 'You can do it, Steve,' he gently encourages.

I hesitate, a train has just pulled out of Acton Central and a few people are making their way along the pavement. I'll have to walk through them or stand and wait until they've passed. I freeze, my fingers grip onto the car door handle. 'Steady, mate, just sit here until it's clear. They won't hurt you, they're just making their way home. They aren't interested in us.' Jacobs calmness and soothing tone helps a lot. I quickly thank him and practically sprint to the door, the second that there's a break in the small crowd. I fumble for my keys, drop them, pick them up again, and finally fling open the front door.

'Same time tomorrow? Jacob shouts from his rolled down window.

'Yeah, why not. Cheers for that, mate.'

My new friend gives me a cheery wave and drives off. I did it. I only bloody well went and did it. I feel a great need to tell someone, but not Helen. She's asked me to leave her alone, and I will. I switch on the kettle and leave a voicemail for Jenny to call me. I do deserve a beer for that, but I'm most definitely not going to have one until teatime.

Chapter Eleven
Helen

How on earth did Steve know about the kittens? The only reasonable conclusion I can come to is that he has some cop buddy spying on me. That really was the icing on the cake. I have left him and he has no right to interfere in my business. Why can't he just leave me alone to get on with my life? Incredibly, I was civil enough in my message, I know how fragile he is and I really don't need to make things worse than they are. Still, I really had to hold back from what I actually wanted to say.

"It's a bit late to be attentive now, Steve. This ship has sailed, so stop stalking me. God forbid you do anything constructive with your life, like get sober or overcome your agoraphobia. You have caused this break-up. I refuse to take responsibility for it. I have done everything for you, for years, for nothing in return. Now piss off and leave me alone."

I had typed this out, then deleted it. It gave me some small therapeutic benefit, but it wasn't enough to de-stress me totally. So, I headed to the pool at first light, while I actually could swim up and down uninterrupted. I did fifty lengths and as I clambered out, legs shaking like jelly, I felt cleansed. The frustrations had subsided and now I simply pitied my husband. I hate saying that, Steve was once a towering man. He was full of confidence and bravery, and not in an egotistical way. I miss the man I married. He's now just a sad and complicated shadow of his former self.

A creepy feeling comes over me, as I think about that last part of his latest text. I thought I was anonymous here but now I'm not so sure. It has completely caught me off guard. I take a furtive glance around me, to see if I'm being watched. It could be anyone. That guy at the table next to me, sat on his own. He keeps smiling over at me and I've had to stop catching his eye because of it.

"Anyway, I hear congratulations are in order. We both know that little ones are always a blessing. I hope you're enjoying your time away."

What the actual fuck? I haven't told anyone at home that I'm working at the vet practice, yet he knows about the little ones. He also knows I'm on holiday. I had been firm but gentle in my reply. "It turns out it's twins," it was just enough information to acknowledge him and not be a complete cow. But I need him to know that there will be no reconciliation. I won't be going back to him. Much as it pains me to admit it, we will have to sell the house. I guesstimate that there are two to three months of mortgage repayments left in the joint account, plus enough for bills if he actually puts the bloody lights off for once. Part of this fear he has means he likes most of the lights on in the house, all evening. I think it's to put off intruders, make the house look occupied and they won't even attempt to break in. It's like Blackpool illuminations round our gaff. In fact, I'd probably prefer their electricity bill to ours. Anyway, I refuse to pay for a home that I can no longer live in, therefore I have no choice but to enforce a sale, the second I get back to London. My stomach lurches at the thought. It's our family home, it holds so many treasured memories for us. It was in our front room, the first Christmas we put the tree up in the bay window, that Steve went down on one knee and proposed to me. I went into labour with my babies there too, and it was there that I cradled and comforted them, made all the silly mistakes a first-time mother makes. The ghosts of their childlike laughter still resonates in the rooms, I swear I could hear it if I was still enough. The walls hold our memories and know all our secrets, ones they will never tell. It's not just my past that I'm selling, it's all of ours. I don't feel I have a right to do that. I thought I'd help my grandchildren learn to ride their bikes up and down the back garden path, like Matt and Jenny did. I thought their sticky little fingers would leave their marks on the walls, just like their parents before them. When I give the place up,

I sell all that too. It's not just a house, it's a home, full of our memories and hopes for the future.

On a practical side, when we bought it, it was dirt cheap. Yes, it will have increased in value, but so have all the one bedroomed places. Trust me, I've looked often enough, you're easily a quarter of a million for a shoebox.

I think back to just over five years ago. I had almost managed to convince Steve that moving abroad would be a great idea. He was about to start his promoted role and I was all set for increasing our mortgage repayments, to pay the house off more quickly. Then I was planning to start a retirement fund so we could afford a bar with a flat above it, overseas somewhere. We both loved the Canary Islands so that seemed the obvious choice. When Steve quit the force, my dreams came crashing down around me. There was no escape from the dreary life I'd been living anymore, and it was like the light in me went off. Of course, he didn't see it that way, he accused me of counting my chickens too soon and said that he wasn't just some cash source, there for my benefit. That really pissed me off, because although he earned more, I had paid for half of everything we owned and just had less pocket money for myself. Nursing wages hadn't gone up in forever and I was gutted that he had turned down this opportunity to invest in our future.

So, you can see how annoying it is to have swung from visions of early retirement in sunnier climes, to becoming a singleton hunting around for a tiny flat that I can barely afford. This is not how I imagined my life to be. I don't know that on a nurse's pittance I could even afford to live in the city on my own. I'd have to move way out into the sticks and that would mean a longer commute, or I'd have to buy another car. Even though he doesn't even drive it, Steve would never part with the pile of rust sat outside our front door. God forbid I'd have to house share, I like my own space too much. I also remember well that Jenny had to have a fridge in her room and a lock on her door, when she stayed in a house of multiple occupancy as a student. I guess Steve will go to his nan's old flat. He will likely make Matt get a job to supplement his art degree and let him sleep on the sofa bed. That way Steve can still have money to pay bills and have someone to shop for him. He will get some state benefits, so he won't starve. That's a small comfort to me. Mind you, anything could've happened to Matt's decision about his course, given his track record. He could be here right now, having yet another half-arsed attempt at being a DJ, but in Kavos this time. Could he be the spy? No, I shake the thought off. Matt couldn't afford the flight over and Steve certainly couldn't pay for it. There's no way Jenny would help her brother out. Besides, her Chiswick mortgage repayments are crippling, even on her substantial income. I could possibly afford a place of my own if we sold Steve's nan's flat too, and pooled all the money, but it doesn't seem fair. He owned that place before I came along. Although I'm legally entitled to half and I do need the money, I couldn't see him potentially homeless if he pisses his share against the wall. The likelihood of that is startling. My mind goes round and round in circles as I sit in the restaurant and wait for Tom.

I had a lovely day with the cats, Miss Tilly is very protective of her new babies, but Tom had briefly managed to get them away from her to check them over. We have a boy and a girl. 'Just like me,' I had smiled at the mama cat, as she suspiciously watched me give her son and daughter a quick snuggle. They are adorable. So very tiny, because their mother is so young herself, but they're feeding well and thriving nonetheless. She's a good mum, in fact she puts me to shame. I had voiced my concerns about taking them away from her once she'd completed her job of feeding and training these little scraps, but Tom said that cats tend to chase off their young eventually anyway. That made me chuckle, Tilly and I have more in common than I thought. Feral cats do live in packs for protection, but they tend to be rather particular about the company they keep. There's no guarantee that her offspring will be part of her feral family. Cats don't appear to have the same emotional ties that humans do. Tilly will stay with us until her babies are ready to fend for themselves, remarkably, this happens at only eight weeks. Take note, Matthew, I had thought on hearing that. It wasn't a particularly safe area that Tom found this particular cat in, she was up near a notoriously busy road. He explained that she'd likely have lost her scent for going back there now. He prefers her to be close by, where he knows she will be given twice daily meals at the feeding station. He's a big softie and I know he's grown fond of her. I wouldn't be surprised if he takes her home. I understand how he feels; I don't know how I'm going to leave them all in just over a week. I've been here for four days now; the time is flying by and my stomach sinks at the thought of leaving. It's not just the cats that I've grown fond of. A certain vet has been giving me some very abashed looks when he thinks I can't see him. I know he's having thoughts that he thinks he has no right to have. For one, because I'm married, but also because I suspect he feels like he's betraying his wife's memory. He did tell me he hadn't felt he could move on from her yet, and that it may never happen.

'I have my cats,' he had shrugged, with a sad little smile. I felt sorry for him, but also secure in the knowledge that he wouldn't try anything on with me. It's not that I don't find Tom attractive, I just haven't been in a place where I could commit to anyone new yet. There has been a gradual shift in that department. The more I get to know him, the more I like him. Although, I can see the appeal of his cats and why he struggles to let them go. They're a safe replacement for unpredictable human love and he has made these creatures his whole life.

'Hi, Helen. I see you've ordered a bottle of our usual red,' Tom chuckles as he takes the seat opposite me. Our usual, the familiarity of his comment made me bite back a smile. We talk about Tilly and the other cats. Some of the older kittens are ready to be neutered and released near the feeding station. We talk about building a few feral shelters on the grounds of the surgery, there's a decent sized yard that could be fitted with little nesting style boxes, with access to the great outdoors. We could have a fence around it with cat flaps in it, to let the kitties in, but to keep out the stray dogs. The one thing that Tom hates about his job is letting the cats out into the wild. They would be feral anyway without his help, but he struggles to let them go off into the world and fend for themselves once they've been a part of his life. There's a natural lull in our conversation, a comfortable silence falls over us.

'You're such a refreshing change from Steve,' I smile. 'You and I can chat for hours about nothing.'

'I think it's probably nothing more than me being someone different. You and Steve have probably long since said all you have to say to each other. You've been together a long time, I remember my wife and I being the same.' Tom gives a soft chuckle.

'Maybe, I don't think me moving into my son's old room helped, but I got sick of seething at the back of his head like a serial killer at five in the morning. I lost respect for him that could've been salvaged had he cooked and cleaned. It could have been so easily resolved if he had pulled his weight. I remember going into the bathroom after him and he had left an empty toilet roll tube on the holder. How many men does it take to change a loo roll? That's what I thought. Then I realised there was actually no punchline, it was the fact that I had expected him to do it in the first place that was the fucking joke.'

Tom throws his head back and gives a proper belly laugh. He wipes his eyes and high fives me across the table.

'You crack me up, Helen, he smiles.

'Yeah, well if you didn't laugh at life's annoyances you'd go insane, I reckon.'

I tell Tom about how it had taken Steve three years to get the new kitchen cooker installed. It had sat in the shed for ages, until it was completely out of warranty. Thank goodness it actually worked. I remember the day I came home, expecting to see the tiny electric hob. It drove me insane; it was either burning things to a crisp or doing nothing at all. In its place was my eight ring gas range. I was delighted, but it annoyed me that Steve was so smug about finally getting it installed.

'Cooker, meet kitchen,' he had shouted, triumphantly.

'They know each other,' was my sarcastic reply. 'They've been in a long-term relationship since 2011.'

'Helen, you should consider a career change to stand up,' Tom chuckled.

'I think I'll stick to cats for now, thanks. I've always been told that I crack jokes once I get to know someone well, so at least it shows that I feel comfortable with you.'

'That's nice to hear, thank you for saying that. Right, let's order. I'm famished and feeling a bit pissed after half that bottle on an empty stomach.' Tom picks up his menu and scans it, although we both know he will choose one of his two favourites. It's funny how I know him so well after just a few days.

You know, instead of scraping around for pennies back in London and returning to my backbreaking job, I *could* always move here permanently. There's nothing to stop me. I could take my share of the house sale and buy a property here. It would be way more affordable than London, and I'd have year-round sun and a wonderful new occupation. Tom has said when he moves islands that the veterinary nurse's job would be a paid role. Why can't that be me? It would save him having to find someone to take over from him. He and the cats know me now; I'd be the obvious choice. I keep this to myself, there is way too much to plan before I even consider my next move. The temptation to blurt out what I'm thinking increases with the next bottle of wine the waiter brings. It makes me unable to trust myself to talk, so I let Tom fill the blanks in conversation. I eventually realise that he has noticed my quiet demeanour, but my silence doesn't seem to faze him.

'Helen, I know what you're thinking, and I know why you don't want to commit. It goes without saying you'd be my number one choice as the fulltime nurse, but I also know that you have so much to sort out.'

'You have this uncanny knack of knowing what I'm thinking,' I laugh.

'I think it comes from working with animals,' Tom smiles.

'Oh, thank you,' I raise my glass to him. 'You're right though, there's not much difference between me and an old sow.'

'That's not what I meant,' Tom admonishes affectionately. 'I mean I'm good at reading non-verbal signs. Animals can't tell me what's wrong with them so I have to try and read them.'

'You bloody old hippie, cheers to you.' I raise my glass again and clink it against Tom's. 'I will let you know if I think I can. I really want to say I will, but I've no idea how long it'll take to sell the house and pack up my London life.'

'I'll be here,' Tom smiles. 'I can always get a temp in to cover. Don't worry, I wouldn't be leaving you until we had gone through some intensive training on handling the cats, taking temperatures and giving injections. It's not hugely different from what you already do, on humans. Animals get many of the same diseases that people do, but also a lot that we don't. Neither the cats, nor you, will be put at any risk. I won't move on until you're ready and I'll always just be a boat ride away if there's something you're not sure of. We can even do a remote video consultation. Technology never makes one feel too far away from anything, nowadays.'

'Thanks, Tom. It would be amazing to live here permanently. You're so lucky to call this island your home. I'm going to do some serious thinking over the next few days and I'll let you know as soon as I can.'

I head back to my hotel room and stare up at the ceiling fan whirring above me. It's a hypnotic sound, and mixed with the wine, it soothes me. So what if we haven't sold up in a couple of weeks. I could easily take the job here and live off my savings, in a rented property. It's a paid role and I know it will be minimal. The nurse's wage will be coming directly out of the amounts raised for the cats, from the charity tins. I wouldn't expect, nor would I accept, a large salary. How much do I really need to live on? It's not too pricey here, even for eating out. I could certainly commit to a year, given my savings. Surely the house would be sold by then and I could buy somewhere in Corfu. I smile into the half-light; it all suddenly seems very clear. Also, considering that I may one day want more than a friendship with Tom, that's making me want to stay here too. It seems very spur of the moment and frivolous, but I'm so over making plans. Look where that's got me in life, fast hurtling towards fifty, with a drunken, soon-to-be ex-husband, and offspring that don't want anything to do with me unless they need cash. By that I mean Matt, not Jenny, she just doesn't bother seeing me, full stop. My working life consists of either very early starts or late finishes, nursing now floors me by the end of a shift, and my back has more than the odd twinge these days. That Dr Forbes recently resurfaced from my distant past and that had only served to piss me off more. The agency sent me to a hospital he now works in, he wasn't a patch on how good looking he was all those years ago. Strangely, he still acted like he was. I saw him flirting with a young nurse, she was giggling at something he had whispered to her. I had walked straight up to him, my belly pulled in, of course.

'My goodness, Dr Forbes. How are you? How are your wife and children?'

The young nurse hadn't appreciated the interruption and scathingly looked me up and down. Clearly he had gotten older, but his type hadn't. It seems he hadn't got any the wiser either.

'My word, Helen, is that you? I haven't seen you in years, you haven't aged a bit,' he gushed. He had turned away from the nurse he was chatting up and she stormed off, throwing me a filthy look. I've done you a favour, love. I smiled to myself. Now, keep walking away from him and save yourself a lot of hassle and grief.

Peter and I chatted for a bit and he let me see a photograph in his wallet. It was a family group one. Olivia, still beautiful and now elegant in her fifties, the two children all grown up. The son was very much like Peter once was. The daughter looked just like a younger version of Olivia, she had a little girl of around three clinging to her arm and a baby on her lap. What a good looking family, I had thought. Can you imagine the time I would have wasted hanging around with a married man? Hoping he'd leave his wife for me, after finally discovering the truth. Why have I managed to repeatedly go for the wrong types? I mean, at least Steve isn't a player of a man, just an ignorant and selfish one. Even before my husband, I'd end up with the biggest losers and cheats. They weren't serious relationships, but still, my judgement has been consistently off my entire life. Well, I'm done with men like all of them now. I have no idea if Tom is even ready for a relationship, let alone interested in me for anything more than a friendship, but he is very much the right type. Time will tell, and given my recent all clear, time is something that definitely seems more on my side.

Chapter Twelve
Steve

It's been seven days since Helen left me and I've managed to have two completely alcohol free days in that time. When I have had a drink, it's only been a couple of beers maximum. Every single day I've been out in the car with Jacob, for a little longer and going a bit further afield each time. Yesterday we drove all round Richmond, through the stunning deer park and along by the riverside. The previous journey was to Chiswick, along the High Road and down the A4. The day before that we went out towards Park Royal, just a quiet drive around the industrial estate.

I'm feeling a little apprehensive about our outing today. Yesterday, on telling Jacob that I wanted to quit smoking, he suggested I try an ecig. I thought it was a great idea, so he decided that today's trip would involve getting out of the car and going into the vape shop along the high road. It would do me good to mix with someone new, he said. I guess he's right, but I'm nervous about stepping out of the safety of the car. I'm not quite sure I'm ready for this; It's the biggest step yet, being out in the street and vulnerable.

I've distracted myself with boxsets all day, old classic comedies that I've always enjoyed. Fawlty Towers had taken me back to the days at Nan's, where we'd sit with our dinner on our lap trays and chortle along to our favourite telly programmes. The highlight of our day was circling what we wanted to see that evening, in the TV Times. Nan always loved the Saturday night variety shows. We had a penchant for Tales of the Unexpected and Hammer House of Horrors, but anything would do. We weren't as dissatisfied as my kids were when they were growing up, I refused to believe them when they said that there was nothing on five hundred and odd channels. They didn't know they were born.

Christmas was me and Nan's favourite TV Times edition. I would run triumphantly up the hall shouting that it was here, after almost taking the hand off the paperboy for it.

My grandmother would put the kettle on, this was an occasion for the best biscuits. No rich tea or digestives for us today, Christmas had officially arrived and the lid was prised from the Family Circle box. We would clutch our mugs and pore over the four channel lists greedily. Then I'd go up in the loft and bring down the tree and decorations. I fondly remember all the brightly coloured foils that we'd string across the ceiling. I'd expertly locate the same pin holes every year whilst putting them up. It was a joyous occasion and it brings a smile to my face still, to remember Nan looking up fondly at me as she supervised. She was tiny anyway, not even five foot of her, but from up on one of the kitchen chairs, she looked miniscule. I actually still have those same decorations and tree up our attic. Helen didn't like them, she said they were outdated and tacky. She wanted a real, six-foot pine in the bay window. If Helen doesn't come back this year, I'm having Christmas Nan style. It will feel like she's here with me, rather than being all alone.

I may have been a nanny's boy, but I did go out too. I would go with mates to watch Fulham play and I'd join them for five-a-side on a Sunday morning. Then we'd go for a burger and chips at the Wimpy after. They eventually stopped bugging me to go clubbing. When they hit the pubs, I'd head home to Nan's. I really did enjoy the company of my mates, but only when sober, otherwise they were a bunch of irritating, lecherous twats.

New Year was another favourite time for Nan and me. Her being of Scottish stock, we would sit up after the bells, waiting on the neighbours to first foot us. Together we'd toast the evening: me with a ginger beer, Nan with an advocaat. We'd make up cheese, pickles and pineapple, on cocktails sticks, pushing them into half an orange to make a hedgehog. We'd lay out bowls of twiglets and nuts, Nan always made her legendary shortbread and tablet too. We had such a laugh with her friends, with me being barman and providing the entertainment. I'd make them a jug of snowball and play old Scottish songs on my guitar, whilst we all sang along. Nan always made me sing Wild Mountain Thyme, which was her favourite. She and her friends would all join in.

'Will ye go, lassie, go,' they always made me smile. She always wanted Danny Boy, for my Dad. She used to sing it to him as a baby, and she'd get this far away look in her sparkly, blue eyes when I played it. In his younger years and after a couple of whiskies, Dad would sing Auld Scots Mother Mine, to Nan, and waltz her round the front room. I learned it one year, as a surprise. She said it was the best gift ever. Although a close second, was the fluorescent bingo dabber set I'd got her for Christmas, the week before. I'd pass round the party Susan, full of drunk, old lady treats, and keep their glasses well filled.

We had an absolute ball.

It was because of my love of banter and being sociable, that my grandmother suggested I leave my job in the newsagents and get a pub job. She said I'd never find my wife popping in for a newspaper or rolls, just old biddies like her. It was because of Nan that I went on to meet Helen. I will forever be grateful to her for that. She died when I was in my early twenties. She never saw me become a cop or got to attend my passing out parade. Although, being from the Highlands and proudly claiming spaewife status, she said that she knew for a fact that our spirits never die. Nan told me she would see every wonderful event of my life, and be there for me through the bad times too. I believed her. She was very spiritual, and by that I don't necessarily mean religious. She had an old soul knowledge and a look in her eyes that said she'd been here before. I miss my wonderful Nan, so much still.

After devouring all that Basil and Cybil had to offer on boxset, I found more and more old favourites. I had cringed at the rampant sexism and racism, casually flung around in the 1970s. Jesus, that was actually what the world was like back then and everyone just seemed to accept the fact. I've been so consumed with reflecting on the past that I haven't even gamed much in the past few days. I've not missed it one bit. In fact, I think it actually seems to raise my stress levels further, perhaps it's the constant cycle of defeat and having to restart levels that makes my angst increase. Just like real life, when you work so hard and yet you never seem to progress. Anyway, whatever caused it, I feel calmer without gaming. I've kept on top of the household chores and have ordered some more cook from scratch items, that Ocado will bring later. It's exciting to have this change in routine. Jacob says it's the lack of booze that's making my positivity increase, as well as causing my anxiety to decrease. I'm also sleeping so much better without it, a straight through seven hours a night now. No waking up in a panic or stressing out about what I'm doing, or rather not doing, with my life. I haven't woken at the dreaded hour of 4am in days. No palpations and adrenaline coursing through my body. How on earth did I manage to cope with that for so long? The constant cycle of drinking and being hungover. God only knows what state my liver is in after so many years of abuse. Well, that's all going to change from now on. I'm going back to a slightly more fun version of the old me. Someone who can have a small glass of red, or the occasional beer, and stop there.

At 4pm, I hear a toot from outside. We decided two days ago that Jacob would just give a blast on the horn instead of coming to the door. It was all a plan to build up my confidence. It's working. Today I walked boldly out to the car without any surreptitious glances along the street. I even heard a train pull into the station and didn't feel the need to break into the kind of sprint that would make Mo Farah envious. I shouted a friendly hello to the neighbour, putting out his bin. I even noticed cat's arse face glancing curiously out from behind her voile curtains. Sandra stared in shock at the sight of me, for not only being out of the house but for getting into an unknown man's car. See, I do have mates, you old boot. I smirk to myself as I give her a wave, for no other reason than so she knows that I've spotted her curtain twitching. Jacob chats away amiably as we make our way along to the supermarket car park. The vape shop is on the High Street, so we have a few minutes of walking to get there. On sensing my anxiety rising, Jacob starts to talk about random topics to distract me. 'What you making for dinner tonight, mate? I need some inspiration.'

'I could really go an Indian, actually,' I glance enviously into the restaurant we're passing.

'Sounds good to me. I was actually thinking of having a takeaway too. I can't really be bothered with cooking today. You heard from Helen? Any idea if she's definitely in Scotland?' Jacob chatters away and before I even realise it, we are right outside the shop.

Fifteen minutes later and I'm the proud owner of an ecig, a spare battery, a variety of fluids and a charger. It all looks a little complicated, but the guy in the shop says before long it'll become second nature. As we walk past the Indian restaurant again, Jacob glances at his watch.

'It's a little early, but do you fancy having dinner with me? You said you wanted a curry, and I'd like to challenge you into staying out a little bit longer today.'

I smile warily, could I really be that brave?

'Only if you don't embarrass me with ordering a mild one. I won't be seen out with some korma eating wimp.'

'Is that a challenge?' Jacob chuckles, jokingly squaring up to me.

'Sure is, pal. Bring it on, if you're man enough, 'I retort.

We head inside and take our seats. The smells emanating from the kitchen are amazing. I haven't had a proper curry in years. I haven't had a lot that isn't convenience food and I've missed it. We order a Madras and a Vindaloo, deciding to share. Man curries, Jacob declares them as. He orders a coke and I hesitate over the drinks menu.

'We both know you want a beer, so have one,' Jacob smiles.

'Are you sure?' I exhale my relief. 'I don't like to be boozing it up when you're doing so well at not drinking. I've only had a couple a day, bar two days where I had nothing at all. Is that normal?'

'It wouldn't be good for me,' he shrugs. 'I have a couple of mates who now manage to drink moderately, after being daily bingers. You'll figure that out for yourself, Steve. You have come a long way this week. Don't beat yourself up, Rome wasn't built in a day.'

I order a beer and decide I like Jacob even more. Ordering a coke while I have an alcoholic drink isn't fazing him one bit. I ask about this and he shrugs nonchalantly.

'I still go down the local with my mates, it's honestly been so long that I don't even think about it now. If I sat home alone, I'd feel I was really missing out. It's the company I like, doing all that without the booze is actually a bonus. No hangovers and I can be up at 7am, bright and breezy.'

'I wonder if I'll ever be in that place again,' I muse. 'Although, I'd really like to be able to have just one or two.'

'I think for most people who once drank heavily, it's not an option. Deciding you'll have none is easier than saying you'll have just a couple. It's stopping at that point that's difficult for many of us in recovery. That's where the phrase comes from: one drink is too many, a thousand is not enough. I don't miss it one bit now that I'm a few years down the sobriety road. It's the same freedom I felt when I quit smoking. I couldn't imagine having to do that anymore. The sense of release from my addictions is exhilarating enough.'

'I see what you mean, I may well give it a try. So far, I'm doing ok, maybe I have found my off switch. I never want to touch hard liquor again, that's for sure. I poured three quarters of a bottle of whisky down the sink the other day. A couple of beers or a glass of wine don't feel too bad to me. There's something about spirits that feels wrong. I think it's the alcohol percentage. It's hard-core stuff that hits me fast.'

'I hear you, mate. I used to slam the vodka for a quick return. Now I like an alcohol-free beer for socialising, I usually have a few of those down my local. Nobody questions it either. I'm not ashamed of my drinking past, but I don't feel the need to have to explain to strangers, when they ask why I'm only on Coke. I'm not the only nondrinker now, one of my mates gave up too. There's definitely a strength in numbers aspect to sobriety. When I first quit, I felt very alone. That's why I went to AA. At the time I thought I needed to see that others were suffering. I didn't realise back then that they weren't, not one bit. The only reason many of them did go to the meetings was to support others through their issues, not to commiserate with how shit sobriety was.'

'Interesting, I'll put some alcohol-free beers on my shopping list. Cheers Jacob,' I smile. 'You really have done me the power of good. A week ago I would never have contemplated walking next door. Now look at me.'

'You're very welcome, Steve.' Jacob clinks glasses with me. 'You've no idea how happy it makes me to see you out and about. It's my new buzz in place of booze, being drunk all the time was never this fulfilling. To think, I wasted all those years trying to find my purpose in the bottom of a vodka bottle. It was out there all along, waiting patiently for me to discover it.'

'You've done amazing, I can't even imagine what you'd be like drunk,' I shake my head in awe of my friend.

'Well, we'd be abandoning the car and I'd be on coke for real. The snorting kind, I mean. We'd be in the pub until the early hours having a lock-in. After that, I'd be bribing some corner shop dude for a bottle of vodka, and before we knew it, we'd be waking up in Great Yarmouth train station, getting lifted by your old crew.'

I give a loud snort but Jacob looks nonplussed.

'Steve, that's exactly what happened, the last time I decided I could probably handle a couple.'

By the time I get home I am absolutely buzzing. I'm so bloody proud of myself for getting out of the car, going into a shop, and having dinner with a mate in a restaurant. Just like a normal bloke. Helen would be astounded by this news. After Jacob dropped me off, I even ventured the five minutes down to the corner shop, to pick up some alcohol-free beers. They were good too. I texted Jacob to tell him I went out by myself, he sent me back a high five GIF and told me I was a fucking legend. I glance around the clean living room with deep satisfaction. I thought my world had ended when Helen walked out, instead it was the shake-up I needed. I would never have got my arse into gear had she still been here. I put so much on my poor wife, I can see that now. I basically forced her into enabling my self-obsessed and entitled behaviour. Poor woman, I'm actually beginning to wonder how she managed to stay as long as she did.

Tomorrow, Jacob has decided we should leave his car at my house and I try driving mine. He thinks it's the next natural step. The following day we will try a walk on Acton Common, he thinks it's important that I don't go from being inside the house all the time, only to get into the habit of being in the safety of the car. I love that he's setting me small, achievable targets. I could never have done this alone. I'm so chuffed to have a new mate too; you'd think we'd known each other for years. It makes me realise that I've actually been pretty lonely since I quit the force. I should have at least had friends round, but getting close to people had seemed impossible back then. I wanted to close off the world. I shut them all out years ago and eventually they stopped calling. It was too difficult to get close to any of my colleagues again after the devastation of losing my partner. Isolating myself kept it from feeling real. If I pushed everyone away, then I wouldn't feel the loss of them if anything bad happened. I had forgotten how good company feels. Maybe I'll get back in touch with some of the Met guys again. I could organise a barbeque and invite Jacob too. I had deleted everyone except Helen and the kids off of social media, but with a new surge of positivity, I open up my laptop and set about finding my old pals once more.

Chapter Thirteen
Helen

Tom has spent the past couple of days training me up to potentially take over the role of veterinary nurse. At first, I'm really worried about performing many of the procedures. These days, we don't tend to stick thermometers up a human's arse, for example. But after a few nervous attempts, my confidence grows and soon I'm handling the cats expertly. It will only be felines that I'll care for, any other animals will involve Tom sailing or flying back from whichever island he is currently on. That's a relief to me. I wouldn't fancy trying to take the temperature of a horse or a cow. I've always been a little anxious around dogs, after one snapped at me as a child, when I went to pet it. I still haven't completely decided that I'll be taking on the job here, I need to see the state of play back home first. I haven't heard from Steve in a week now and that has been a relief. It helped me keep a clear head with my decision making. Matt has given up trying to badger me for money. I do get a daily email update from Jenny and it's more contact than I've had from my daughter in years. I begin to look forward to her news, she's a positive little ray of sunshine, thanks to this this new bloke on the scene. It also means I know that no catastrophes have occurred back home.

I now have only four days left before I have to fly back, I can't say I'm looking forward to it. God only knows what kind of state Steve has let himself and our house get into. I assume Jenny has been shopping for him, her emails don't say too much about her father. She's quick to brag about anything he does do well, so I can only assume he's still in the same shit state I left him in, possibly worse. My plan is to return home to London, but to stay in Chiswick, in the spare room at Jenny's. I'll then head over to speak to Steve, get the house tidied up and put it on the market. Then I'll issue a stern warning to my husband to only smoke at the door, to not make a mess, and *definitely* do not drink when viewers come around. If he won't comply then I'll ship him off to his nan's and leave my key with the agent. I don't care if he's too terrified to go out. I will just have to get him pissed and drive him there. I'm taking no prisoners now. I want my money from the house sale and he will just have to suck it up. Once I've got all that in place, I will be able to make a decision about my next move. I'm seventy-five per cent sure, maybe a little more, that I'll be back to Corfu within the week. I can't imagine going back to my dreary life in London now, or the endless nursing shifts. I certainly can't imagine having to live with Steve again. I feel a surge of irritation as I think of the car chase drone of his games, and the smell of stale cigarettes and whisky. I just can't understand it. My husband doesn't have a life; he has an existence. It's not something I can bring myself to stand by anymore.

Miss Tilly brought her babies over to me today, I was absolutely thrilled with the young mum's gesture. Tom says it's the ultimate compliment. I had petted her gently and said thank you for her trust. It's like she senses her little ones with have a better life if they're socialised. Humans are recognised as a supplier of food and shelter to her now. Cats are incredibly smart and intuitive creatures, way more so than many humans I know. I spend a lovely day with the kittens in the nursery. I can see so much difference in their growth, although I've only been here ten days. I'm going to miss them so much. I'd take every single one home with me if I could. It's fascinating to see their little personalities develop, just like human babies. I smile wistfully as I remember my two as little children. Like this little ginger tabby on my lap now, Matt was my snuggle bunny. He would follow me around continuously, begging to be picked up and carried everywhere. Of course, I indulged him, he was a very pandered to first child. He never liked the rough and tumble that Steve had hoped a son would enjoy. He wasn't a fan of football, or any activity in which he thought he may be hurt. Matt was such a mummy's boy, he hated me being out of his sight. I remember the pure devastation of his first day of reception class. He clung to me and stared at the teacher like she was the big, bad wolf. He had to be physically prised from me and it broke my heart. That first day he had bawled non-stop, setting off quite a few of the other children too. If Matthew was this upset, there must be something very bad about this place, they no doubt thought. I had anxiously paced the living room that day, with the phone in my hand, trying to resist calling the school to see if he had settled. It took him until the middle of the school year to stop getting distraught about having to be away from me. Luckily, after the first week he at least calmed down once he got into school, but the handover in the morning continued to be a challenge for him. The utter relief when he saw me at pick up time made me feel terribly guilty, I even considered home schooling him at one point. He hated any kind of change back then, which is why it was so shocking to me that he has switched career and course, so many times. I still worry about him, even though he is the eldest. He's pretty flaky and doesn't take great care of himself.

Jenny, on the other hand, was never a huggy child. She'd squirm to get away from Steve and I, and always had this air of maturity about her, even as a youngster. She had a very rational mind and a fixation for learning. From the age of three she was asking how long it was before she could go to school. She could count and do basic sums from three and a half, it's no surprise that she's now a chartered accountant. She was reading year two books when she began reception. The teachers were awed by this smart child. She could be pretty intimidating too, by eight years old she was challenging teachers about facts that she was being taught. She was a nightmare in Sunday school. How could Moses part the sea? Was Jesus a magician that he could conjure up all those loaves and fishes? The minister's wife was at her wits end with her constant questioning. We had to take her out in the end. Jenny's mind was cynical, she liked hard

facts and proof. She was a keen saver as a kid too, taking ten pence from of her pocket money for sweets, all the rest went in her piggy bank. From the moment she left uni, Jenny was saving for a deposit on a home. Security in life was of the utmost importance to her. She had a good eye for a bargain and even though Chiswick is pricey, my daughter bagged herself a doer upper and doubled its value within six months. She's like that little tuxedo kitten over there. She won't be cuddled either and is always off on some adventure of her own. Her quizzical nature makes me smile.
'Ready to go?' Tom pops his head around the door. I look down at my little Matthew cat on my lap.
'Five more minutes?' I whisper.
Tom shakes his head and disappears back to the surgery.
'Big softie,' I hear him chuckle as the door closes.

Tom and I headed down to our usual restaurant for dinner. We ended up chatting for hours to a couple from Scarborough, who had just arrived on holiday. The wife was lovely, so warm and genuinely interested in conversing with us. I found her husband to be patronising and full of himself. He talked about his multiple businesses in the car industry, simultaneously saying how he hates people digging around to find out how much he's worth, then ten minutes later, telling us precisely how much. Try as we might to distance ourselves, this couple were set on chatting to us. They didn't take any strong hints, such as Tom and I politely answering their questions then continuing with our own conversation. On ordering his first round, the man at the next table was extremely rude to the waiter. Overcome with wanting to give this idiot a dressing down, I ended up biting my lip until I drew blood. We waved off his request for another bottle of wine for us, charged to his bill. He insisted anyway, and my stomach sank at the thought of now having to be embroiled with him for even more of the evening. He used an extremely racist word to describe the Greek people, and by that point, it really was a struggle for me to keep a civil tongue in my head.

I got a little irate at Tom too, who smiled calmly and told me to chill.

'The opinions of others don't matter to the Greeks. They're a confident and self-assured race,' he smiled warmly.

I had opened my mouth to protest, but Tom silenced me again.

Now, anyone who knows me will tell you, that I am not one to be told what to do, by any man. I smarted indignantly at this and was just about to give Tom a piece of my mind.

'Helen, you know the Greek people are hospitable and non-judgemental, a man as important as your friend here, he must *clearly* be a friend of Stavros.'

Tom smiled at me slyly across the table, before telling the bigoted prick all about how he could bag himself a bargain and special treatment.

I grinned over at the idiot, nodding my head enthusiastically.

'It's true, I couldn't believe what happened as a result.'

'Here, boy!' Ignoring me, as his sort do, the man had snapped his fingers irately at the waiter serving a few tables away.

Tom and I could barely contain our mirth as he told the young man who had sent him.

'You say who sent you, Sir? You are sure?'

'Yes, I said Stavros,' he bellowed, self-importantly. 'Are you stupid, boy?'

As the music kicked off, Tom and I snuck off to pay our bill, before heading down to the Irish bar along the road. We clung to each other and laughed. The utter horror we saw on the man's face as he was pulled from his chair, I will never tire of thinking about it. Even better, was the sly wink his wife gave us, as she saw us leave.

For the first time since I got here, I have way too much to drink. This really isn't like me at all. With Steve becoming a very heavy drinker, I had toned mine down massively, as a result. I always wanted there to be one responsible adult in the house, in case of an emergency. Even after the children had left. Not being in control made me anxious, particularly with Steve often falling asleep mid cigarette.

Given the amount I drank, I'm not surprised to awaken the following morning confused and disorientated. Then it dawns on me, I'm not in my hotel room. Where am I? My head pounds and my vision seems blurry. Am I in a hospital? What the fuck?

'Hello?' I call out, cautiously. The door swings open and a nurse walks in.

'You are awake,' she says in broken English. 'How is your head?'

'What happened to me? I don't remember how I got here.'

'You had a bump but is nothing to worry about. A scan has showed that you are OK. Your husband called an ambulance. He just went out for coffee.'

'My husband is here?' How much *did* I have to drink if I don't remember Steve turning up?

'Yes, of course. He tells me you stop the man from breaking into the surgery.'

I did what? I have a vague recollection of leaving the restaurant and badgering Tom to let me see my babies. I recall checking in on the cats and eventually leaving the building with Tom. Yes, someone approached us. Then what? The nurse busies herself with tucking in my sheets and writing something on the chart at the bottom of my bed. The door opens again and Tom walks in.

'Thank goodness, you're alive,' he hurries over to my bedside. 'Bloody have-a-go hero that you are.'

'You're going to have to remind me of what happened. Is my husband here? The nurse says he is.'

'I think she assumes that I'm your husband, she's just come on shift. Well, I finally managed to get your drunken arse away from the little ginger kitten that you kept calling Matthew. I was just locking up when this man came out of nowhere and demanded money and any drugs we had in the surgery. You told him that unless he had fleas or worms, we couldn't help him, and you blocked the door with your body so he couldn't get in. I was trying to negotiate with him, but he was clearly high on something. He grabbed your bag and you took off after him. I followed on and kept trying to get you to leave it, I had no idea if he was armed. Anyway, you tripped over a kerb and bashed your head.'

'What an idiot, that's so embarrassing. Will they let me out today? What about the cats?'

'The cats are fine. I managed all this time on my own and I need you to just to get better now,' Tom pats my hand gently.

'I have no purse or phone? How am I going to contact my children?' I gasp.

'Don't panic, you can call them from my mobile.'

'But I don't know their phone numbers. God, isn't that dreadful, I can only just remember my home phone number, now that everything is stored in my contacts list.'

'Your land line is a good place to start. Would you like me to call your husband?' Tom smiles. 'Your family should really know you're in hospital. I'm quite sure they will want to fly out and see you.'

'No, Tom, please just leave it. It's best I don't worry them. I'm heading home in a few days anyway, as long as they allow me to fly, that is. My documents are in my room, thank goodness I thought to take some insurance out.'

'Well, if you're sure. I've given a description and statement to the police. Hopefully they'll manage to track this guy down.' Tom stands to leave. 'I'll go and do the rounds at the clinic. I'll pop back and see you later, Helen. Get some sleep and you'll be out before you know it.'

Chapter Fourteen
Steve

Jacob arrives at one in the afternoon the following day. I called him last night to see if we could drive to Jenny's office and surprise her. I had given her a call and asked if she fancied having lunch with her old dad. Of course, she assumed that I meant for her to come to me.

'I'm really sorry, Dad. I won't manage to get away at all today. I have such a heavy workload that I'm only planning on popping to the deli next door and eating at my desk. I can maybe pop by and see you on my way home, one night through the week.'

I told her it was no problem and that we'd catch up soon. I only wanted to find out where she would be. If she was meeting a client, then I'd likely not see her at all. I know the office closes between one and two for lunch, so I plan to wait outside and surprise her when she pops out to buy a sandwich. I give a small chuckle to myself when I think of the shock I'll see on my youngest child's face. I just know it'll filter back to Helen too; she will be stunned by the news. What else has changed about Steve? That's what she'll wonder. Maybe he wasn't so bad after all.

By five past one, Jacob and I are sat in my car, whilst I familiarise myself once more with the mechanics of driving. It's been over five years since I've driven anywhere and I'm more than a little rusty. So is the car, I noticed, when I gave it a quick once over before I got in. There's also a dent in the back where Helen has obviously reversed into something and omitted to tell me. That was sneaky, she obviously knew I wouldn't be out in it and thought she'd get away with that one. Jacob gives a booming laugh, as I attempt to turn on the indicator and instead the wipers go on full pelt. My first attempt to pull out of the parking space results in a stall.

'Don't worry, you'll soon get the hang of it again. This is good for you, Steve. You won't be focusing on the fact you are out, because you'll be too busy concentrating on the driving,' he smiles over at me proudly.

He's right too. After a few more stalls and some kangaroo petrol moments, I'm up and running like I'd sat in the driver's seat yesterday. Things have changed a little, around Acton, there's a new crossing outside the local school and a set of lights have moved up the street a bit, to a busier spot. A bus route has changed which throws me off. Having expected it to turn left, it turned right. I was about to overtake and luckily just stopped in time. At least it wiped the smirk off of Jacob's face.

'Anyone ever told you that you scream like a girl?' I enquired.

'Anyone ever told you that you drive like one?' He batted back.

I give a throaty chuckle. I'd like to see him try and say that to my daughter.

By the time we reach Ealing, I'm expertly negotiating the traffic like I'm back in my cop car. We find a space just a little along from Jenny's office, but then comes the challenge. It's a tight spot and I need several attempts at learning how to parallel park again, much to my friend's amusement. Twice I hit the kerb, then I nearly backed into the car at the rear of me. I had no idea that the reverse sensors had stopped working. I only realised when they never warned me of my close proximity. I damn near shat myself, when a loud beep from the irate bloke sat in the driver's seat of said car, alerted me to it. They'll have been buggered from when Helen twatted it into something, no doubt. She always claimed to be a great driver, but I've seen her in action, many times. She used to utterly terrify me on the M1 and M6, but that wasn't a patch on what she was like on those winding, highland roads. It was like being on a high-speed rollercoaster, but without the reassurance that you were likely to get out of it alive. It was like the one in *Final Destination*, you were pretty sure something horrible was about to happen, you just didn't know when.

I finally manage to position the vehicle in a more acceptable manner, Jacob and I get out and wait patiently by the deli. Around ten minutes later, I see my daughter come out of her office and lock the door behind her. She's busy focusing on her phone and hasn't seen me watching her, with a huge grin plastered on my face. She pops her phone back in her bag and struts down the street towards us. She's the absolute spit of her mother. Not just her looks, but the confidence, walk and mannerisms too. An elegant, professional woman-about-town, my heart swells with pride as I watch her. She gets to the door of the sandwich shop and glances at me, before pulling open the door. I give a soft laugh as she freezes, before turning slowly back and peering at me curiously.

'Dad? Is that you?' She stares in shock as she looks from me to Jacob. 'You're out of the house? How? What the…?'

'I thought I'd buy my daughter lunch, that's all.' I give a nonchalant shrug, as if me being out of the house was no big deal. 'You got ten minutes to spare your old dad from your busy schedule?'

Jenny gives me the hugest hug.

'Of course I do. I'm so proud of you, I had no idea you were getting out and about again.'

'It's a fairly recent thing, I've been building up my confidence with a few short trips. It's no big deal,' I smile.

'Are you kidding me? It's a huge deal. Well done, Dad. Is this all your doing?' My daughter beams at Jacob.

'Nope, not at all. This is all your father's idea, Jenny. He has put in so much hard work this week. I'm quite sure he will tell you all about it.'

Jacob's phone rings and he pulls it from his pocket.

'It's my daughter, excuse me a moment,' he smiles, before turning away. 'Hello, love. How are you?'

'Look at you, Dad. I really can't believe your standing here,' Jenny makes light conversation, so it doesn't look like we're listening in to Jacob's call.

'I'm so sorry, Lily, I won't be able to pick her up,' my friend says, apologetically.

'I'm helping a mate at the moment. Is her dad not free? Ah, he's in meetings.'

'Do you need to go?' I whisper. 'I'll be fine driving back, I'm OK in the car.' Other people may not be, with my lack of practice, but I'm sure I'll make it home in one piece.

'Hang on, Lily.' Jacob turns to me. 'Are you sure, Steve? My granddaughter isn't feeling well and needs picking up. My daughter can't get away from work and her husband can't be reached at the moment.'

'Sure, you go. It'll be good practice for me,' I smile.

'Her school isn't far from here; I'll hop on the bus and pop by later for my car.' Jacob gives us a wave and heads off in the direction of the bus stop.

Jenny and I head into the café and take a seat. I pick up a menu, acting like it's is a completely normal occurrence. We order our food and I relax back into my seat. I can't quite believe how chilled out I'm feeling after all those years of confinement. It's just like someone flicked a switch and took away all my fears.

'God, Dad, I'm so pleased that you're out and about again. You're acting like it's nothing, but you're hugely underestimating this. How many times have you been out?'

'Thanks, Jenny. A few times now, today it's the first time I've actually driven, normally Jacob does. I've been working on other areas of self-improvement too. I've had only ten beers in total this week, no whisky, and given up the fags as well.' I pull the ecig from my pocket and hold it out for her to see.

'Wow, can I tell Mum? She's going to be so impressed. That's a lot to conquer in just one week,' Jenny stares at me in awe. It's been a long time since I saw that look on my daughter's face. Probably the last time was when I bought her that Barbie house, for her birthday. She's not one that impresses easily, so it does mean a lot to me.

'If you want, she may not be interested, love.'

'Don't be silly, of course she will be. Have you still no idea where she is?' Jenny takes a delicate bite of her sandwich, that the waitress just brought over.

'Scotland, I think. Probably at your great-nan's old, family home. All our money is still in the joint account so she can't have gone too far. It has to be somewhere she hasn't had to pay for,' I shrug.

'Where does the find my phone function on her tablet say she is?'

The fuck? I cannot believe I didn't think of that.

'Jenny, you are an absolute genius. I had forgotten all about enabling that. Now I can track your mother and find out her exact location. Quick, we need to finish our lunch because I'm dying to know,' I laugh.

'I didn't even think of it myself, until now,' Jenny shrugs off my compliment. Hey, have you spoken to Matt recently?'

'No, why? I have suspected that he's up to something. It's usually what it means when he goes incommunicado.' I eye my daughter suspiciously. 'What do you know?'

'Oh, nothing. He may have some news for you, that's all.' A smug smile flashes across her face.

Half an hour later and I'm confidently driving home. Intrigued by what Jenny said and excited to know where Helen has holed up. What an amazing distraction it has been, knowing that I can find out in just a few swipes where my wife is. How had I not thought of it myself? It's not like I never knew it was there, I was the one who set the function up for Helen. She was notoriously bad for losing her mobiles and this was the perfect solution. It would track her phone, be it lost or stolen, to the precise location. Also, this thing about Matt, my daughter was not for budging on it. I knew it wasn't about university, and it wasn't that he'd got another job. Those were the most likely scenarios when it came to Matt. Jenny looked like she could barely keep the news to herself. My children have always enjoyed pointing the finger of blame at the other sibling. It was their favourite pastime when they were growing up. I remember those tell-tale voices so well.

'Muuuu-uuuum, Daaaa-aaaad!' They'd yell loudly, with combined undertones of disbelief and excitement. Then I'd dash upstairs to discover Matt had tried to flush a whole loo roll down the toilet. Or Jenny had raided her mum's make-up bag, and had spilled an entire bottle of expensive foundation on the new bedroom carpet. The only thing worse was complete silence. It fills me with suspicion to this day. It meant that, combined, they were up to no good. I knew that Matt had been unnervingly quiet. No requests at all for money, these past few days, that's most unusual. Apparently, this gossip was far too good for Jenny to share, which means it must be really bad. Something that she would only enjoy more by viewing Matt's discomfort in telling me. I had to let her know the second Matt told me he was coming round for a chat. Her brown eyes had sparked when she said that, like a mischievous, little elf.

By some miracle, I make it home unscathed, and without anyone beeping at me. I park up expertly, in front of the house, and make a dash for the front door. For all the right reasons this time, not through fear.

'Oh, Stee-eeve,' a voice sings out.

Fuck. As much as I've wanted to pick Sandra's tiny, shopping obsessed brain over the past week, I really can't be arsed with her right now. She won't tell me anything, and I won't give her the satisfaction of asking her.

'Sandra.' I stop, smiling in what I hope is a breezy but business-like manner. 'What can I do for you?'

'I just wondered if you'd heard from Helen is all. I've sent her a few messages but she hasn't got back to me. I'm beginning to feel a bit concerned about her.'

'Hmm, that's surprising, I thought you and Helen were quite close friends.' I just couldn't resist the dig. 'Don't worry, we've all heard from her and she's grand. I'll be sure to let her know that you're asking after her.'

'Oh, and Steve, I haven't seen that man before. The one that's round your house every day. You been hiding a little secret from Helen, have you?' She gives a tinkling laugh.

'He's just a friend, Sandra. I'm afraid there's no juicy gossip for you there.'

'I'm, kidding, of course, you know I'm not a gossip,' she raises her eyebrows in mock innocence. 'But really, how are you keeping, Steve? You're out and about again, I see.' She glances at the car and then back at me. 'Are you sure that you're OK to drive?'

'Well, I have a license and insurance, so I shouldn't see why not,' I bat back. I know what she means, she's implying that I must be perpetually over the limit.

'Anyway, I must dash, Sandra. I have a lot to get on with. I'll let Helen know that you've sent your regards.'

I leave her standing there, gaping like a fish, disappointed that I gave her nothing to pass on to her gossipy, mum chums. She will find something to add arms and legs to, no doubt. Cheeky bitch that she is too, I have never been a drink driver. I wouldn't even go out in the car the day *after* a session.

I give a soft chuckle, I enjoyed giving her no information, even though I don't know anything yet myself. For her to admit she hadn't heard from Helen either, that has pleased me no end. I bet that stuck in her craw, as my nan would have said.

I take great delight in the fact that I never approached Sandra to ask about Helen's whereabouts. I know that she would have made out that she knew everything, but couldn't possibly tell me to protect Helen's privacy. Checkmate to me, you silly, old bag.

I quickly locate my wife's tablet, sighing with disappointment when I see that the battery's flat. I rummage around in the Welsh dresser drawer, for a cable that will fit. Christ, there must be fifteen in there, along with remote controls for tellies we no longer have, a pile of batteries, and an ancient pad of post-its notes that have lost their sticky. I finally locate a charge lead and wait impatiently as the battery symbol appears. Make a coffee and calm down, Steve. You've waited this long, what's a few more minutes. No, if I go to the kitchen right now, I may be tempted by worse than coffee. I'll stay put. I drum my fingers on the dining room table for what feels like an eternity. I'll call Matt, that's what I'll do while I'm waiting. He was my next port of call anyway. The phone rings out for ages, I can almost sense him looking at it and deciding if he should answer or not. He's never off it when I see him, there's no way it's not in his hand, right at this very moment. Finally, he picks up.

'Uhhh, hi Dad. How are you?'

'I'm good, son. How's yourself?' I say breezily. 'You've been rather quiet this past week, what's the gossip? You heard anything from your mum?'

'No, she's mostly been ignoring me. I haven't been quiet, dunno what you're talking about.' he mutters defensively.

That voice says it all, he's definitely guilty of something. I don't even have to see the face that accompanies the voice, but I know it will be wide-eyed with mock innocence.

'When you coming to visit your old man?' I press on.

'Well, I do have something to tell you, some news. *Good* news,' he blusters.

'Matthew, that's wonderful. Well, I'm free tonight, how about you?' I've got him now and I'm not letting go. If he doesn't come round, I'll drive over there myself. The shock will make him come out with whatever it is that he's hiding.

'Uh, possibly...' he sounds far off, like he's taken the phone away from his mouth and is whispering to someone. After a little back and forth, he returns. 'Er, yeah, tonight would be good, Dad. Is seven OK?'

'Seven is great, son. See you then.' I hang up the phone and turn my attention back to the tablet. To my utter joy, the logo appears on the screen. I am seconds away from knowing the whereabouts of my errant wife.

Chapter Fifteen
Helen

I've been let out of the hospital and I'm now recuperating, back in the hotel room. I only have two days left here and I'm desperate to get back to my cats and kittens. I've missed them so much. My holiday has passed by so quickly; I now have a dull feeling of dread in the pit of my stomach. I don't want to go back. I will miss the fragrant air, that gorgeous mix of sea and flora. Any doubts I had about coming back here now seem to have lifted, the bop on the head seems to have knocked some sense into me, for sure. I can't leave this island and those tiny creatures. They've managed to tumble and claw their way right into my heart. I'm increasingly realising that I don't want to leave Tom either. We have struck up a great friendship, even if nothing more ever came of it, that would be fine.

With this in mind, I start to plan out exactly what will happen when I get home. I'll ask Jenny to fetch me from Stanstead when my plane lands, I think that's around half seven in the evening. I'll go to hers for the night and then head over to my old house, first thing in the morning. I'll break the news to Steve that I want to sell up and get a divorce, then list the house with the estate agents and go back and gut the whole place. I'll get rid of anything I don't need and store the rest up Jenny's attic. It's something I've been meaning to do for years. We have stuff up there from when the kids were little. Cots, prams, all their baby clothes. I'm actually surprised the attic flooring hasn't collapsed down onto our heads by now. Then I'll let Steve deal with the viewings, pack myself up, and head back to Corfu. The thought of making a permanent move here makes me smile. I walk out to my small balcony and glance around at my surroundings, savouring the memories to keep me going until I return. I'll have to rent until the money from the house sale comes through, then I'll buy somewhere. It will give me time to get a feel for the island, that could actually be a blessing. When I do find a permanent residence, I will do up my new home in all the beautiful, natural colours of the island. Sea blue, terracotta, and the shades of the bougainvillea flowers. I'll take a couple of the cats home with me, and I already know exactly which two. Me and my little family will blissfully enjoy our new abode. We will have a little stove fireplace for chilly, winter nights. A digital radio for listening to some calming, classical music. Do you know, I've always fancied trying my hand at writing and painting, and I'll learn the local language too. I will make souvlaki on my little stove, with breads and healthy salads, and pour myself a glass of red wine. I'll have a little terrace with a patio, for warm evenings and al fresco dining. Friends will pop round for barbeques, we'll sit outside chatting and watching the stunning sunsets over the sea. It sounds like perfection to me and I congratulate myself on taking the decision to come out here for this holiday. I certainly can't take full credit for that. Sandra's words echo back to me, that I wouldn't want to come back home once I'd seen what's out there. She was so right, I'm glad she gave me the confidence and push that I needed. She's a smart woman, because it's thanks to her encouraging me to see it as a holiday and not leaving my husband, that made me even consider it. That reminds me, I haven't got around to replying to her messages. I wonder what the weather is like back home. Maybe twelve or fifteen degrees? The thought of freezing, drizzly mornings now makes me shudder. I imagine waking up for an early shift and taking an ass haul journey to whatever hospital I'm currently working in. The prospect of weekend rail replacement, of either having to take the bus an hour earlier or trawl through traffic in that rust heap. Even at seven on a Sunday morning, the roads are fairly busy. Or the more favourable scenario: my cats and kittens, working only a few hours a day, my beautiful new home that I'm already mentally decorating. Temperatures that rarely drop below ten degrees. I've seen so-called summer days in London reach not much more than that. I can be near Tom, my kind, generous and handsome friend. I have been pushing away any thoughts of him and I, but they creep back in when I least expect them to. He's a good man, we get on so well and have so much in common. There's no getting away from it, I really do care about him. Regardless of any potential romance, I know now that I want him in my life.

Actually, speaking of Tom, he paid me a visit earlier. The most bizarre thing happened at work today. Steve rang the veterinary practice and left a message. I have tried to call our house number several times from the hotel room telephone, but there's been no answer. Tom swears he didn't contact my husband and I believe him. How could he have? My passport with the emergency contact details was in my hotel room, and he has no way of knowing my home phone number. Does he even know my surname? I'm not sure I've even told him what it is. How on earth has Steve tracked me here? Was it his cop friend spying on me? Also, where the fuck is he? He doesn't go out anywhere and yet he's not answering the house phone. I just know something terrible has happened, because I can't reach Jenny either. I got Tom to Google her work number so I could try and catch her there. I feel helpless without my mobile. I know only my house phone number by heart, but no mobile ones. The other emergency contact on my passport is my daughter's old number, one that she changed several years ago to shake off a guy she went on one date with who turned out to be a creep.

What now? I've left messages, but there's nothing I can do but sit and wait until Jenny or Steve get back to me. If my daughter does indeed go into the office. Her emails have often spoken about working remotely, so she can get peace from the constant questions from her staff. I knew something like this would happen. Didn't I almost turn straight back and fly home? I should have trusted my instincts.

Oh, my God, was there a fire in my house? Did Steve fall asleep and leave a burning cigarette dangling from his fingers, just like I thought he would? I know he's alive, because he left a message, but he is most likely in hospital. It's the only possible reason for him being out of the house. How can I sell our home now, when it's probably just a burnt-out shell? I don't even know Sandra's home phone number. I'm completely stuck with nothing but the horror of my imagination to keep me occupied.

I need to get out of here, I know I'm supposed to rest but they've said I'm not concussed. All the memory of that evening has come back now. It was just a little blip after being knocked out. I pull myself out of bed and take a shower. I need to see Tom and my cats. I want to hear the message that Steve left on the surgery answering machine. If there is the slightest element in his voice that sounds ashamed, then I'll know if he's done something stupid. Actually, I could email Jenny, that's the answer. She checks her mail several times a day, even at weekends. The clinic has a computer; I know Tom won't mind me using it. With a renewed surge of urgency, I get dressed and head out to the practice. Knowing now that contact with my family is just a few clicks away is such a huge relief. I am never going to put myself in a position like this again. I will memorise every single important phone number from now on.

I walk along the now familiar streets, saying hello to a few of the locals who have started to recognise me. A couple of them call out to ask how I am. News travels fast in a small community like this. Tom told me it was a most unusual occurrence; people have good moral fibre around here and there isn't much in the way of crime. One elderly shop keeper told Tom it must have been a British person, as it was always the bloody foreigners who caused the trouble. We do seem to have a bit of a reputation around here. No doubt from the young crowd, like that lot on the beach, with the girl who passed out. I'm quite sure the Greeks wouldn't be doing shots for breakfast, even if they were on holiday. Culture, family, good food. That's what they're all about.

I arrive at the surgery and Tom looks surprised to see me.

'Helen, you really shouldn't be up and about yet. What are you doing here?' He walks quickly from examining Tilly, to my side. He shines his torch into my eyes and stares at my pupils intently.

'I couldn't stand being in that stuffy hotel room any longer,' I reply, with a grimace. 'Get that bloody light out of my eyes, you're giving me a headache. I can't get into Greek soaps when I don't know what they're saying, I'm bored and I want my cats. I also want to hear the message from Steve, please. I don't know what he's done but this doesn't sound good.'

'Of course you can.' Tom smiles. He presses a button on the answering machine and I hear my husband's voice. Steve sounds strange and so distant. There's a slight edge of concern to it that I haven't heard in years, this both reassures and confuses me. He can't have burnt the house down, he sounded worried about me, not guilty of having done something wrong. I listen intently, looking for any underlying clues. You can't be the wife of a cop for this long and not pick up a few investigative skills. Actually, being a wife already gives you a good head start on that anyway.

'Hi, I'm looking for Helen Brown. It's Steve, her husband. Her tablet tracked her to this location and I understand you may be a doctor's surgery. Anyway, I don't know if whoever receives this can get in touch with her, but if you can, please pass this message on. I'm worried that she is sick or in hospital, none of the family can seem to reach her. I just want to check that everything is OK with her. Helen, if you hear this, we are all fine, but we do miss you. I have a lot of big news to tell you. We can't seem to get you on your mobile, but if you can, please call.' There's a bit of a pause before he continues. 'I love you, Helen. Please come home.'

'He sounds like he means it.' Tom looks at me kindly.

'I know,' I sigh. 'I sound like a complete bitch, but I don't want him back, there's too much water under the bridge. I know now that my marriage is definitely over. We've been together for such a long time and I'm ready for a fresh start. I may stay single or I may eventually move on and find someone new. I'm not exactly elderly, so I'm not quite ready for a life of being alone.

I certainly don't want to stay with the wrong man either. Forget it, it doesn't matter, I shouldn't be bothering you with the drama that is my personal life.

Tom, can I please check my email?' I sigh. 'I need to try and get in touch with my daughter.'

'Of course.' He has been watching me intently, with a look that I can't quite identify. I turn away from him and take a seat in front of the dusty, old computer. It makes me wonder if this could be one of Greece's famous, ancient relics. I wait impatiently as the browser attempts to load. After ten minutes, I type my email address into the log-in page.

I freeze, as I remember that I changed my password to keep Steve out. The new one was long and complicated, I kept it in the notes section of my phone. Shit, I don't know it. It was just a random jumble of letters, numbers and symbols. Defeated, I shut down the computer and stare sadly at the keyboard, as if the characters required will somehow jump out at me. I have absolutely no way to contact my family now, other than to keep trying the land lines that I do have.

The kittens seem to have put on their greatest performances to cheer me up today. They are super cute and silly. My little Matthew cat heads straight over for cuddles. As he settles onto my lap, I ponder on how I should break the news to my husband that I want a divorce. I'm a bit annoyed with myself for blurting out that I maybe saw something happening with someone new. I didn't mention any names, but I saw it in Tom's eyes, we both knew who I meant. I'll blame the bump on the head for that one. We have kind of avoided each other a bit since. I did the temperatures and injections earlier, and I could sense him watching me. Not in a creepy way, just an awareness of his eyes and close proximity. I clearly wasn't paying enough attention to my nursing duties, because I got a little nip from Hector. My hands were shaking and I think he perceived that as a lack of confidence. Tom checked me over and it made me a little uncomfortable. He was close enough that I could smell his light spritz of aftershave. I told him I was fine and awkwardly pulled my hand away, with an apologetic smile. There's a tension hanging in the air, the residue of my words. I think about saying I can't do dinner tonight but I know it'll only make things feel even more uneasy tomorrow. I also don't have an excuse, what else could I possibly be doing? Anyway, I'm sick of the sight of that hotel room and it's my second last night on holiday.

I try both Jenny and Steve again, at closing up time. Where on earth is my husband? At least I feel calmer after hearing his voice message, I can sense that he's not in any trouble and I know every side of Steve. He was concerned. He had that tone he would have back when we first met, that there was nothing that could possibly be wrong with me that he couldn't fix. It's a pity he didn't try and fix our crumbling marriage before it was too late.

Tom and I walk wordlessly along the terrace towards the little row of restaurants. The silence hangs in the air between us. As we take our seats, I'm quicker than usual to order our favourite bottle of wine, desperate to diffuse the awkwardness. Tom finally breaks the atmosphere.

'I was thinking, some of the kittens are ready to rehome now, Helen. I'm going to put some posters in the shop windows, if you want to help out.'

I glance up with a smile.

'Of course I will, I'd be delighted to. Oh, what lovely news. Those lucky owners to be don't even know how much love is heading their way. Please, not my ginger tabby and tuxedo cats. I want them for myself, if I come back.'

Tom gives me a huge grin.

'I'll keep a hold of them for you. You'll need to point out which ones and I'll put collars on them, to say they're reserved.'

'No pressure then, if they're booked then I definitely have to return,' I smile.

'Helen, are you saying what I think you're saying?' Tom gives me a sly grin.

'I've thought of nothing else for days now. I'm coming back and I'm going to accept the job. I do need to wrap things up at home and get the house on the market. Can you please give me two weeks to tie up some loose ends?'

'Of course I can. Do you want me to look around for some digs for you while you're away? I do have a spare room at mine, which you'd be more than welcome to use, in the meantime.' he smiles awkwardly.

'My goodness, that's very generous of you, but I couldn't possibly impose. I'll give you my email address and if you see anything, please do send the details on. Oh, the wine's here, thank goodness,' I blurt out. I can't make a decision to live with Tom just yet, that's a step too far. It would appear that he does like me, given his offer. No, I need to get my head together before even thinking about becoming involved with someone else. I feel dreadfully guilty for even having thoughts about a potential new relationship whilst I'm still married. I know for a fact that I'd be pretty gutted if I knew Steve was seeing someone else already. Tom does know the island well, so I do trust his judgement on making suggestions for me. He will choose a lovely and safe location for me and the kittens, I'm sure. Close to work so I don't need a car, there's no way I'd even attempt to drive here. Well away from the tourist hotspots and busy roads, to protect my precious babies.

Tom laughs and clinks his glass against mine.

'To being permanent colleagues,' he toasts.

'To being permanent colleagues,' I echo.

God, I really do hope I'm doing the right thing.

Chapter Sixteen
Steve

My wife is in Corfu and I'm on my way to be with her. Yes, call me crazy but I have to see Helen. It's a bold move and I have no idea if I'm anywhere near ready for this, but I sense that Helen needs me. I have to push my fears to one side and man up to the challenge. I travelled all over the world before I ended up housebound, but this is really going to test my nerve. What the fuck she's doing in Corfu, I have no idea. I left a message on some answerphone, I assume it's a doctor's surgery. The recording said the name of a practice and in the event of an emergency to call this mobile number. For all other enquiries, leave a name and contact details. I couldn't bring myself to call the mobile number given; it was an emergency to me, but not a medical one. I know only too well not to waste the vital time of these services. I've seen that often enough from my cop days, you'd be amazed at what some people consider an emergency. Some idiot's internet connection was down and he called us. A woman lost her house keys and she called the station, instead of a locksmith. Of course, we would hang up immediately and clear the line for someone in real need. The fact that these pillocks thought they should take precedence over a real crime, that was beyond my understanding. It was a Godsend when they stopped giving out direct numbers of police stations. It was mainly for counter terrorism purposes, but it did filter out many of the time wasters too.

I did wonder if perhaps Helen is unwell. Is it something to do with her pregnancy? Twins can be high risk at any age, let alone what they would class as a geriatric mother. It could be just a check-up, but her phone did track her to a surgery. That made me need to be there. I know her new babies aren't mine, but I won't leave my wife alone and scared, regardless of how many men she's been shagging behind my back. Maybe she's not alone at all, perhaps her boyfriend is there too. I didn't think of that before I booked my flights. Oh well, I guess I'll just have to graciously piss off if he is. At least I will know what's going on. Surely she wouldn't have me fly all the way out there, then refuse to at least have a civil discussion with me about our future, even if there isn't one for us as a couple. I would then know it was time to begin a new life as a single man. The thought makes me sad, and a little angry, but I can hardly blame my wife for refusing to put up with me anymore. It was a long time coming, there's nothing I can do but accept her decision with good grace and fly home to break the news to our children.

Jacob is driving me to the airport. I am absolutely shitting myself about getting on a plane. Quite literally as it turns out. We were driving out towards the airport when I felt an urgent call of nature. We had to make a detour by his house, after my nerves got the better of me. Having kindly stopped off to allow me the use of his facilities, Jacob had announced that he couldn't believe he'd been the victim of a shit-and-run. I apologised profusely, commenting that I did at least open the window a little and had a good spray of air freshener after.

Greater London whizzes by me. I contemplate on just how far on I've come since Helen left me.

Last week, I was delighted to have walked to the bottom of the front path. After that, my little driving trips felt like a big deal. To go out for lunch with my daughter, and have dinner with Jacob, that was my most amazing achievement to date. Nothing is a patch on what I'm about to do now. I have to go into an airport and take a flight, land somewhere I've never been before, and hunt for my wife. I must be insane. I would have got one of the kids to come with me, but then I looked at our dwindling account. With no income coming in from Helen now, I realised I had no choice but to go it alone. Jenny wouldn't be able to take the time off at such short notice. Matt would have been as much use as a button on a sock. He hates flying more than I do. He probably would've ended up freaking me out even more.

One panic-stricken person on board a tin can hurtling through the air, is plenty. I brought Helen's tablet so I can keep track of her whereabouts. I checked an hour ago and she's now in another part of Corfu. Quite a bit away from the surgery, according to the map. That was reassuring, she must be OK and is recuperating somewhere. I glance out at parts of the city I haven't seen in the longest time. I think back to Matt's bombshell last night. At just after seven, my son had sheepishly skulked in. He was closely followed by a rather posh looking, young woman, of around his age. Jenny had arrived half an hour before and taken a front row seat, bristling with anticipation. Again, she would tell me nothing.

'Dad, this is Tara,' Matt said sulkily. He had taken a seat at the furthest point away from me and stared sullenly at the floor.

'Charmed to meet you, Mr Brown.' Tara air kissed my cheeks, three times. She was incredibly polished and smelled expensive. I'm certainly no expert, but those clothes looked designer. She had glossy blonde curls and the brightest blue eyes I've ever seen.

'Please, call me Steve,' I had smiled, using my best telephone voice.

'Thank you, Steve. I just wanted to dash in and meet you, but I'm afraid I can't stop,' she announced. 'Your son speaks so highly of you, so I thought I'd pop in and say hi, while Giles was dropping Matthew off.'

Tara says off like "orf."

Who on earth is Giles? I glance outside the window to see a glossy black Mercedes, with a man in a black cap in the front, scrolling through his phone.

Anyway, it was delightful to meet you, Steve,' she smiles warmly, as she says my name.' I'm having dinner at Mummy and Daddy's, over in Chelsea, and I'm afraid I'm frightfully late.'

'No problem, it's nice to meet you,' I had smiled back graciously, despite my confusion. Where the fuck did my dosser, stoner son meet this chick? That's what I was thinking in that moment. I had glanced over at Jenny, who was viewing her brother's great discomfort with glee. This is it? This was what she was so excited for me to find out? I mean, it is surprising that my son has pulled a bird as fit and loaded as this one, but it's not exactly breaking news. The young woman had given Matthew a little wave and a peck on both cheeks.

'I'll see you later, Matty.' With that, she glanced around the room with a critical eye, before showing herself out.

I raised an eyebrow at my son.

'Matty, who is that lady?' I enquired.

'That's Tara Plinky-Plonkington,' Jenny interjected, in a very posh voice.

'It's Tara Pearce-Pilkington,' Matt glared at his sister.

'What was the reason for her flying visit?' I'd smiled, beginning to suspect that there was more to this story.

'Go on then, Matt. Tell Dad the *real* reason that Tara popped round.' My daughter was now on the edge of her seat, barely able to contain her delight at her brother's awkwardness. 'She's your girlfriend, isn't she?' Jenny prompted.

'No!' Matt grunted, aghast. 'Well, I suppose she will have to be now, won't she?' he'd shrugged.

'So, she just wanted to meet me when she dropped you off, is that all?'

God, it was like pulling teeth trying to get any information from my son.

'Oh, please,' Jenny squealed excitedly. 'Do let me be the one to say it.'

Matt shrugged his reply.

'Dad,' my daughter beamed. 'Brace yourself, you're going to be a Granddad.'

I stared at my youngest in shock.

'You?' I could barely get the words out.

'God, no. Not me. I don't want brats, you know that.' Jenny stared at me in utter horror.

'Because you're too selfish,' Matt batted back. 'That's fine, I'm happy to take all the glory in providing the grandchildren for Mum and Dad.'

'Oh, Please, Matthew. You don't measure success by your ability to breed. Or would you like me to get in touch with Kylie Minogue and Jennifer Aniston, and let them know what dreadful failures they are?'

'Guys, please?' I had shouted above them both. 'I can barely hear myself think. Am I clear on this? Is Tara having your baby?' I took a seat next to Matt, who cowered away from me.

'Uh, so she says,' he answered carefully. His relief was palpable, when I held out my hand to congratulate him. Jenny, on the other hand, seemed most dismayed that I wasn't reading her brother the riot act.

'Father, can you actually *imagine* him having a child? Have you forgotten about the year of the backyard Barbie massacre? He's a psychopath. Who puts their little sister's dolls on a lit barbeque, whilst taking great pleasure in her screaming at him to stop?'

She had a point. We had to take him to see a child psychologist after that.

'Jennifer, I'm quite sure he's grown out of that,' I attempted to soothe my twenty-two-year old's temper tantrum. Matt fanned the flames by giving his sister the V sign, which I just caught in my peripheral vision.

'You can't even look after yourself, Matt. You don't even have a job,' Jenny bounded over towards her brother. I placed myself between them. Things could still get physical, even nowadays.

'I'll not need to get a job, Tara's fucking loaded. I can probably leave the kid here and go take courses in whatever I like, for the rest of my life.' Matt smirked and dodged behind me, as his sister took a swipe.

'This is so typical of you, Matthew. I've worked my arse off for what I have. You just fanny around your entire life, only to land on your feet after a one-night stand,' Jenny screeched.

'What can I say? It's an art form,' my son raised his eyebrows mockingly.

'Matt, you're not helping things,' I interjected gently.

'So, you're planning to continue pissing about, whilst offloading your nut-sack gremlin on our parents? They should be looking forward to their retirement, Matt, not raising your spawn for you.' Jenny picked up her coat and car keys, jabbing them into the air, dangerously close to her brother's face.

'Don't go calling your niece or nephew a nut-sack gremlin,' I'd scolded gently.

'I'm not staying here to listen to this. Fuck you, Matt.' With that my daughter stormed out of the house, slamming the front door behind her. My son stared at me warily, waiting to see if it was all just for Jenny's sake and he really was in trouble.

'A granddad?' I finally found the words.

'Uh, I guess so. Sorry 'bout that.'

'How far on is she?' I'd shrugged off my quickly disappearing visions of eternal youth. Until I'd found out this news, I had actually been considering getting a motorbike and tickets to Glastonbury. Maybe a pipe and slippers would be more apt now. I suppose turning Matt's room into a weight studio is a stupid idea too.

'Six months,' Matt replied quietly.

'Six months? Christ alive, your Mum's twins with be aunts or uncles before they're even born. That's not weird at all.' I shook my head in disbelief.

'Yeah, I thought this family wasn't quite dysfunctional enough,' Matt chortled. 'I'm glad I could make a further contribution to our fucked-upness.'

My God, I could use a whisky for the shock, I had mused to myself. Of course, I didn't have one, I just booked a flight to Corfu and called Jacob. He was little concerned I was biting off more than I could chew, it's still in the very early days of me getting back out there. He was worried that it would hinder my recovery more than it would help. I have to admit that I did too, but in all honesty, I feel that I have more than enough to distract myself with. In these past two weeks alone, it seems like the whole fucking circus has come to town.

I sit anxiously in my plane seat, trying to control my breathing, as the air stewards do their safety demos. I really don't want the humiliation of having a full-on panic attack, mid-air. I suspect it may well happen if I don't stay focused. The cop in me had done some visual scoping of the other passengers to seek out anything suspicious. Anyone could be a terror suspect in my book. I'm not going to lie; I did have a wine or two in the airport bar. I wouldn't be sat here if I hadn't. This is my biggest test, so far, and I'm completely aware that this could be a totally wasted trip. I have to accept that my wife may not want to see me, in fact, she may be extremely pissed off at the intrusion. She could be shacked up quite happily with her huge, Greek boyfriend, who will want to beat me to a pulp on sight. On the other hand, it may just show her how much I do care. It could be that she has secretly been hoping for some grand, romantic gesture, in a last-ditch attempt to patch up our floundering marriage. It's a leap of faith, but it's one that I'm willing to take.

The jets of the plane switch on. I grasp the arm rests until my knuckles turn white. After we finally level out in the air, I open my eyes to see the stewardess strapped into the seat facing me. The relief I felt when I was offered a front seat with extra leg room, was palpable. I detest the closed in feeling of being back in the rows, particularly if I'm stuck in by the window.

'You OK?' The stewardess smiles warmly at me. I give a quick nod and attempt a smile back, which is probably more of a grimace. It's only a few hours to Corfu. I've done South America before, so I'm sure I can handle this. Think of Helen, she could be all alone and frightened. Think of your grandchild, you're going to want to take the little one to Disneyland. You can't do that if you continue to be the total pussy that you've been these past few years. You have to be a role model again and not show fear. I glance over at the tot opposite me. She must be only fifteen months old. She gives me a beaming smile. I wave to her and she waves back. She's not frightened, the young are fearless. They don't expect anything to go wrong and only respond to what's happening in their lives right at that moment. What a good way to be. I know it's only lack of experience that makes them so assured of their safety, but still, it would be wonderful to be like that again.

I distract myself with thinking about Matt's news. It's reassuring to hear of something positive associated with my son, for once. I will love being a granddad, I just know it. Once I've overcome the shock of realising that I'm old enough to be one. Of course, I knew it was possible, but Mother Nature has now reliably informed me that I am officially over the hill. Thanks for that.

Matt has given me permission to let Helen know, I can't wait to see her face. I think he's happy for me to take any freak out reactions, he will see his mother when she's calmed down and come to terms with it. Helen will be fine, probably horrified to be a nan before the age of fifty, but she will get over it. Especially since she's having her own too. Hopefully, being a Mum again will make her still feel young and distract from the fact that she's a grandmother. It makes me sad to think of my wife having children with another man. If it really is the case, I know that we can't get back together. However, I am concerned for her safety and I want to be there if she needs me. I don't want any awkwardness. It would be good to know that we could be civil and still do Christmas dinners with our own children too.

After a nerve-wracking but otherwise smooth landing, we finally arrive in Corfu. I immediately switch on Helen's tablet to see that she's changed location again. A quick look at maps on my phone shows that her location is around twenty-four miles away. I give her a quick ring, just to see if she will answer. Still nothing. I call Jenny and she answers straight away.

'Hi Dad, how are you?'

I haven't told my son or daughter that I'm taking this trip. Now is the time to let them know.

'Well, I've landed safely.'

'Landed safely, where?' Jenny ask accusingly, after a short silence. I can feel her exasperation over the miles.

'Oh, did I not mention it to you? I thought I'd pop over to Corfu, I've tracked your Mum's phone to here and I decided to go and see her.'

'What? Dad, have you completely lost the plot?' She hisses. 'You've been housebound with agoraphobia for years, now all of a sudden I can't bloody well find you when I'm looking for you.'

'I think you'll find that I'm in complete possession of the plot, young lady. I do not need a row from my daughter, thank you very much. I want to know what's going on with my wife. I have a right to know.'

'Jesus wept,' she exclaims. 'This family has turned into a bloody pantomime. Am I the only normal one left in it? Call me as soon as you find her. I need to speak to my mother. I've had no texts, no calls, no email replies. Tell her from me that this is most unfair.'

I hold the phone a foot away from my ear and let her rant it out.

'Bye Jenny-henny. Love you.' When she finally takes a breath, I grab my opportunity to hang up.

I head out towards the taxi rank queue, I only brought hand luggage so I could skip the baggage collection and get to Helen as soon as I could. I call my son to let him know where I am. For once, he answers immediately.

'Hi Matt, it's Dad. How are you? How's your girlfriend and my grandchild-to-be?'

'Fine. Got a scan tomorrow, gonna find out what flavour it is.'

I chuckle at my son's silliness.

'That's great, son. I'm in Corfu looking for your Mum. I'll give you a call when I find her. Let me know how the scan goes.'

'OK, Dad. Have fun.'

No concern or grief at all from the boy wonder. I don't understand why Jenny's so highly strung these days. Me and her used to have a great laugh together. She's turned into a right little prissy pants, since she became a partner. I miss the chilled out, silly girl, who used to take the piss out of everyone.

I jump in a taxi and show the driver the location on the tablet. He pulls out of the space abruptly and I quickly put on my seatbelt.

'Jesus, slow down,' I mutter to myself. Never mind, the quicker I get to Helen, the better. It's been so long since I've been abroad that I had totally forgotten how hot it could be. I probably should've freshened up a bit before I see Helen, but it's too late now. I mull over what I'll say to my wife, as a distraction from being driven dangerously close to a cliff edge. This whole experience has tested my nerves to the max, I can't quite believe that I'm really here. The only thing keeping me from a full on freak-out is the thought of my wife's beautiful face at the other side of this. Even if it may show me that I'm about as welcome as a fart in a lift.

We finally pull up at a dilapidated looking building and the driver eyes me cautiously.

'Who are you meeting here?' He glances at the building with a frown.

'My wife, supposedly. Although it doesn't look like the sort of place she would stay. This is the location her tablet says her phone is.'

'Be careful, this area is not good.' the driver warns as I get out of the cab.

I give a couple of sharp raps on the rickety door.

'Helen? Can you hear me? It's me, Steve,' I yell. There's no answer so I bang a little louder. I hear someone shout something aggressively in Greek and the door swings open. A rough looking man stands in front of me, shirtless, wearing only jeans. Surely this can't be the boyfriend. I know I'm no chuffing oil painting, but seriously? I give my competitor a critical glance over.

'I'd like to speak to my wife, please.' I begin, assertively.

'I don't have your wife,' The man looks at me in confusion. He towers above me menacingly, I'm not far off six foot but this guy seems like a giant to me.

'My wife's phone is here. I've tracked it, this is the exact location.'

'You accuse me of stealing your wife?' He pulls himself higher still.

'No, but you must have her phone,' I reply with a boldness I don't feel.

Shit, of all the times for my anxiety to make a reappearance, it's now. I place my hand on the door frame to stop my head from spinning, it's a gesture that he interprets as a threat. My breathing quickens and my eyes blur. Don't pass out, do not lose consciousness around this huge man who could do anything to you while you are out cold. Pull yourself together and embrace your inner cop, I silently scold.

I hear a voice behind me and glance round to see the taxi driver, who is shouting something in Greek. The shirtless man retaliates, and an argument ensues, one that I'm physically stuck in the middle of. The tempers escalate until they are right up in each other's faces, finally I can squeeze myself safely out of the way. That's when I see it; a glint of metal that catches the sun. A gleaming blade in the taxi driver's hand. It's the final straw for my nerves. The last thing I see before I pass out, is a flashback to my partner, lying on the ground while his murderer towers above him. The irony doesn't escape me, as I feel my eyes closing. Karma has got me and it's all I deserve. This too is how I will die.

Chapter Seventeen
Helen

I sit by my husband's side, feeling rather uncomfortable with being stared at, by an imposing looking Greek man. This scary looking bloke in the chair opposite, has point blank refused to go along with our numerous requests to call the police. He says that things are now dealt with. It all sounds rather ominous, so I haven't asked him to go into any details. I think I'd probably rather not know. He says that I have my phone back and he has returned my husband to my care. That should be enough. He just wants to stick around and make sure that Steve is going to be OK. I still can't quite believe that my husband, who hasn't been out of the house in over five years, is here in Corfu. He's gone from terrified recluse, to taking on a huge man, and getting my mobile back for me.

Steve is denying any involvement in tackling the guy who robbed me, he says he fainted, and when he came around there was no sign of the thief. By then, the taxi driver had my phone and brought him here, to the surgery. We got the opposite story from the Greek guy. He said Steve went storming up to the door and confronted the thief, completely unarmed. Although he was knocked to the ground and briefly did lose consciousness, he says it was all my husband's bravery that made the difference. I don't know which version of events is the right one. I guess it doesn't really matter as long as everyone is safe. Anyway, this is why we are now in Tom's office, for Steve to be checked over by a vet. You honestly couldn't make this shit up. I give a small chuckle at the thought of all the strange events that have occurred over the past two weeks. I really can't take any more shocks, so this had better be the last of them.

Steve didn't take out insurance for his hastily organised dash. Because we never go anywhere, he hasn't got a European health care card either.

The taxi driver had brought Steve to us, after he'd mentioned that my tablet had checked me into this location. Neither thought they'd find themselves in a veterinary clinic, surrounded by cats. They had assumed it was a doctor's surgery. Anyway, they thought here was a good place to start. If I wasn't here, at least the surgery may know my whereabouts. It didn't occur to me to switch off the tracking on my phone. I had completely forgotten that Steve enabled it. In hindsight, it's lucky that I didn't. I would never have seen it again.

Tom shines a torch into my husband's eyes, moving it to the side occasionally to make sure his pupils are equal and reacting. Steve hasn't vomited, he has no nausea or blurring of his vision, no headache either. He does have a lump on the back of his head, but I personally always find those lumps reassuring. You want any swelling to come out the way, not in, as that can cause intracranial pressure.

'I'd say you're fine, mate,' Tom concludes, standing up from his crouched position in front of my husband.

'No fleas or worms?' Steve jokes. 'I'm just relieved that you didn't stick a thermometer up my arse.'

We all give an awkward laugh. The Greek man gives me a poignant stare, before saying he will be on his way. What's his problem? I imagine that Steve told him that I'd left him and he doesn't approve. I thank him for his assistance but he shrugs away my gesture. Tom goes to see him out. Steve gives me an awkward glance; we haven't been totally on our own yet and I'm unsure where to start. Tom returns and the atmosphere turns even more awkward. What now?

'Helen, feel free to take your husband back to the hotel room and see him settled in,' Tom breaks the silence hanging over us.

Shit, I hadn't actually thought about where Steve would stay. I suppose it makes sense that he'd go to the same hotel as me. God, am I going to have to share a bed with him? I hadn't bargained on that. How awkward, we haven't shared a room in years. We may be married, but it just seems too intimate after all this time. Even more so now that I've left him.

'Uh, I guess that's what we should do,' I finally answer. I really don't want the discomfort of having to bunk up with my husband, but I do have a duty to look after him now that he's here, with a minor head injury. I would much prefer to come back and sleep in the kitten nursery, but that seems rather callous. I don't want Tom to think I'm a complete cow. I'm actually pretty irritated that Steve has probably just spent our monthly mortgage repayment on a flight. I hadn't accounted for that extra cost disappearing from our joint account budget. That means there's even more of an urgency to sell up.

'You guys head off, 'Tom smiles graciously at Steve and me. 'Hey, you should take your husband to that great restaurant along the road, Helen. I bet he'd love it.'

My heart sinks. I know this is Tom's way of saying that it's OK with him that our usual dinner date is off the cards. I just want things to go back to how they were when I woke up this morning. I was prepared for dealing with this back at home, but not here. I feel like I've been forced into facing things before I'm completely ready. I know it sounds churlish, but I feel that Steve has backed me into a corner.

'I suppose we'd better go then,' I sigh. 'I'll just say goodbye to the babies and we'll make a move.'

I stand in the nursery and look around at what has been my life, for almost two weeks. I really can't bear to leave here. Maybe I don't have to. I could tell Steve it's over now, without even having to go home. Perhaps in that sense, he's done me a favour and saved me from having to go back at all. No, I need to see my kids and sort out the house myself. Steve has a rather haphazard opinion of what's important and what's not. I imagine him holding up Matthew's little sailor outfit he had as a baby, or Jenny's teeny party dresses. 'Well, I don't think these will fit now,' that's what he'd say, before piling my treasured memories on the chuck heap. Old drawings that I've saved from their first scribbles. Tabatha, the cat I had as a student, I still have her old collar and I could never part with that. Birthday cards, Christmas cards, the cork from the bottle of champagne on our engagement, that I wrote the date on. The thought of leaving Steve in charge of what's important and what is tat, is horrifying. I have to be the one to do it. I give a resigned sigh. I do have to leave my beloved, new home for a little while. It'll still be here. I can say goodbye to my kids and my London friends properly, I can eat one last time in my favourite restaurants. One more week in my home, absorbing every precious memory from it. I'll lay on the sofa where I nursed my babies, I'll lie in a bath full of bubbles where they used to splash around together. It won't all be bad going back. It will be closure. A proper ending to that particular chapter of my life.

I'm suddenly aware that I've left my husband and friend together, no doubt desperately trying to find some light conversation to fill the awkwardness. I can't quite pull myself away from the nursery just yet. I scoop up my little Matthew cat, who had begun to climb his way up my long skirt.

'Hi, baby,' I lift him up and snuggle him to my face, deeply inhaling his adorable kitteny smell. 'Mummy just needed a moment to gather herself from this crazy pantomime that her life has become. I am going to miss you so much, please don't forget about me.' I try to lift him from my shoulder, but he clings on. It tugs at my heart. He's just like my original Matthew, on a school morning.

'Come and see your sister, she is going to show you how to be independent. You can learn a lot from her. I place the ginger kitten next to the little tuxedo girl. They immediately launch into a play fight. Just like my other children, although that wasn't always playful. I watch them for a few moments, unable to tear myself away from the adorable twosome.

'I promise, I will come back for you both and we will have a beautiful home together. I love you, my babies.' I give them a little pat on the head each, and make my way to the door. I can't look back; I can't bear to see those little eyes pleading with me to stay. Matthew cat, of course, not Jenny. I head back into the coolness of the surgery. In my absence, it seems like some male bonding has been taking place, as Tom and my husband guffaw at some joke they are sharing. 'I was just saying to Tom that he should join us for dinner. He's been telling me all about what a great help you've been with the cats. Although, I don't know that it's safe for you to do so. Toxoplasmosis can be very serious for unborn babies. I hope you at least wore gloves.'

Tom's eyes shoot urgently to mine, then down to my stomach area.

'Wow, Helen. I had no idea,' I can almost visibly see his guard come up with every word spoken.

'Steve, what are you talking about?' I shake my head in confusion.

'It's OK, Helen. I know everything. Don't worry, we can talk about it back at the hotel. I have a lot to tell you too.'

Tom smiles broadly at us both, but his eyes now tell a different story. There's a sadness in them that fills me with guilt. I know I shouldn't feel that way; I haven't once led him to believe that anything could happen between us. Although, there was some kind of unspoken agreement there from the beginning, I don't think either of us could deny it. I felt it and I know he did too.

'You guys enjoy your dinner out. It's very kind of you to invite me along, Steve. Maybe another time, I have a ton of paperwork to get through.' Tom indicates to the computer table, before realising there are only around five sheets of A4 on it, at best. To save his embarrassment, we act like there are stacks of files sat there.

'No problem, I'll see you tomorrow, then?' I ask hopefully.

'You take the day off, Helen. It's the last day before you fly home and your help has been invaluable to me and the furry people. You've earned a day of fun and relaxation.'

For the second time, my heart feels like it's plummeted to my stomach. No, I can't bear not to be coming back here tomorrow. Steve and I make our way to the door, I indicate for my husband to go before me. I look back one last time to glance at Tom.

'It's OK,' he smiles, a little sadly. 'Everything is going to be fine, Helen. You'll see.'

I stare into my wine glass in shock, as Steve begins to relay all the information he has gathered on me over the past two weeks, none of which has any truth to it at all. Thank goodness for Jenny. Without her, the two men in my life would have tied themselves in knots over all this silly nonsense.

'The twins I was referring to are the cats, Steve. Miss Tilly had two kittens.'

He shows me the message on his phone where I apparently admitted I was pregnant.

'Really, that's all you had to go on to create that bonkers philosophy? The sun was probably in my eyes and I put a full stop where there should have been a comma,' I shrug. 'Jenny was right, it's a simple error of punctuation.'

'What a relief,' Steve visibly relaxes and takes a sip of his pint. I was so impressed to hear him order an alcohol free one. Although there was no way I wasn't having something stronger, given the shock of having my housebound husband track me down and appear from out of nowhere.

'I don't know what your plans are, Helen, or if we even do have some hope of a reconciliation. I really have missed you and I'm desperately hoping that you'll say our marriage isn't over. If you want me back, then I can probably get over the other men. I admit that it won't be easy, but I've hardly been a picnic to live with. I guess I can somewhat understand why you did what you did, and I take responsibility for that. Maybe we could go to couples' therapy? You would have to agree to stop the affairs and try with me. Do you think that's something you could do?'

I stop fiddling with the bread basket and stare at Steve in confusion.

'What? I haven't had one single affair behind your back, let alone several. I have never been unfaithful to you. Was it

Matt that said this too? Honestly, I do worry about that boy. You really need to stop listening to him, he's off in cloud cuckoo land most of the time.' I give an irate tut at my son's melodrama.

'That brings me to another point...' Steve looks like he can hardly contain his mirth.

'Oh Christ, what fresh hell is this?' I mutter, putting my face in my hands. I pour up another glass to dull the pain of whatever godforsaken announcement this is about to be.

'What would you prefer to be called, Nan or Granny? Helen, the wine!' Steve makes a grab for the bottle, as it overflows in my glass. The waiter rushes over with a cloth and begins cleaning up around me.

'Steve, what the fuck? Is Jenny expecting? I thought she didn't want kids.'

'Nope, I thought it was her too, at first. You should've heard the abuse I got from her for even suggesting it. Go on, try again,' he chuckles.

'Matthew. Shit.' Oh, dear God, as much as I love my son, he can barely care for himself. 'How did this happen? The boy dresses like a walking charity shop reject, he can't even get eye contact properly with us and we've known him since conception. I'm far too young to be a grandmother, Steve.' I shake my head in denial of my imminently looming fifties. 'Matthew can't even earn enough to support himself, let alone a child. Do we know who the mother is?' I give a helpless shake of the head.

'Yes, I've met her. Tanya or Tara something,' Steve shrugs. 'She has a double-barrelled name and is well posh. She's from Chelsea,' my husband gives me an approving raise of an eyebrow.

'Well, that's something, I suppose,' I reply sarcastically. In my head I was stood aghast, alongside Davina McCall, as the contents of my dwindling bank account just suddenly opened up and fell. Like on *The 100k Drop*. I can barely afford life as it currently is, without another two mouths to feed.

'They're going to move in together, she's six months gone and they're finding out the sex at her scan tomorrow. They didn't want to know at first but they've changed their minds. She's getting one of those fancy 3D ones, I believe.'

'Six months?' I screeched. 'Why hasn't he said anything until now? I don't know how you can be so blasé about this, Steve.'

'Because it's Matt,' he gives a nonchalant shrug. 'Nothing that boy does would surprise me.'

Just when I think my life can't possibly get any weirder, the third round of shit hits the fan. Now I have got to go home for a bit. I can't not meet this girl and see Matt to congratulate him personally. Or wring his bloody neck for giving me the shock of my life.

'Is he happy about it?' I finally find some words.

'It's Matthew, who the fuck knows.' Steve rips a bread roll in half and dips it in oil and rock salt. 'He looked like he was about to get the bollocking of his life from me. You know what he's like, always assuming he's in trouble for something. He will adapt, this may make him finally grow up.'

I stare at my husband across the table. He seems like a different man to me, and not just because the location has changed. The old Steve swagger is back, the one he had when we first met. That cheeky glint in his eye. I can almost see him like I did then, across the bar, handing me a beermat with his phone number on it and tossing his long, permed hair back. It's like the last five years never happened. With all the new thoughts and information buzzing around my head, I'm seriously wondering if I imagined the whole thing. The drinking, the agoraphobia. Have I entered a parallel universe? I glance over at the waiter, currently serving at the table next to us. An idea occurs to me. So, my husband thinks he can just rock up and drop every bombshell under the sun on me? He can go from hermit to hero, flying out in what he thinks is my hour of need. Then inform me he's quit smoking and almost completely given up the booze. He has me down as some scarlet woman, carrying another man's twin babies. Not only that, he then plays me the grandmother card.

Well, I don't bloody think so, he's not getting away with this lightly. I lean across the table and whisper to him.

'Hey, Steve, you want to know a secret that only the locals know about?'

'Sure,' he beams back at me, leaning in further so that I can whisper to him.

'It's amazing, you get a discount and a special menu that the tourists don't get. None of the regular bottles of wine either, only the best stuff from the private cellar. Tom told me all about it, he's lived here for years.'

'Yes, of course I want to know. Don't leave me hanging, Helen,' he urges.

I smile benevolently at my husband over the table.

'It's quite simple, I tried it one of my first nights here and it changed everything. All you have to do, is tell the waiter that Stavros sent you.'

'Stavros sent me?' Steve looks across the table at me cynically. 'Who is he? I don't know the guy.'

'Trust me, it doesn't matter,' I urge. Quick, here he comes, Steve. Go on, tell him.'

I lie in the dark next to my sleeping husband, noticing how he doesn't snore when he hasn't been drinking. It's a relief to finally have peace to process the thoughts whirling incessantly around my head. A grandmother, me? I know that at my age I should half expect it, but Jenny doesn't want kids and Matt is just so flaky. He can't commit to a college course, let alone a girlfriend. It also complicates thing a lot for me. Can I come back here, now there will be a little one on the scene? I don't know if I could. I love it on the island, and I promised I'd take the kittens. I really don't want to go home, but I do want to be around Matt's child. I guess I can fly back to the UK every couple of months. Is that wrong of me? What sort of person would not want to see their grandchild every weekend? To be on hand to do school pick-ups and to snuggle them when they're all snotty and full of the cold. I should be there to care for my baby's baby. He won't have the first clue what to do and I can help him. I also wouldn't want the child to forget who I am if they don't see me often, I couldn't bear to see them turn away from their own nan, like she was a stranger. Maybe I could take the cats home. No, wouldn't they need to go into quarantine for six months? Then I'd let them out right next to a railway station? I shudder at the thought of my precious babies crossing the lines. Or being lonely, scared and locked in a cage for six months, due to my selfishness. Stop thinking about it and the answers will come, I chastise myself.

I distract myself with thinking about Steve. He's done a remarkable job in overcoming his fears. I'd have never in a million years have expected to see him here, in Corfu. He's stopped smoking, practically stopped drinking, overcome his agoraphobia and lost a stone. All in the space of two weeks. I should've left years ago; he would have motivated himself long before now. We'd also still have some money left. He looks so much better for a good overhaul of his life. Almost, dare I say it, *attractive* again. For God's sake, Helen, get a grip. I scold myself. You're overtired and have had a lot to take in. It's just your imagination playing tricks on you. I've already decided that my marriage is over, I at least need the comfort of having one definite decision made. I need to try and get some sleep, everything will be clearer in the morning. I turn to face the other way, towards the window. The breeze blows the light curtains in and I catch a glimpse of the starry sky. Everything will be OK, that's what Tom said earlier. Steve's arm snakes sleepily around my waist. I have no idea if he's awake or not, but he's looking for comfort, for me to tell him that I appreciate all he's doing. I can't. It's too late.

Don't, Steve, I silently plead. Please don't make this any more difficult for me than it has to be.

Chapter Eighteen
Steve

I wake up momentarily disorientated, before remembering that I came out to Greece, all on my own. I roll over in the double bed to see an empty space where my wife should be. There's a note propped up against the lamp. I scramble over Helen's side to pick it up.

Good morning, Steve. I couldn't sleep, so I've popped out to the surgery to see the cats. See you later. H.

It's an encouraging sign. No usual two kisses after the H, but at least she's gone from seemingly disappearing off the face of the earth, to leaving a note. It's a start. I'll take anything I can get.

I roll back onto the bed and glance at the whirling ceiling fan above me. When I saw Helen yesterday, she seemed a little awe-struck. Not only for me being there in Greece, but for stopping smoking and almost stopping drinking. I suspect she was shocked at how much better I looked. I was aware that my appearance had improved dramatically in only two weeks. The puffiness has gone down considerably, I look a good bit younger without all those nasty toxins swirling about my body. The tiredness has gone from my eyes now that I don't have constant sleep disruption and hangovers. I actually do feel more like the old me, the twenty-four-year-old lad that Helen first knew. There was a look in my wife's eyes that I haven't seen in a long time. A kind of admiration, and dare I say it, I think she maybe fancied me a little bit. It's quite ironic that I look years younger than I did, just as I find out I'm going to be a Grandpa. It was wonderful sharing a bed with Helen again. I even chanced a little hug, and although I could feel her tense up, she didn't push me away. It was comforting to have close contact with her again. I had the best sleep I have had since before the dreadful event with Luke.

I pull myself out of the double bed and take a shower. I did bring a couple of spare sets of clothes with me in my hand luggage, but I didn't think to try anything on before I left.

Barely drinking means I've eaten hardly any shit, while I've been sat in front of the telly. The weight has started to fall off me. I imagine that a big part of it is losing pounds of fluid retention too. I looked at myself in the hall mirror at home yesterday, and for the first time in years, I actually smiled at my reflection. Because I never go out anywhere, I haven't worn my summer stuff in years and it's all pretty loose on me now. Imagine that, going from not being able to zip up my jacket, to being smaller than I was five years ago. Mind you, hasn't Helen always sworn by wearing a size bigger than she is. She says it takes pounds off you. She's right too, never go by the label, that's her rule. Her friends would all try to cram into a smaller dress size, one that only they knew about, but their clothes would cling to every bit of them. It made them look larger than they really were. Helen loved the bagginess of a size up, it made her feel petite. Not that she's in the slightest way fat, although I'm sure she would say otherwise. If anything, I thought she was more attractive with a few extra pounds on. It plumped out her face a bit, making her look even more youthful than she already does. The weather here is certainly agreeing with her. Or perhaps she's loved up? Oh, God, I never thought of that. I wonder if there's something going on with her and this Tom guy. The atmosphere felt tense yesterday, when they were both in the room. Maybe she's gone to tell him that she and I are giving things another try. Perhaps she's gone so they can work out how to break the news to me that they are a couple. Stop it, Steve. Didn't Helen tell you yesterday that she hasn't ever been unfaithful? I was over the moon to hear this news, and also to discover that Helen's twins were kittens. I still wonder why she ended up here, in particular. I know she says she hasn't cheated, and I do believe her, but what if she met Tom online and thought they'd meet up and see if they'd get on?

I still have so many questions for her but I'm trying not to be too pushy.

I make myself a coffee and take a seat out on our balcony. My phone gives a notification ping and I pick it up from the table. It's a message from Matt.

"Hey Daddy-o, you ready to find out if you're going to be a nanny or a grandpa?"

An unexpected burst of laughter escapes me. I glance at the veranda next door; the two women smile indulgently at the mad bloke laughing like a loon on his own. God, that lad is a daft one. Wait, I hope he is actually joking and he doesn't really think...oh, he's sent a scan picture, with a caption.

"It's a boy! Surprise, you're a grandpa"

I gaze in awe at the perfect 3D image of my first grandchild. You can make out every part of his sweet face, his tiny clenched fists and his little toes. I feel a surge of pride in my son.

"Well done, Matt. He is absolutely gorgeous. Congratulations to you both," I type back.

I feel like I could burst with pride. I stand on the balcony and look down at the holidaymakers relaxing by the pool. A gentle breeze catches the palm trees and creates a soft whoosh by me and into the room. It makes me feel uplifted, like a sudden rush of positivity. Everything is going to be all right, I can feel it.

I head down to breakfast alone, wishing my wife was sat opposite me, like the other husbands. I mindlessly stir my coffee and ponder on the great leaps and bounds I've made these past two weeks. I very much hope it makes some difference in my marriage. I glance at the couple at the table next to me and the woman smiles, before glancing apologetically at the empty chair opposite. I'm not normally one for telling fibs but I cannot abide the pity of her thinking I'm alone.

'She's having a lie-in, a little too much wine last night.' I smile back, making a drinking motion and a silly face.

'Oh, I see,' the lady replies, giving a soft laugh. I resist the urge to blurt out our happy news to this complete stranger, but once I've shown Helen the scan, I'm letting everyone I meet see it. This is such a blessing to us, surely there's no chance that Helen won't want to get back together now. We are going to have a new reason to celebrate soon. It's been a long time coming. It feels like someone has opened the window in a dark, stagnant room, revealing beautiful sunshine and a breath of fresh air. I think Jenny is the only one not delighted by this news, but only because she's so competitive with her sibling. Any success of her brother's, she needs to draw a comparison with. She doesn't even want kids but I know this will make her feel inadequate in some way. She'll probably get a couple of dogs and call them our grandpuppies, just to even out the balance.

For most of the morning and early afternoon, I sit by the pool bar, waiting for Helen to return to the hotel. It's taking all my patience not to run down to the surgery and show her the picture that Matt sent. Oh, and to ever so casually see what's going on down there too. I had been pleased that Tom had suggested we spend the day together and I'm disappointed, but not surprised, that Helen didn't choose to. I have to suck it up and give her the space she needs, allowing her to tie up whatever loose ends there are left here. So, she was planning on returning tomorrow after all. I wish I'd known that, although the ultimate test of traveling alone has paid off. I had no time to think about it or stress over it, I just went. It won't be so scary in the future and now we can take those trips away that she's always dreamed of, if we are indeed getting back together. I watch the holidaymakers around me enviously. Couples looking like they haven't a care in the world, even though statistically a third of them will divorce, eventually. Or is it half? I can't quite remember. Hopefully that won't be Helen and me.
A vision of beauty appears at the top of the stairs to the pool area. Wow, she really takes my breath away. My wife looks like a goddess in her flowing, white sundress. It's one I haven't seen before, so I assume it must be new. The sea breeze catches her long, brown hair and it floats around her,

like a halo. The sun has warmed her skin to a gorgeous, olive colour. I am the luckiest man alive and I had completely forgotten that. I had the good fortune to marry the woman that no man can currently tear his eyes from. She's been in my life for almost three decades, what an absolute arse of a man I am to have stopped noticing. I give her a welcoming smile and stand to pull out a chair for her. She walks over towards me and I can't help but notice a few envious looks from some nearby blokes, and a few raised eyebrows from the women. Who does she think she is? I can almost hear their thoughts. Helen thinks she's nothing special, and that makes her even more attractive. The most wonderful thing about my wife is that she has no idea of her air of presence. She walks into a room and people notice. I had initially thought it was just me who saw it, but a few friends of ours have commented on it too. She draws you in and makes you want to be close to her.

'Let me get you a drink, love. How are the cats today?' I take my wife's hand and usher her to the seat.

'They're good, thanks. It was really difficult to say goodbye to them, I'm going to miss them all so much,' she smiles sadly.

'I bet it was. You've grown so fond of them, I can tell. I'll be right back with a drink for you and you can tell me all about it.' I grab my wallet from the table and head to the bar. I overhear one woman nearby, hissing to her husband about how attentive I am, and how he should take note.

'If you looked like her, I probably would,' he casually replies.

Fuck mate, run, I want to shout. Instead he chortles and clutches his sides. I see Helen glancing their way curiously. The woman shouts that he's a bloody idiot, following it up with a swift pouring of her cocktail, onto the top of his head. He gasps as a trickle of slushy liquid makes its way down the back his t-shirt. The barman and I exchange a look. He got what he deserved there, seems to be our unspoken agreement.

I walk back over to our table, with a glass of white wine for Helen and an alcohol-free beer for me. I open up Matt's message and place the phone in front of my wife, trying to stop myself from blurting out what she's seeing.

She gives a little squeal of delight and beams at me.

'Is this who I think it is?'

'It sure is. Our little grandson.'

Helen stares in awe at the image.

'I've never seen a scan picture so clear, our two resembled kidney beans with legs. I feel like I know him already. Three months we have to wait to see this little one for real.' She can't take her eyes off my phone and I can almost feel the bond between us deepening with every second that ticks by.

'You can get to know his mother in the meantime,' I smile.

'That's true,' Helen sighs and goes back to the picture. 'Can you send this to me, please?'

'Of course.' I take the phone back from her and forward it on.

'I can't wait to give my son a big hug,' Helen smiles affectionately. I know parents shouldn't have favourites, but I know Helen's is Matt. Jenny and I share a similar sense of humour, so I've always had a particular soft spot for her. I guess as long as we don't both favour the same kid, it's OK.

'This will be the making of him, Steve. I just know it,' Helen continues, still staring at her screen. 'He's never been able to find his way before, but I just feel that fatherhood is what he's destined for.'

I love it when Helen speaks like this. She reminds me of my Nan, with all her talk of destiny and callings.

'You could well be right, Helen. He's never settled into any course or job, in spite of being more than intelligent enough. Maybe he will become a stay at home Dad.'

'What's she like, this girl?' Helen leans forward conspiratorially.

'Shall we do a bit of snooping?' I chuckle. 'She's bound to be on Matt's Facebook friends list.' With a sly glance between us, we both make a grab for our phones, in a race to be the first to locate Tara.

'Scroll through to the Ts, Helen,' I urge.

'Found her,' Helen declares within seconds. 'Tara Pearce-Pilkington. Oh, wow, she is gorgeous. Look at those eyes, you can tell she hasn't even used a filter on these photos. What a beautiful son they will have, with their combined genes. Hey look, she's a fashion designer. I wonder if she'll give me some style tips. Dammit, she has her security settings too high, I can see nothing else. Let's Google her.'

Helen laughs as I pull my chair round to hers and we load up the browser.

'She goes all over the world,' I say in wonder. 'Look, there she's in Milan, this other pic is from New York Fashion Week.'

'Jenny is going to hate her,' Helen declares.

'Oh, you bet. She already had a serious go at Matt about him landing on his feet. She has a point, our girl has worked so hard to get where she is, and her brother strikes out as a soon-to-be-rich, baby daddy. It looks like you need another drink. You keep searching.' I get up and head back to the bar. I hear a squeal from the table and give a wide smile my wife's way. She's probably just found Tara's parents and discovered just how loaded they really are.

'There's an article on her parents in Hello magazine,' she bellows across to the bar. 'You need to see this house in Chelsea, they have an indoor to outdoor pool.'

I smile warmly across at my wife, noticing that others are listening in to hear what else this mystery couple have in their home.

This is the best thing that could've happened to Helen and me. This tiny, new family member is already bringing us closer than we have been in decades. Tomorrow, we will make our way back home, with a new purpose and lease of life in our relationship. I know Helen will miss Corfu and her cats, but we can always come back over for a holiday. It's certainly beautiful here, but I cannot wait to get back to London and start properly planning our future again.

Chapter Nineteen
Helen

There's absolutely no way that I'm staying in London any longer than I reasonably have to. Sure, Steve and I are getting on much better, but nothing has changed. I'm still having my home here and I'm most definitely coming back for my cats. I've said nothing for now, it's not the right time to break the news to Steve. I don't want any awkwardness when I have no spare room to escape to. We had a chilled out last evening before flying home. I feel so much calmer now I've made the decision, also the fact that I'm only taking myself into consideration for once. Steve has to think that it's all business as usual for now, but he owes me big style for all those years that I cooked and cleaned and supported him.

My cats, my new job, and my lovely, little Greek hideaway. That's my new future and this is non-negotiable. Of course, I'm over the moon to be a nan soon, but I'm not putting my life on hold to do so. It may sound selfish, but I have to let my son be a grown up and take responsibility for his own family. I can see what the future will be if I stay. I would become a daily, unpaid babysitter, while he continues to fanny about, dropping in and out of courses. He needs to step up now and by removing my potential childcare services, it will ensure he has to. Steve and I can't afford to live in London and not work, that is if Steve was to go back to some kind of employment. I know for sure now that I definitely want to retire from nursing. I haven't had any longer than a few days off at a time, in years. The agency doesn't pay holidays so there really was no choice but to keep on going. Taking this week off has shown me that there is so much more to life, than continually working, whilst simultaneously getting nowhere. I'm like a hamster on a wheel. The money comes in; the money goes out. I'm exhausted with it all. Matthew will be fine, I'm sure Tara can afford a nanny, if she chooses to indulge Matthew in all his latest flash-in-the-pan ideas. They can all come over to

Greece and visit as often as they like. I can fly over every few months for a holiday and go home for Christmas too. I agreed all of this with Tom, this morning. He's delighted that I'm going to come back, although he did feel a bit bad that Steve flying out hadn't changed my mind one bit.

It was a heart-wrenching decision I had to make, one that had seen me awake for most of the night. Leaving my family in the UK, or leaving my furry brood and new life here. When I arrived at the surgery, first thing in the morning, Tom had looked behind me questioningly to see where Steve was. I had to see him alone, I couldn't go back to London without finding out how the land lay with our plans. Nothing had changed on Tom's side. Although he was still reeling with shock over my alleged pregnancy, and how a nurse expecting twins could sink all that wine, seemingly without guilt.

'I left Steve in bed, it's just me,' I'd smiled. He looked pleased about that.

'Tom, I still would like to sell up in London and come back, if you still want me for the nurse's role.'

'Of course, Helen,' he was delighted with my decision. 'What about your pregnancy? Steve is right, toxoplasmosis can be hazardous for unborn children.' He'd said warily.

'There is no pregnancy, my son got the wrong end of the stick, as usual. I spoke of the twins, Tilly's twins, and somehow they thought they were mine,' I'd shrugged.

'Well, that's a relief. Or not, perhaps? I'm sorry, I don't know why I said that,' Tom grimaced.

He was relieved at the news that I wasn't expecting. I knew then for sure that he had seen something potentially happening between us.

'I know why you said it,' I'd smiled. 'I think we both thought that something may have developed between us at some point, or I may be making a complete fool of myself in assuming. What is they say? Don't assume, it makes an ass of you and me,' I laugh nervously. 'You know, because ass, u and me, spell assume? Oh, never mind,' I warbled on endlessly, much to my embarrassment. I hate the verbal diarrhoea that I get when I'm nervous. Tom stared at me with a little smile playing on his lips.

'I think you should try again with your husband,' he finally said.

'I'm glad you said that, Tom. I didn't want to be the one to bring it up,' I'd sighed. 'I have no idea if I'm making the right decision, but I do feel we have to at least give it a go. Given that Matt's baby is on his way, and the fact that Steve has made such a huge effort to get his life back on track. I couldn't bear to see him spiral back into that depressing hole he was in. You do understand, don't you, Tom?'

'Helen, if some miracle occurred and my wife walked back through those doors. Do you know what I'd do?'

'I wouldn't have a look-in, would I?' I grinned.

'As lovely, kind and beautiful as you are? No, you would not,' Tom shook his head and looked longingly at the door. As if somehow his words could manifest such an occurrence.

'Thank you for making that easy for me, Tom. Steve and I are going to be grandparents; I can't spoil Matt's happy news with a divorce. I also do want to see how things pan out, now that Steve has made all this effort. We always dreamed of living overseas. Of course, we will be back and forth to the UK as often as we can, but I would like to come back out here and bring Steve with me. I'll need to find him something to do out here, but I have a few ideas.'

'I wholeheartedly agree with what you're doing, Helen. I wouldn't have it any other way,' Tom stated decisively.

'Can I see my babies, please?' I glanced hopefully at the nursery door.

'Go on then, get a cuddle fix to last you the next week or so,' he chuckled.

I sat on the floor with my little Matthew and Jenny cats, one in each hand, feeling their warm, baby fur against my face.

'Mummy and Daddy will be back soon. Uncle Tom is going to look after you just now. Be good for him, please. I will come and take you home, as soon as I find us one.'

As usual, Jenny cat wriggled to get away, the independent little thing that she is. Matt cat snuggled into my shoulder and I could hear his soft, quick breath in my ear. I'm going to miss all these little scraps back in the UK. Strangely, I have already stopped referring to it as home now.

'Right, babies, we best go and let Tom know that you two are the ones not to rehome. Come with me and we will get him to take a photograph of us all, so he knows you're both mine. He can send it to me and then I can see you every day until I get back.'

I paused in the vestibule between the nursery and the surgery. I didn't intend to overhear Tom, but I accidentally did.

'Well, Miss Tilly, I guess it's just going to be you and me at our house now. Will we take the babies too? Would you like to take your children home with you?'

I heard a soft meow that Tom took as an affirmative.

'Good, it's agreed, let's do that. I know we hoped that Helen would one day end up with us too, but it's not to be. We will still be a happy family, you'll see.'

To announce my presence, I deliberately went back out and in again, making a bit of a racket coming into the room.

'Tom, these two kittens are the ones I'd like you to keep aside for me, please. I'm so going to miss them. I was hoping you'd take a photo and send it to my phone. Mummy will look at you every day, my little darlings.' I pulled the pashmina from my shoulders. 'Can I leave this too, so they don't forget my scent? I feel silly for asking, but I want them to remember me.'

'Of course, what are their names?' He scooped up the little tuxedo girl and struggled with her to put a collar on. 'Here, you're a feisty madam, aren't you? Ow, she just caught me nicely with a claw,' he announced, as she took another swipe.

'Yeah, she does that,' I'd shrugged. 'Well, I've always called her Jenny cat but that won't do. I think after what you've just said, I shall call her Clawdette.'

Tom gave a booming laugh.

'I love it; Clawdette she is. What about the boy?'

'Hmm, I have been calling him Matt cat, but let's think of what he's natured like. He's shy and gentle, of all the kittens, he's the one who gives me the maximum number of cuddles,' I pause to think.

'Max? Short for maximum?'

'Of course, Clawdette and Max. Don't they suit their names too? I'm so pleased they have some now. It makes me feel like they're really mine,' I handed Max to Tom, for his collar. He sat there so patiently, my clever boy.

'They are really yours now, so you have to come back.'

'Even if Steve refuses, I'm still in. I'm willing to give us another chance but it has to be on my terms. He doesn't just get away with his lackadaisical attitude towards me all these years. The PTSD aside, he could've done more in the house instead of all that time drinking and gaming.'

'Sounds fair to me, Helen. Look, you go and enjoy your day and we'll see you in a week or so. There's no rush, but I know you'll be itching to get back to these two. Talking of which, I'll flea, worm, and neuter them for you, and make sure they're ready to go.'

'Thanks, Tom.' There was an awkward moment between us in which so much felt left unsaid. Do we hug? Do we shake hands? I pick up my bag and settle on a smile. Tom looks relieved, I imagine he was having the same dilemma.

How would things have turned out, had I made a different choice? I know it's what we were both thinking.

Chapter Twenty
Steve

London feels Baltic and noisy after the tranquillity of Corfu. Being home has immediately dredged up so many dark feelings for me, ones that no longer seem to belong. It almost feels like I've stepped into a stranger's house. That uncomfortable feeling of staying over somewhere new where you don't feel quite at home in yet. I know what it is, it's the ghosts of the past, the ones that I drank to avoid all that time. Those same ones that I've already worked through, with Jacob. Why have they come back? Is it this house that's triggering the memories? It's like a residue of a sadness, like when you visit a place that you know something dreadful happened in. This has confused me great deal, this house was my solace for so many years. Well, instead of drinking the ghosts away, I now know that bringing them out into the open exorcises them, and they lose their power. With this in mind, I voice my thoughts to Helen.

'I know exactly what you mean, Steve. I'm actually glad you feel that way too. There's something I want to ask you. Let's dish up dinner first and then we will chat.'

Helen turns back to the kitchen counter and unwraps the takeaway we ordered. She uncorks a bottle of red and pours up two glasses.

'Oh, shit, I forgot you don't drink any more. It's just force of habit.' She smiles apologetically.

'I have the odd one now and again. It's being out of control that I don't want. I won't be partaking every day and no more than a couple at a time, when I do.'

Helen gives me a warm smile and hands me the glass. She takes our plates over to the table and comes back for her drink. I'm so enjoying this time together. It declined so gradually that I never even noticed it going.

'First of all, I haven't told you how proud I am of you, Steve. You have overcome so much, and I'm so impressed with all your achievements. I don't know how you made such a quick turnaround, but you should be so proud of your strength.'

I clink my wife's glass with mine and we take a seat at the dining table. I dish up Helen's Indian food first and she raises an approving eyebrow at my attentiveness. It isn't put on, now I've got my head out of my arse again, I've realised just what was in front of me all this time. A wonderful, hardworking and generous lady. Bloody gorgeous too, how on earth did I stop noticing?

The kids are coming over later; Matt says he has something he wants to discuss with us. Helen had rolled her eyes when I told her this news. What fresh hell is this? I know it's what we were both thinking.

'So, Helen, what is this thing that you wanted to ask me?' I take a huge bite of my peshwari naan bread, so that I'm not tempted to interrupt. It's a previous bad habit of mine and I'm trying to make sure I do nothing to upset the equilibrium between us.

'I've adopted two cats,' she states, matter of fact.

I nod approvingly. I've been waiting on this announcement and I congratulate myself on knowing my wife so well. I knew that working with them these past two weeks would renew her interest in wanting some of her own. Although she always said she would never have cats so close to the overground station, the neighbourhood felines are pretty street-smart. I'm sure ours will be OK too.

'I've also taken on a new job. Still in nursing but not the same sort,' she hesitates, watching my reaction closely.

'That's fantastic, Helen. Are you planning on moving from general to a different department?'

'Well, actually its veterinary nursing.'

'That's a great idea. How long do you have to train for that? Are you going to go see the practice along the road about a job?'

'No, Steve. I'm going back to Corfu.'

My stomach flips over, is my wife saying it's over between us? Please don't let it be so. I hardly dare breathe, in case the next words out of her mouth are that she's in a relationship with Tom.

'I want to sell this house, Steve. I want you and I to start a new life away from it all, the life I always wanted us to have. It's something I've needed desperately for so many years, but I just kept saying that one day we'd get around to it. That day is here. What do you think?' Helen smiles warily. She looks so fragile, like a no from me would see all her dreams crashing around her.

'With me? Are you sure that's what you want?' I look around the kitchen as if it's the last time I'm ever going to see it.

'Yes, I've thought long and hard about it and it was the circumstances that were all wrong, perhaps not necessarily us. I'd like at least the chance to see if things could be different now.'

'I am well up for going to Corfu,' I smile. 'I really enjoyed my very short time there. To see you so happy, that made me happy too.'

'Really?' Helen beams.

'Really. Although, should we consider renting out this place? What if one day we want to come back? We'd never afford somewhere like this place now.'

Helen chews thoughtfully as she mulls this over.

'We have your Nan's place. If we do ever decide to move back, it's probably about time we downsized anyway. God forbid things don't work out for Matt and Tara, and he ends up back here, yet again. If we do let this place, he would fully expect us to cancel any tenancy as soon as possible, so he could live here rent free. We both know he's got previous on that.'

My wife has a point. The boy wonder really does need to get his shit together, so closing off the option of this house is probably a good idea.

'How much do you reckon we'd get?' I muse.

'A million? Give or take a few grand.'

I choke on my wine and stare at Helen in confusion.

'Are you having a laugh?' I haven't even looked at the local house prices since we bought this place. She surely must be joking.

'That's what one of the nurse's got for her three bed place, down the road. It's not even near a tube station or the park.' Helen shrugs.

'We would be loaded, I had no idea we were sat on a goldmine,' I bluster.

'That and the seventeen grand I had stashed away for leaving you,' Helen smirks. 'Oh, I've dipped into it a little these past two weeks, but the majority of it is still in my personal account.'

What the fuck? How long was she planning to leave me? I decide that now is not the time to ask.

'Helen, we could have a bloody castle in Corfu, with that amount of money.'

'Or, we could build a few apartments that you could oversee the rentals of, while I look after the cats. We did talk once about having a pub, but given your new clean living regime, I had a rethink. It's something you'd be great at. You can do so much in the way of building and repairs. Not that you've put it to much use in here.' She raises an eyebrow and looks pointedly at the wires sticking out from the walls. I had actually been planning to see to that this week. No point in saying it, I'm sure she won't believe me. I've said every weekend, for years, that I'd see to them.

Do I even know the woman sat in front of me? She has thought of everything and is now including me in it. I take a large sip of my wine. Me, a property manager? I could totally see myself doing that. I'm warming to the idea, the more I think of it.

A key in the lock distracts me from my thoughts.

'Hello-ooo?' Jenny calls out from down the hallway.

Helen is straight on her feet.

'Jenny, darling. I've missed you so much,' she envelopes her daughter in a warm hug.

'Wow, Mum, you look amazing. Greek weather clearly suits you.' She dumps her coat and bag on a nearby chair and dips a bit of naan bread in Helen's tikka masala.
'I'm starving, mind if I pinch a bit of this?' She pulls a plate out from the cupboard, not waiting for confirmation of her request.
Helen pours Jenny up a wine. She took the train down from her work in Ealing, Tara is driving her home to Chiswick, on her way back to Chelsea.
'So, are we on or are we off?' My daughter glances between her mother and I sternly.
'We are very much on,' I beam.
'Good, about time you pair got your act together. I can't abide being the only sensible one in this house,' she declares.
'Actually, we won't have this house much longer. Your mother and I are selling up and moving to Corfu.'
'What the fuck?' Jenny hold her hands up in exasperation. 'Mum, what about your job? You can't just up and leave London. This house will be worth even more in a few years. It's called an investment, parents.'
'We like the mad notion of investing in our future, of making memories, working less and enjoying life. Jennifer, this house will likely be standing hundreds of years after we're gone,' Helen replies haughtily. 'I'm very sorry if our plans have got in the way of your potential inheritance. If it's all the same to you, I think we're good for unsolicited advice today.'
'Oh, please. I'm not Matthew,' Jenny gives a derisive snort. 'I make my own way in life, but I'm not sure you've feathered that little prick's nest quite enough yet.'
'Oi!' Helen and I both chorus.
'Come on, you know what I mean. That boy has been entitled his entire life. You only exist to fund his various ridiculous ideas and projects. He doesn't even get his wallet out when we all go for dinner. When have either of you seen a birthday card, let alone a gift? He's lived rent free in great-nan's house for over a year now. I have always fended for

myself. Even through university, I'd be up until two in the morning working in bars, then into lectures after just four hours sleep.'

Helen and I exchange a glance. She does have a point.

'Mind you, there's a new cash cow in town, so you're probably off the hook for now. I have no doubt that in time Tara will see right through him. Enjoy your financial freedom in the meantime.'

As if on cue, there's another key in the lock. Helen rushes down the hall to see her firstborn. I follow obediently on behind. Jenny tuts and rolls her eyes at the arrival of the prodigal son.

'Come in, have a seat, Tara,' Helen ushers the young woman to a chair. She smiles lovingly at the bump that contains our grandson.

'Can I fetch you a cup of something?' My wife fusses around like a mother hen. Finally, we're all seated with drinks, and a silence descends. I can feel the frostiness emanating between my children.

'We have an announcement,' I declare, desperate to quell the awkwardness and fill the silence. Tara and Matt look at us expectantly. Jenny gives a loud tut and rolls her eyes.

'Your mother and I are moving to Corfu. We will be selling this house to fund our new life in the sun.'

Matt looks up, alarmed. He looks for all world like that little boy did again, when we'd tell him it was a school day.

'But...what about the baby? What will we all do without you?' He blusters.

'I'll look after you, Matty,' Tara pats my son's hand affectionately.

'Oh, please. I think I'm going to vomit. Man up, Matt, you're twenty-three, for God's sake,' Jenny spits.

'What if we bought the house? This is our home; it can't go to *strangers*.' Matt glances hopefully at his girlfriend.

'We?' Jenny snorts. 'Don't you mean *she*? Where you planning to find your contribution? Anyway, I somehow don't think Tara is going to want to live in Acton, Matthew.'

'I have two words for you, Jennifer,' Matt smirks. 'Gentri fication,' he finishes proudly.

'What? Oh, my God,' Jenny stares at Helen and I, in turn. 'How does he even make it through the day unscathed? That's what I'd like to know.'

'That's one word, darling, but you're right. It is a fantastic idea.' Tara lovingly strokes Matt's face. 'Yes, of course we'll buy it for you,' she declares, giving Matt an indulgent smile. 'That way, Matty still has his childhood home and we have somewhere to raise our baby. You guys get a quick sale without any fees. It's a win-win situation, in my opinion.' Tara gives the kitchen a critical glance over and takes a look out the back window. 'We could probably extend out a fair bit, for a playroom and some nanny quarters,' she smiles approvingly. 'It's a decent enough sized garden.'

'Don't be ridiculous,' Jenny snorts. 'Why on earth would you give up on Chelsea, for a three bedroomed house in Acton?'

'You'd be surprised how up and coming these rather earthy areas are just now, it's happening all over London. This would be a fantastic investment,' Tara smiles warmly at us all.

'See?' Jenny shrugs, glancing at Helen and I, pointedly. 'I told you it's an investment, but nobody listens to silly Jenny. What does she know?'

'Tara knows her stuff too, she's super smart,' Matt says smugly.

'Well, isn't that just as well, Matthew. You sure as shit can't look after yourself. If it wasn't for our parents looking out for you, you'd probably have been living in your car all these years. Oh, no, that's right, you sold it to pay off your dealer, didn't you?'

'No, I never,' Matt looks shocked at his sister's accusations and glances helplessly at Tara to bail him out.

'Matt hasn't smoked weed in months, I simply wouldn't allow it,' she confidently assures us.

So, that is how we come to sell our home. With Helen delighted to be keeping it in the family, and me thrilled at the prospect of escaping my ghosts. We spend the evening looking at rentals in Corfu and booking our flights for the following Friday. In less than a week, our new lives will begin. A new baby, a million quid on its way, and the sun on our backs.

We suddenly have so many reasons to celebrate.

Chapter Twenty-One
Helen

I honestly can't believe it. I am completely gobsmacked by how things have gone so swimmingly for Steve and I. Tara asked how much we wanted for the house, and we gave an answer off the top of our heads, based on an average of what I've seen homes go for around our area in the past year. She looked at us like a million quid was small change from down the back of the sofa.

'Should've said one point five,' Steve chuckled later. He made out it was a joke, but I know my husband better than that.

'We could have at least got it valued,' he tutted.

'They're family,' I shrug. 'Besides, there's that dodgy patch growing in the master bedroom. A survey may well have dropped the price, if that whole side of the house is riddled with damp.'

'True,' Steve laughs. He dumps another case onto the bed and rifles through his wardrobe. 'Think I could still rock this?' He holds out an ancient shell suit for my approval.

'Can you bollocks, mate.' I make a grab for it and Steve sweeps it away from me, like a matador. 'In the sin bin, that's where all the crimes against fashion are going. Those disgusting things have never been stylish.' I point to a black bag, heading for the charity shop. 'Most of these are only good for fancy dress or nineties revivals now.'

'Harsh!' Steve gives me a pained look. 'I looked hot back then.'

'Two words: poodle perm,' I smirk.

'At least that really is two words, unlike gentrification,' Steve snorts.

'Remember when we'd just got home from the maternity ward and we accidentally dropped Matt out of his Moses basket?' I enquire. 'You don't think we did him any damage, do you?'

'We were pretty clumsy first time parents, so I guess it's a possibility. I wouldn't mention it. The little shit would probably sue us if he knew the half. Remember that time you left him in the back of a taxi?' Steve pulls out some ripped jeans and holds them up.

'I was sleep deprived and it was our first barbeque of the summer. Two wines and I was totally floored,' I say, aghast.

'No, you are not keeping those trousers. You could recreate that shredded look with a single fart nowadays. Sin bin.'

I pull out my favourite blue shift dress and glance over it with admiration.

'That's a keeper,' Steve says salaciously.

'Shut up, you sound like a pervert,' I squeal as he makes a grab for my rear.

'Go on, try it on for me,' he wheedles.

'Turn around then.'

'No,' he states defiantly.

I take my sweater off and pull the dress over my head, shimmying out of my tracksuit bottoms under the dress.

'You look just like Jenny did getting changed on the beach in Tenerife, during those prim spinster years,' he laughs.

'God, don't remind me. She was a bloody nightmare, like something out of an Austen or a Brontë novel. My goodness, look at this, my favourite dress fits me again,' I gaze at my reflection in wonder. The woman in the mirror grins back at me. She looks so happy. 'This is a cause to celebrate. We are going out for dinner and drinks, and I will be wearing my blue shift dress. Stuff the packing for today, I'm bored of it anyway.'

Steve follows me obediently downstairs, watching on as I fix my hair and make-up, in the hall mirror.

'I'm loving this new Helen,' he smiles wistfully. 'She's bubbly and confident. I haven't seen her in so long. I feel like we only just met.'

'Meh, I'm way hotter now,' I shrug.

'You know; I do believe you are.' He snuggles up behind me and kisses the top of my head.

Since we've got back from Corfu, we've acted like newly-weds again. The kids have been round quite a bit, Matt to measure up for curtains and furnishings, Jenny to moan about her brother, mostly. We hadn't realised quite how soppy and gushy we'd been until the chorus of, 'Oh, my God, *gross*,' had kicked up again. It had been absent for many years from our offspring's vocabulary. They did it all the time as kids, at any slight gesture of romance between Steve and me. He did once ask them how they thought they had got here in the first place. I thought they were actually going to vomit at the thought.

A key turns in the lock, Jenny and Joseph walk in.

'Seriously? Can you two not get a room,' she wrinkles her nose and gives us that look she gives Steve, when he farts in her vicinity.

'Oh, pardon us for enjoying our own home. Can you two not knock?' Her father sarcastically replies.

'We're just heading out for dinner. Would you care to join us?' I smile.

I'm desperate to spend as much time as possible with my children. We will be stating our new life in Corfu, in just a few days. Jenny, in particular, I've felt a need to be close to. I need to see her chill out a bit. She's so serious about life and I'd love to see her cut loose. The past twenty-seven years with Steve have passed by in a heartbeat. She has everything she really needs and wants in life; she really could do with taking a little time out to enjoy herself. Life is far too short.

'Hmm, we really needed to go over that new case,' she glances over at Joseph.

'I guess we could get up an hour earlier tomorrow?'

'Or, how about we start keeping work where it belongs, in the office,' Joseph smiles wearily. 'Sorry, I know work is crazy busy and important to us. Seeing your Mum and Dad enjoying their lives, this week, it's made me feel we may be missing out a little.'

Jenny gives her boyfriend a curious glance over. As if the thought of having fun hadn't occurred to her.

'OK, I guess we'll be joining you,' she shrugs.

We head down to the Thai restaurant, along the opposite end of Acton High Street. I intentionally take a seat next to my daughter, who looks fraught and distracted, no doubt with thoughts of her case load. We order a bottle of wine and I top up her glass first. I had insisted on her taking the car home, while I followed on and gave her a lift back from Chiswick. It's Sunday tomorrow and we are having a family dinner before we leave. I want to see my daughter enjoy a full and proper weekend for once. Joseph also looks exhausted from working all the time, my daughter is perpetually like a tightly coiled spring. I'm afraid that if she doesn't have some fun and downtime, that her boyfriend is going to tire of her soon. Either that, or she'll give herself an ulcer. It's not even been a month that Jenny and Joseph have been together, they should still be in the first flush of those hedonistic realms that is a new relationship. At least Steve and I had a couple of years of messing about before settling down to the serious stuff.

'Jenny, do you know, I wish your father and I had taken more time out to have fun before now. After you and your brother left home, we did nothing together. It ended up being quite a lonely existence for us both. Do you remember how bad things got between him and I?'

'Of course I remember, it was only a couple of weeks ago that you were barely talking,' she tuts irately.

'Don't be so grumpy, darling. Not everything people say has to have a scathing reply. All I'm saying, is don't make the same mistakes that we did. I didn't tell any of you, but I was under investigations recently, for cancer.'

'Mum,' she says in alarm. 'Why didn't you tell us? Did they find anything? Does Dad know?'

'He does now, he didn't at the time. I hadn't seen you or your brother in so long. You never came round to visit; it wasn't something I could really say in an email. Matt, well he only wanted money from me. Your Dad was only interested in his gaming and drinking. Nobody asked how I was, so I didn't tell anyone.'

'Oh, Mum, I feel so awful. I guess I just get caught up doing my own thing. I was preoccupied with my cases, with decorating the study at home and getting the garden landscaped. I had no idea you were going through that on your own.'

'Don't worry, you weren't the only one. What I'm trying to say, badly, is take time out, go on holiday. Be a couple, be present for Joseph. He looks for all the world like he could do with jumping on a plane right now. Why don't you both take next week off and fly out with us? You can help us house hunt, I've always admired your good judgement.'

'A whole week with Matt? No thanks,' she shudders.

'Tara is in her last trimester; she can't fly anywhere. She's Matt's comfort blanket and he will go nowhere without her,' I smile, conspiratorially. 'It'll be just us four. Think what fun we'll have, lying on the beach, sipping wine down at the bars, out for dinner every night. Come on, I really do need your expertise on a decent location to buy land for our holiday homes. I have no clue about how to negotiate on price, or what a plot would even be worth over there. You're the financial expert in this family, and your choice of location is always spot on. We should look into how to design the interiors too. I was thinking of a traditional Greek style décor. What do you think? We both know your father's taste is in his arse, there's no point in asking him.'

'Apart from in women,' my daughter gives me a cynical smile.

'Obviously,' I laugh. 'Listen to me, please. You work so hard, my darling. You always have done, and you're rather serious with it.' I put on a mock frown, so typical of my youngest. 'Take a break and recharge your batteries. You're a partner in the company, so get them all told. I do genuinely need your help.'

'It does sound good,' a shadow of a smile plays on my daughter's lips. 'I do love a new challenge. Let me look into property prices and locations there, over the next few days. You don't want something too touristy, but it has to be reasonably close to civilisation. There's nothing worse than going on holiday and finding there's only the resort there, with nothing around for miles. I'll look into the real estate market too and I'll make sure I negotiate you a good deal.'

We shake hands under the table, so the boys don't see. I pull Jenny into my arms. Already I can feel the tension going from her shoulders. Hugging my daughter is often like embracing a stick.

'Thanks Mum, sometimes parents do seem to know best. Who knew? Hey, Joseph, how would you like to take a trip with me next week? Mum needs a bit of help choosing a property in Corfu.'

Joseph beams at my daughter, the tiredness across his eyes dissipating a little, at the mere thought of a holiday.

'I guess we should really do your accounts for you too,' Jenny smiles. 'You're going to need someone you can trust to look after your affairs.'

Steve's head shoots round at the mention of affairs.

'Not that kind, father. We've been over this already. Mum is not a cheat.' She turns to me. 'Christ, the apple really didn't fall far from that tree when you had Matthew, did it?' She rolls her eyes, dramatically.

'Well, isn't it just as well that you and I have so much common sense,' I lean into whisper.

Jenny needs this, the camaraderie and the bonding. I need it too; I've felt estranged from my own daughter for longer than I can remember. I know that Matt's announcement has made her feel inadequate in some way. She really shouldn't, Jenny has made it no secret that she doesn't want children and that's fine. Her insecurities will pass; she just needs to see that she has so much value to me in all the other ways possible. The one thing I always wanted for my kids, was that they live their lives being honest to their desires and to fulfil their life's dreams.

Nothing more, nothing less.

My girl is a huge success and has been for years. I have a gut feeling, a mother's instinct, that my son is just about to finally find out what he was put on this earth for too.

Jean
Christmas 2019

I gaze on proudly at the baby boy in the pram, what a bonnie bairn he is. He stirs in his sleep as I stroke his little hand. Uh-oh, I'll be in trouble now, it took them ages to get him to drop off. I chuckle softly to myself. His eyes open and he looks up at me in innocent wonder, making a grab for the brooch on my cardigan.
'No, baby. You can't play with that, you're too little.'
He has his mother's beautiful, blue eyes, but otherwise looks just like my Stephen did, when he was a wee tot. Matthew was the spit of his Dad too, the spaver connection in this family is evident.
Lorcan is just a cuddly as his father was too, when he was little. They're not going to get a foot turned for that lad, just like Helen couldn't, when Matthew was young. We are so lucky to be blessed with this precious bundle of joy. I've not been able to keep away from him since he was born. As soon as he could focus, he recognised me. I saw his first smile too, although I certainly wouldn't tell them that. Every parent has to be the one who sees the first step, find the first tooth, and see the first smile. Even though his great-great-nan did, really.
'You do know that you were the glue that stuck this family back together, don't you?' I whisper to the child. 'I dread to think what would have happened to them all, without you in their lives. Wasn't that clever of you to come along at just the right time. Now they're happy and back together again.'
The baby gurgles and gives me a wide grin. There's a tiny glint of white there in his gum. I try to avert my eyes from it. Tara will be relieved. She was concerned that at five months old, Lorcan had no hair or teeth yet. It's perfectly normal at that age. They were always on their way, but she envisaged having to take him to school as a wee gummy baldy.
'Lorcan's a bloody nutcase, just like you, Matt,' Jenny observes. 'Look at the little fella, grinning and waving at

nothing. Maybe all those years of taking drugs affected your nut-sack.'

'Shut up, Jenny,' Matt yells at his sister.

He may be a father now, but he still acts like a toddler himself, at times.

'Mu-uuum, tell her,' he shrieks, as his sister takes a swipe at him.

'Stop it, the pair of you. Do not make me come over there,' Steven scolds. 'Try and set a good example to Lorcan, show him how siblings *should* behave, just in case he ever has one.'

Helen walks over and pulls Matt from his chair. She places him around the opposite side of the table from his sister.

'Sit here,' she orders. 'I cannot believe the pair of you are in your twenties and I'm still having to separate you. Are you kicking him under the table?'

Jenny looks sheepishly at her mother, as Matthew rubs his shins.

I give a small laugh at the endless banter. They certainly keep me very entertained, although I do often have to turn a deaf ear to some of their rather choice language. It's wonderful to see my whole family here, happy and together. It looked like it was all going to go so wrong for them at one point. They were all scattered off in different directions, but they held it together in the end, and their love for each other pulled them through. Yes, even Matt and Jenny. For all their fighting, they wouldn't see another person dare hurt their sibling.

Steven, laughing as usual, flips burgers on the barbeque. He's always been a wonderful cook and the perfect host. I remember well the lovely food he made, he makes a mean snowball too, thanks to his old nan and her rowdy New Year parties. My boy looks right at home in his new surroundings. The colour is back in his cheeks and he smiles easily again. It's good to see, I was extremely worried about him at one point. It wasn't a good road he was traveling down. He has the occasional drink now, but he's got it under control. His coping mechanism these days is laughter, just like when he was a boy. It's a much healthier way to be.

All around the Greek cottage, are foil Christmas decorations. An old, dilapidated tree stands in the bay window. Helen insisted their new property have one, it's good to see that she's brought a little bit of home with her. They've done so well for themselves. Ten apartments they managed to build on their land.

That clever girl of ours, Jenny, negotiated a brilliant deal with a local farmer. She got that plot for a song. This is the last weekend that Helen and Steve will have free in ages now. The holidaymakers will arrive on Monday and the business is going to be successful beyond their wildest dreams.

Don't get me wrong, there are challenges heading their way too. For the whole world, in fact. Very soon, there will be a terrible affliction that sweeps the globe. It will frighten everyone, and we will have many new souls coming to join us up here. It will feel like it will never pass.

Helen will go back to nursing humans for a few months. Steve will put the time to good use in expanding their portfolio. All will settle back down again, eventually. People will begin to examine, in great detail, what truly makes them happy. It's the greatest change that will come out of the whole thing.

The world will heal. People will learn to love again, themselves and each other.

Jenny, in particular, will be much more fun-loving as a result. The family will all drift this way too, keen to be closer to one another. Matt and Tara will keep the family home in Acton, as a base for them all. Jenny will rent out her beautiful Chiswick house. Joseph will move over to be with her and they'll have a beautiful wedding ceremony, next year, in that little church up the road there.

The family's ambitions to expand their properties across the island, will mean that all hands are required on deck in the not too distant future. Tara will put her design experience into creating a five-star, boutique resort. None of them have any clue about the wonderful times heading their way, just because they were brave enough to take a leap of faith. I'm proud of them all for that. It's so easy to sit back and let life pass you by, to be scared of grabbing every opportunity.

I have Helen to thank for instigating that. That woman is brave and strong, she fears nothing.

I knew she was good for Steve, which is why I sent her to the club he worked in. She and that friend of hers, Susan, way back when. They were walking by to go somewhere else, when Helen paused.

'Why don't we try here for a change? It looks like a fun place.'

Susan wrinkled her nose. Her idea of cool was anywhere that the good-looking men were, not some wee backstreet nightclub. She had a rather scathing view of Helen, but my girl was always streets ahead of her. Academically, Susan had the better results, but I know who the greater nurse is.

In they went to Steven's place of work and the rest is history. I knew once my laddie had set eyes on her, he wouldn't want to let her go. Even soulmates sometimes need a little nudge in the right direction. Helen took a bit of convincing, but I knew my boy would charm her in the end.

Helen laughs at something that Steven whispers to her and the children roll their eyes. She tops up the wine glasses on the table and smiles at whatever naughty comment my grandson just made. I don't want to know, thank you very much. This move has been the making of Helen, she was tired and drawn back in London. Her poor body ached for a rest from the physical toil of nursing, her soul craved love and acknowledgement. She has all that now. She smiles a lot easier these days and finally sleeps well again. Helen smooths her hands down the blue shift dress she's wearing. Such a handsome woman she is; those curves are the envy of all the island's ladies. She gets car toots from strange men, everywhere she goes. Greek lads love curves. Although she's far from fat, I'm glad that Helen has given up the notion of wanting to be skinnier than an anorexic stick insect. I give an irate tut at the thought and Stephen looks my way.

'Oh, never mind me, lad. I'm fine here watching the baby and taking some shade, you carry on with your cooking.'

'Dad! The cat,' shouts Jennifer, pulling his attention away from me. I glance up to see the cheeky tuxedo kitty making a swipe for a sausage. That's the naughty one. Clawdette, they call her. She runs off through the house with her prize. Matthew's chair scrapes back to make chase.

'Oh, let her have it,' Helen smiles indulgently. 'Do you really want a sausage that a cat has just had in her mouth? It was only ten minutes ago she was sat on the table cleaning her arse.'

'*Mum,*' Matthew admonishes. 'Babies are very quick to pick up words, he's at a crucial stage of language development. Do you really want that to be your grandson's first word?'

'I'm sorry, son. It's the wine talking. Anyway, Lorcan's first word will obviously be nana,' Helen shrugs.

Jennifer leans over her nephew, we are just inches apart, almost nose to nose. I'm close enough to look right into her beautiful, brown eyes. She is so like her mother at that age.

'Auntie Jenny, that will be your first words,' she whispers to the baby. 'Go on, Lorcan, say Jen-ny.' She tickles the baby's cheek with a lock of her hair. He gives her a wide smile.

'No way, is that what I think it is? Has Auntie Jenny just found your first tooth?'

'Shhh,' I whisper, and Jennifer glances up. She stares right at my face, but I know she can't see me. This is her way of achieving one-upmanship on her brother. She wants to discover everything new that Lorcan does, and then tell his father about it.

'Little besom,' I chuckle.

I have huge admiration for this young lady. She has the presence and strength of her mother, combined with the humour of her father. What a beautiful mix-mash to place into one soul. In the beginning, I wasn't too sure if that

Joseph lad could quite handle the little firecracker she is, but he does try to hold his own. He's really quite smitten with the wee lass and she's smart enough to know it. No man will ever walk all over that one. That fire in her belly made her a partner at the firm she works for, and her boyfriend admires her for it. Her lifestyle does sound exhausting to me, but she seems to have boundless energy. She will need it once she's over here, trying to keep up with all the new business accounts they're going to have. She will, but she will also find a good balance of down time too.

Matthew, oh now, what can I say about that young man. He has certainly found his calling. He became a registered childminder back in London. He currently stays home with his son and another baby, he does a school run to pick up another couple of kids in the afternoon too. He is going to adore running the children's club, here on the island. I really don't know how they all didn't spot it before. The eternal big kid was always perfect for looking after the little ones. He's responsible, obviously, and a good role model. It's his sense of wonder in the world that has created this love of all things childlike. Luckily, he never found the escapism he needed in the occasional joints of marijuana he had. That could have led him down a completely different and unsavoury road. He's also lucky that he was never caught with it, as that could have completely put the kibosh on his future career. He was never as bad as they all thought anyway, he hasn't touched the stuff in over a year now. Still, we all keep schtum about his dabbles in the past. Except Jennifer, who loves to point out during arguments that he wasn't always the perfect family man. To her, he's still the same bad boy who chargrilled her Barbie dolls. She doesn't even remember the half, he used to blame her for everything when she was little. He was rather naughty back then, but Helen could not see past those big, brown eyes. She still can't now. Becoming a nan has made her happy beyond belief, although when she takes Lorcan out, nobody believes she could possibly be his grandmother. They can barely make it ten paces without one of the Greek people stopping to admire the baby. They're very family orientated as a race. My lot fit in perfectly with that ethos.

Matthew has already been pestering Tara for another baby. She currently jet sets all over the world and says not yet, but I've seen what's going on. I miss nothing. She's grown tired of the crazy lifestyle she leads and is already thinking of scaling it back massively. Their trips out to the island have led her to see that life is not all about the material world, or how much money she makes. I could have told her that. Enough to live on is all you need; the rest of life is all about the people you love. Tara sees that now. Her parents loved her, of course, but they showed her it in the way of ponies, the best school, and Caribbean holidays. The wee lass didn't really know pure joy until she had her own little one. She adores the two boys in her life and being away from them tears at her heart. She spends every night away in lonely hotel rooms, dreaming of being back with them. She's a proper Acton girl now. She proudly carries her Poundland bags to her car and marvels at just how much a tenner can buy you. I could have told her that too.

Anyway, back to this secret that I know. Tara is already due another little one, and she's about to announce it after dinner. They have all questioned why she's refusing wine. She says she can't drink in the sunshine; it makes her dehydrated. Not even Matthew knows yet, she wants to surprise them all as one.

Wee Max jumps up onto Helen's lap. She looks down adoringly at the little cat and feeds him pieces of chicken from her plate. He's spoilt rotten, that one, but he is a cutie. He sleeps on Helen's pillow, every single night. She has definitely found her happy space with these creatures. She adores working at the surgery and will continue to do so, on a voluntary basis soon, so that they can expand their rescue centres throughout the Greek islands. She and Tom now laugh at the thought that there could ever have been anything between them. Steve often jokingly squares up to him about any thoughts of, "cutting his grass," whatever that means. Talking of Tom…

'Here he is, the main man,' Stephen announces. 'Grab yourself a beer, mate,' he shouts to his friend.

These two have become great pals, Stephen has announced on numerous occasions that he's going to fix Helen's boss up with a bird.

A bird, not a word that I find attractive. A lady would be more apt. Anyway, the woman for Tom, she's on her way. He will have to wait a few months yet for the sad widow heading into his life. She still has a bit of recovering to do from the sudden loss of her husband. He caught the nasty virus, but he's perfectly fine up here in the spirit world. There's not a scratch on anybody once they come home. Although Tom's lady doesn't know that. None of them know what it's really like.

My family all take their seats at the table. Helen places bowls of salad, potatoes and coleslaw in the centre. She hands Steve the platters to fill up with barbequed food. Well, it's about time I head back now, let them have their dinner and enjoy each other's company. I just need to hear the big announcement from Tara. I'm still the same nosy, old bugger that I always was, after all.

'Tara, are you having a wine yet?' Helen proffers the bottle to her soon to be daughter-in-law.

'No, I'm good, thanks. Actually, I have something I want to say. This will also come as a surprise to my fiancé.'

Matthew give Tara a puzzled look.

'I'm sorry, my darling, I wanted everyone to see your reaction too.'

A hush falls across the group as they all look expectantly at the young woman.

'I'm thrilled to announce that we are going to be joined by baby number two, in seven months.' She smiles broadly at their shocked faces.

My family all rise from the table, hugging each other and gazing in wonder at Tara's tummy. Matt looks like a goldfish and his expression makes me laugh.

I stand a little away from them, smiling fondly at their strength and unity. Each one such a different soul, but each one precious and extraordinary in their own unique way.

'Congratulations. I'm so happy for all of you. A little girl to keep her father on his toes, and by golly, she will too. The poor lad doesn't know what's about to hit him.'

I smile around at the noisy group, each yelling louder than the other to be heard.

'You thought I'd gone years ago, but I've been here for you all along, just like I promised I would. Steven, do you remember that old lady you helped when she got mugged? You never did see her face, did you? You just heard the shout and took off after that lad, who incidentally, has managed to stop nicking from people, now that he's cured his drug habit. You needed the confidence to join the Metropolitan Police and I was the one to give it to you.

When Helen told nobody of her cancer scare, she went alone to her hospital appointment. Except she wasn't on her own. I said I was there to support my granddaughter, and I was. My beautiful, strong, independent granddaughter-in-law. I would never have dreamed of letting her go through that without support. I was pleased to see that she pressed my little sprig of white heather. It's brought her luck over the years, as was my intention.

Oh, and those numerous occasions that I had to waken you, Stephen. Many, many times when you had passed out with those cigarettes burning in your fingers. You nearly drove your poor nan demented. Those pesky foxes that had taken courtship in your garden, they came in pretty handy. Animals are very sensitive to spirit, you didn't know I was there, but they certainly did. I'm sure they weren't too thrilled at me for the coitus interruptus, but needs must.

I was there too when Luke, your partner, was taken from this life? I couldn't stop it happening, but I could send help. Your back-up colleagues were there for an elderly lady who fell down an escalator. Strangely, she had gone by the time they arrived, but they were there for *you*, in your moment of need. That's what's important.

Oh yes, and that local Highlander out walking her dog, when Matthew went missing that night. Have a guess who that was?

Then there were those eerie feelings that came over Helen, when she decided to get out of bed and check on you. She could feel someone urging her to do it. I didn't want to scare the poor girl, but it was important that she knew the risks. The comforting hand that held yours through all those desperate, awful times, when you felt so sad and lost. I sat with you too, when you watched all our old, favourite sitcoms. It was wonderful to see your body and mind healing; to hear you proper belly laugh for the first time in so many years.

I was that backseat driver, urging you on when you took your trips out with Jacob. I always have and always will be there for you and your family, Stephen.

Although, I've never yet needed to be there for little Miss independent, Jennifer. I will be, if she ever needs me. I am so proud of all of you, you have achieved so much in your lives. This really is only the beginning of your adventures. You have no idea about all the amazing experiences heading your way.

You see, you may have said goodbye to me physically, Stephen, but your old nan has never really left you. Just like you were there for me, I will always be there for you.'

I take a glance around the festive scene in front of me, the ancient string of foils strewn all around the house, just like they were in mine. You're making new pinholes to find in your own home now. It makes me smile to see you honouring me. I need to go now, but I'll be back.

'Merry Christmas, son. Thank you for putting up my Christmas decorations. It means more to me than you'll ever know.'

Louise Burness was born in 1971 and raised in the Scottish town of Arbroath. She spent several years living in Edinburgh and Fife, traveling around Australia and South East Asia, and eight years living in West London. Louise has currently moved back home to be a full-time writer.

After many an entertaining conversation concerning Louise's latest love life disaster, her friends encouraged her to write her experiences down. What began as a humorous, cathartic exercise, gained the approval of family and friends.
'Crappily Ever After,' was born.

Louise has also written three other fiction humour novels, *Ivy Eff*, *Falling from Grace*, (which are both now available on Audible) and UK kindle bestseller, *Crappily Ever After*.

Printed in Great Britain
by Amazon

85706566R00129